Swerve

Swerve

Inglath Cooper

Contents

Copyright Paperback

Books by Inglath Cooper

Melville Quote

"Swerve me? ye cannot swerve me, else ye swerve
yourselves! man has ye there. Swerve me? The path to my
fixed purpose is laid with iron rails, whereon my soul is
grooved to run. Over unsounded gorges, through the rifled
hearts of mountains, under torrents' beds, unerringly I
rush! Naught's an obstacle, naught's an angle to the iron
way!"

— **Herman Melville**

Emory

"Every person has free choice. Free to obey or disobey the Natural Laws. Your choice determines the consequences. Nobody ever did, or ever will, escape the consequences of his choices."
—Alfred A. Montapert

"DAMN."

The coffee pot is empty.

I drop my head back, exhale at the ceiling and ask myself whether it's worth the seven minute wait for a new pot to brew.

"Did I just hear profanity in the breakroom?"

I glance over my shoulder to find Dr. Ian Maverick staring at me with an amused look on his over-the-top good-looking face. And yes, his name really is Maverick.

"Ah, I'm so sorry," I say, gushing my apology. "I was really looking forward to that cup of coffee."

"Four more hours on your shift?" he asks, glancing at his watch.

"Yes. My seven a.m. cup has obviously worn off."

"We better make some more then."

I watch with some surprise as he picks up the glass carafe, rinses out the old coffee, then lets it fill with fresh water while he puts in a new filter. Once the carafe is full, he pours the water into the machine and sets the pot on its burner.

"You've gotta let the experts handle these things," he

1

says, turning a high-wattage smile on her. "I got through med school on Maxwell House."

For a moment, I'm caught in the blinding headlights of physical attraction. Dr. Maverick has earned a reputation in psychiatric medicine that reaches beyond Johns Hopkins notoriety. I've found it difficult to meet eyes with him when we pass in the hospital hallways. He's the doctor most whispered about at the nurses's stations. And he's not married.

Which by all laws of rational thinking makes no sense. Maybe it's the long hours that have taken marriage off the table. Or the fact that he spends his days with people whose problems aren't easily solved. If ever solved.

I stop myself there with a mental shake. Me. Second year psych resident. Nearly bottom of food chain. Him. Department head. Top of food chain.

"I'll blame my verbal slip up on fatigue," I say, noting my own breathlessness, "and hope that you'll forgive the faux pas."

"Verbal slip up?" he asks, as if he has no idea what I'm talking about.

Is he flirting with me?

Admittedly, my radar is rusty. I'm twenty-seven and haven't had a boyfriend in three years. Two in total. And neither one lasted beyond six months. Medical school and Mia are all I've had time for.

"Mind if I join you for a cup?" Dr. Maverick asks. "I have an eight o'clock meeting so I have a little time to kill."

"The fact that you made it means it will be drinkable, so how could I mind?"

He pulls two white mugs from the cabinet above the pot, then removes the carafe from the burner to let the coffee pour directly into each mug.

"I'm not a patient man," he explains, turning a startling grin on me as he hands me the cup.

I forgo the cream and sugar, taking a quick sip from the mug's rim and burning myself in the process. "Ouch," I say, putting a finger to my now-throbbing lip.

"You could mainline it," he says, smiling at me over the rim of his cup.

"If only," I say.

"When I was in med school, I considered it." He waves a hand at two leather chairs by the window. "Come and sit."

"I should get back." I'm aware that I'm standing somewhere near a line here, if not altogether crossing it. "I'm on call for the ER."

"Five minutes. They'll page you if you're needed."

Reason waves its flag again, but he is the head of the department, so who am I to argue?

I take the chair, my mug wedged between my hands, tempted to follow the path of small talk, then deciding against it. If there's a reason he's asked me to sit here, I'll leave it up to him to get to it.

"What's the most difficult case you've seen since you've been here?" he asks, sipping from his mug, staring at the skyline outside the large glass window in front of us.

"Um, that would be the naked man who insisted on doing cart wheels in the ER."

"Ah, yes," Dr. Maverick says, smiling. "Hypoglycemic, right?"

"Right. And he had no memory of anything that happened before we gave him the orange juice."

"That one was a bit of a shocker, I have to say."

"What's yours?" I ask.

He visibly ponders, then, "A young woman who suffered from trichotillomania. She had the compulsive urge to pull out and eat her hair as well as her eyelashes."

My eyes widen at this one. "What did you do for her?"

"The amino acid N-acetylcysteine worked wonders. And cognitive therapy. She'd had a traumatic experience during childhood where an adult caretaker had punished her for chewing on her hair by cutting off a chunk and making her eat it."

My stomach dips a bit. Human cruelty still surprises me. Although I'm not sure why. I see evidence of it every day and its lasting effects. "I guess you've heard it all by now."

"Actually, I still get surprised. That's the thing about human beings. We're all unique." He takes another sip of coffee. "What made you decide on Hopkins? We were all glad you did, of course. You were one of our top pics, but I'm always curious as to what tips the scale."

"Columbia would have been my other choice," I say, deciding on honesty. "But I'm my sister's guardian, and she's finishing up high school in D.C. I didn't want to make her move to another place where she wouldn't have the friends she's grown up with."

I can see that my answer isn't what he expected. "That's a pretty enormous load of responsibility."

I shrug. "I don't see it that way. She's my family, the only family I have."

He studies me for a few seconds, visibly rearranging the pieces of information that have until now formed his opinion of me. "Does she have your drive and academic talent?"

"Actually, I think she got the brains in the family."

"You're modest."

"Honest."

Admiration flickers through his scrutiny, and I feel the moment his interest flares to something not appropriate for our positions. I'm conflicted in my response. This beautiful man, and he is beautiful, has noticed me. I've been turning away from potential relationships for so long now that my inclination is to douse the spark of this one before it ever has the chance to flame to life.

But I don't. I don't know why. Common sense mandates that I do. Workplace relationships are always a terrible idea, and in the case of him being department chair, well, terrible wouldn't be a strong enough adjective.

I hold his gaze just long enough to let my recognition of the attraction register. The silence between us becomes full with awareness, and it's then that my phone buzzes. I glance at the screen. "I'm needed in the ER."

"Better go then," he says, his smile again retreating to neutral so that I wonder if I had imagined the attraction.

I set my mug on the table in front of us, stand. "Thanks for the coffee, Dr. Maverick."

"Thanks for the company."

"Have a good night," I say, heading for the door.

"You, too, Dr. Benson," he says, his voice now brisk with professionalism.

Already, he has rethought the wisdom of that detour we'd both considered taking. A single moment of weakness properly rerouted by an ER page. No harm done.

Except for the fact that for the next few hours, I am certain I can still smell the faint scent of his cologne.

~

THE EMERGENCY ROOM page was for a sixteen-year-old girl who attempted suicide with an overdose of her mother's sleeping pills.

These are the cases I struggle with most.

When you've seen first hand how easily life can be extinguished in a person with every desire to live, it's difficult to accept the premise that it's not worth living. Especially from someone so young.

Katie Dare is awake when I walk into the room. She

takes one look at me, the white coat, the notebook under my arm, and turns her head to the wall. "I don't want to talk," she says.

"You don't have to," I say. "Is it okay if I just sit with you for a bit?"

The response surprises her. She lets her eyes meet mine for a moment, then turns back to the wall, her body stiffening with visible resistance.

I force myself to wait out her silence, sitting next to her bed in quiet acceptance of the conditions. A full ten minutes have passed when she finally turns her head back to me and says, "You're wasting your time. Just because it didn't work this time doesn't mean I'm not going to try it again."

"I understand."

She frowns, locking her hands together across her abdomen. "What could you possibly understand? You're a doctor, and you're what? Twenty?"

I smile a little. "Twenty-seven, actually. But I get that a lot."

"What?"

"The fact that I look younger."

"Yeah. You look like you started med school when you were ten."

I laugh. "Good one."

My response again surprises her. "Isn't it a little weird to be laughing at someone who just tried to commit suicide?"

I shrug. "What you said was funny."

"I'm not funny. I'm the opposite of funny."

"In that moment, you were funny."

She stares at me, and I can feel her trying to figure out whether I'm for real or not. "I've been here three other times," she says. "Why have I never met you before?"

"I don't know. Maybe I wasn't on call those times. But I'm glad I am tonight."

"You can't help me. I don't want help. I just want out."

"I get it."

"No, you don't," she snaps, lasering me with a look. "You don't."

"No," I say, holding her gaze in a way that lets her know I'm not backing off. "I really do."

"What? You tried to off yourself?"

I hesitate, and then, "I thought about it when I was a little older than you."

She clearly doesn't believe me. "But why would someone like you—"

"My parents were killed in a head-on with a drunk driver. I was eighteen. I'd had a fight with them right before the accident. Told them I hated them. That I never wanted to see them again. I never got to take that back. My sister was eight, and I was the only family left to raise her."

The girl's eyes widen. I've surprised her. "I'm sorry."

"It sucks. I've had to live with words I can't undo. For a while, I didn't want to live with it."

"Yeah." She's quiet for a bit, glancing off to stare at the corner of the room, as if she's reliving something. Several minutes pass before she finally speaks. "My dad. He was a policeman. A really good one. One night, he was sitting outside this coffee shop, finishing the paperwork for the end of his shift. And these two guys . . . they just walked up to the window of his car and shot him. For no reason. They just . . . killed him."

Shock skips through me. Words rise to my lips, but every one seems completely incapable of expressing anything remotely worthy of her pain. "Oh, Katie. I am so very sorry."

She shrugs.

"Your mom—"

"Will be fine," she bites out.

"Why do you think so?" I ask softly.

"Because she's moved on. Turns out she didn't really need either one of us."

I hear the edge of anger in her voice and realize this isn't a conclusion I'm likely to alter at this point. "So you think it would be easier for her if you weren't here either?"

Katie shrugs, her expression stormy. "Then she could just get on with her new life."

I give her conclusion some consideration. And then, "Have you ever wondered if she might be trying to be strong for you?"

She swings me a glance, immediately dismissing the possibility. "She's strong for herself."

"Did she tell you that?"

"She didn't have to. I can see."

"Tell me what you see."

"She wants to go places. Do things. Be with other people."

"Katie. People have different ways of coping. When it comes to grief though, none of us has any choice but to swim through it. There's no going around it. You can put it off, but the only way to come out on the other end is to swim through the middle. If I had to guess, I would bet your mom doesn't want to add to your grief by letting you see hers. That's what I did for my sister."

She studies me intently now, looking for evidence that I'm telling her the truth.

"I didn't let her see me cry," I say. "I saved that for nighttime after she was in bed. I wonder now if that was the right thing."

"You were trying to protect her," Katie says and then realizes what she's said.

"Yeah," I agree. "But maybe she needed to know I was sad just like she was."

"You think I'm being selfish?" Katie asks quietly.

"I don't think that. I'm sure your mom doesn't either."

"She's angry at me."

"If I had to guess, I'd say she's probably terrified for you."

"She'd be better off without me," Katie says, turning her face to the wall.

I reach out and take her left hand between mine. I wait until she looks at me before I say, "Do you really believe that?"

Tears well in her eyes. She bites her lower lip, shakes her head.

"I suspect you need each other as much as my sister and I needed each other. And still do, in fact."

We sit for a while, Katie holding onto my hand now, as if she doesn't want me to let go. When the time feels right, I say, "Is it okay if I ask your mom to come in now?"

She nods once, and I get up to go outside the room and get her.

An hour later, I leave Katie's bedside feeling optimistic that she will get through this because she's opened the door and let her mother back in. I'm hopeful that they can hold on to each other. They're going to need to.

I'm headed for the nurses' station when my phone beeps. Mia's picture flashes on the screen in a FaceTime call. I step into a nearby linen closet and answer.

"Hey," I say. "Are y'all having a good time?"

"Hey, Em," Mia says, her voice infused with laughter and cotton candy and the kind of teenage fun I'm happy she wants to experience. Witnessing Katie's despair just now makes me realize how unnatural it is for someone their age to be filled with anything other than joy.

Grace sticks her face on screen and says, "Hi, Emory! Wish you could have come. The festival is amazing."

"Glad you're enjoying it, Grace. What's the best thing so far?"

"The lead singer in the first band," Mia pipes up, her sunshine blonde hair glistening under the festival lights behind them. "Oh, and the cotton candy. You should have come with us."

Is the note of accusation my imagination? "You know I would have if I hadn't had to work."

"You always have to work," Mia says with a blend of resignation and disappointment.

"Food on the table," I say.

"Yeah, but you never get to have any fun."

"I'm off this weekend," I say. "Why don't we plan something?"

"Like what?" she says, attempting not to sound too excited. I feel a stab of guilt for the fact that I've made such promises before only to get called in and have to cancel them. "We could go to Virginia Beach. Maybe spend Saturday night?"

"Really?" Mia ditches her indifference now. "That would be awesome. Can Pounce come?"

"You think he'd like the sand?"

"He would if I'm there. And I just got him that cool new cat harness."

"Cats don't like the beach, Mia," Grace chimes in.

"My cat is no ordinary cat," Mia defends.

"I will have to agree with you on that one," I say. "What time will you be home tonight?"

"Is midnight okay?"

"As long as it's no later. You have school tomorrow."

"Will do, Doc."

"I'll be home about eleven-thirty," I say.

"You don't have to wait up," Mia says.

"I will," I say. We both know I have to know she's home before I can go to sleep.

"Okay. Later, sis," Mia says.

Grace pops back on the screen. "Bye, Emory! We won't talk to strangers!"

"Good deal," I say, smiling at her teasing. It's the last thing I always tell Mia before she leaves the house to go out even though we both know it's something of a ridiculous request in an age where they talk to strangers on their phones 24-7. "You two have fun." I click off and put my phone in the pocket of my white coat.

I'm headed back to the ER when I spot Dr. Maverick walking toward me. He's got an entourage of first-year residents in his wake, and I'm surprised when he stops just short of me to ask, "Your page turn out okay?"

"She will be. A bit of a journey ahead, but I think she's up for it."

He nods once, looking as if he wants to say something, but thinks better of it. "Good to hear, Dr. Benson," he says, and then continues down the hall, the neutrality of professionalism notably back in place.

Knox

*"Down is up, up is down. Good is Wicked, Wicked is
Good. The times are changing. This is what Oz has come
to."*
—Danielle Paige

HE WONDERS EXACTLY when it was that the police
became the enemy.

Sitting at a large round table with eleven of his fellow
officers, Knox Helmer listens as Senator Tom Hagan
presents his case for the Metropolitan Police Department's
committed efforts to be at peace with its community.

"These are trying times we live in," Senator Hagan
asserts, his blue-blood inspection skirting the crowd of
officers before him. "The efforts of the police departments
in our country have never been under more scrutiny. I
realize the tremendous pressure you are under when a
situation calls for a quick-thinking response. Many times,
your decision will result in life or death. Unfortunately,
your jobs require that you think beyond the present
moment."

Dawson Healy leans in close to Knox and says in a low
voice, "You mean the part where we're dead?"

Knox tips his head in acknowledgment of the question,
wondering if the senator would expect them to carry out a
military mission with their hands tied behind their backs.

"We in public service," the Senator continues, "must be
aware of our role to set an example for our citizens."

"I guess that example includes the armed security who walked his ass in here. And anyway, I thought our role was to serve and protect," Dawson says now in a less-concealed tone.

"Restraint must serve as the hallmark of your every action," the senator continues.

"Does that include when we have a gun pointed at our heads?" Dawson asks in a voice loud enough that the other officers at the table give him looks that say, "Cool it."

Knox's own blood pressure has started to inch upward. He runs a finger between the collar of his shirt and his neck, wondering why the hook of tonight's invitation had been Appreciation Dinner when it should have read Political Correctness Lecture. He decides a bathroom break is in order and leaves the table to weave his way to the back entrance of the hotel's conference room. He's just stepped into the hallway when the door swings open behind him. Dawson Healy has followed him out.

"Screw that," he says, reaching inside his jacket pocket to pull out a pack of cigarettes. "Join me outside?"

"Sure," Knox says following him across the carpeted floor to a glass door that leads out to a balcony. He lights up, offers Knox one.

"Thanks. I'm good," he says, leaning against the railing to stare out at the lights of downtown Washington, DC.

"When the hell did the good guys become the bad guys?" Dawson asks, pulling in another drag from his cigarette and then expelling the smoke from his lungs on an angry whoosh.

"Damned if I know," Knox says under his breath.

Another drag on the cigarette is followed by, "I'd like to see Senator Priss Pot in his Armani suit make a life-and-death decision with a Glock pointed at his chest. Guess he'd do a quick calculation of the guy's likelihood of having experienced social injustice versus the chance that the bullet will hit within the protection of his vest. He could probably discount the fact that the prick will just go ahead and aim for his forehead."

"He'd probably piss the suit," Knox says, even as he realizes there's little to be gained from indulging in a bitch fest with Healy.

The two of them have worked enough crime scenes together for him to know that Healy is old school. Translation: the general public deserves to live with the reasonable expectation of being able to go to a nightclub on a Saturday night without hiding out in the bathroom to escape the guy intent on killing as many people as he can before someone can shoot him. Or to go to a country music festival without becoming target practice for a psycho.

"You got that right," Healy says. "This shit is upping the likelihood that we're gonna end up giving our lives to the cause. I see guys making calls every single day that aren't based on what we were trained to do. They're making a decision based on whether or not the perp's girlfriend is going to plaster her cell phone video all over Facebook with an edit that makes it look like we created the situation. I swear it's like somebody turned the world upside down, gave it a good shake, and nothing makes a damn lick of sense anymore."

The door behind them opens, and a tall blonde in a designer-obvious black dress that shows off notable cleavage steps outside. "Either of you have a light?" she asks in a silky voice.

Healy pulls his from his shirt pocket, holds it out with a raised eyebrow. "You really smoke, or are you as enthralled with the speech as the two of us?"

She takes the lighter, pulls a cigarette from between her breasts and lights up. She draws in a long drag, as if she's been waiting for the fix before saying, "There's your first answer. As for the second, not exactly enthralled, but he's my husband so I make the effort."

Healy looks as if a spotlight has just hit him square between the eyes. "Oh. Well. Come to think of it, I should probably do the same. See you inside, Knox."

"I should get back in too," Knox says to the senator's wife, starting for the door.

"Stay for a minute," she calls after him.

It would have been the moment to keep walking. He knows it instantly. And he has no idea what makes him turn around. The cleavage. Or the fact that she belongs to the windbag who thought it his place to tell an entire room full of cops how to do their jobs.

Whatever the reason, he does turn around. And walk back. Leans against the wall that offers its view of the city and says, "Smoking's bad for you."

"So I've heard."

"Why do you keep doing it?"

"I have a very short list of things I like to do that might not be so good for me."

Knox has a built-in alarm system for risky situations. It's going off like a sonic boom in his ear. Which in no way explains why he continues with, "Such as?"

"Run with traffic instead of facing it."

"Check."

"I have a tendency to fall asleep in the bathtub with a book."

"Living on the line."

"Oh, and there's one more."

He looks at her then, feeling the physical pull between them. "Yeah? What's that?"

"I like edgy men."

He stares at her for several seconds and then, "That the category you're putting me in?"

She shrugs her narrow shoulders. "I'm guessing I'm right. I noticed you in the conference room. You were sitting at the table across from mine."

He props an elbow against the wall, looking at her intently now. "And you followed me out here?"

"Does that bother you or impress you?"

"I'm not sure yet."

She takes a step closer, puts the cigarette out on the wall next to them. "I'd enjoy having the opportunity to help you make up your mind."

"What if he comes looking for you?" Knox asks, holding her gaze with something closer to curiosity than interest at the moment.

"He won't."

"How do you know?"

"Because if he were interested enough in my whereabouts to come looking for me, I wouldn't be out here trying to seduce you."

"Is that what you're doing?" he asks, his eyes falling to the fullness of her lower lip.

"Awkwardly, and obviously not very well, but yes."

"Maybe you don't give yourself enough credit."

They study each other for several long moments before she places her hand over the zipper of his suit pants, and then concedes, "Maybe I don't."

There was little point in denying it, so he doesn't.

"We could leave," she suggests.

"And go where?"

"I have a place."

"Why doesn't that surprise me?"

She holds his look then, as if acknowledging the next play is his.

He removes her hand from the front of his pants, holds it for a moment in clear indecision. She pins his gaze, as if she knows he is wavering.

He laces their fingers together. She smiles and says, "Follow me."

At the door, she drops his hand, and they walk through the lobby, two people simply going in the same direction. Until they reach the taxi. He opens the door, and she slides in, giving the driver the address.

He hesitates, and there is a moment when they both recognize it as an opportunity to change their minds. "By the way, I'm Savannah."

"Knox," he says.

"Come," she says.

His life has already included a very long string of turning point moments. He realizes this could be one of them. But he also has ample evidence of the fact that doing the right thing doesn't guarantee a good outcome. He's all but sure it doesn't make any difference at all. And without giving himself time to reconsider, he gets in, and the taxi speeds off down the city street.

The Senator

*"The universe is a vast system of exchange. Every artery
of it is in motion, throbbing with reciprocity, from the
planet to the rotting leaf."*
—Edwin Hubbel Chapin

TOM HAGAN WATCHES the video of his wife getting
into the taxi, noting the tall, wide-shouldered man getting
in behind her. Ex-military. You could spot it a mile away. It
wasn't just the build or the haircut. It was the way he held
himself, straight, alert, as if he'd prepared his entire life to
sense when danger was around the next corner.

He plays it through again, noting the smile of invitation
on his wife's face, then sends a text to the assistant who had
messaged him the video.

Find out who he is.

A second later:

On it.

One o'clock in the morning, and he's wide awake. He
sits down at the desk in the middle of the Hart Senate
Office Building and pulls a bottle of Glenfiddich from the
side drawer. He picks up a glass from the round tray at the
corner of the desk and pours himself two inches.

The single malt Scotch burns going down, but he

relishes the sensation and the alcohol's almost immediate ability to smooth the edges of his anger.

Does he have a right to be angry?

By a normal husband's expectations, yes.

But then he isn't exactly a normal husband. Hasn't been for a very long time. And they don't exactly have a normal marriage.

Although it had started out that way.

They'd met in college, both in law school at the University of Virginia. He'd gone to undergrad on an academic scholarship and used college loans to get his law degree. She'd attended as the daughter of one of the university's most noted donors, her family name featured on a plaque on one of the academic buildings.

They'd had absolutely nothing in common other than a passion for the club where they'd met, the Virginia Law Democrats. They'd met at a meeting where students had volunteered to work on a pro bono case for an undocumented family facing deportation. Until that point, their lives could not have appeared more different.

He takes another sip of his Scotch, remembering how passionate they'd both been about winning that case, how it had planted the seed for his own desire to get into politics where he could actually make a difference in the laws that affected such things.

And God, she'd been beautiful. Fresh and full of life. He remembers the first time he realized she was flirting with him. How he'd hardly been able to believe it. Because why would a girl born to everything she'd been born to even look at him?

She'd told him later that it was his passion for the law and his desire to right the wrongs that other people accepted as part of life. By other people she meant the family she had rebelled against, the father she hadn't spoken to in a year.

They were old tobacco money. The South Carolina family home had been built when slaves were still used to harvest the crops. The first time Savannah brought him home with her for a long weekend, he'd felt as if he were walking around in a dream. He'd never met anyone who actually lived in such a setting. The house looked like a set for *Gone with the Wind* with the enormous white columns spanning its front and the four century-old-oak trees marking its entrance.

Until that weekend, he'd had no idea her family was in politics. She'd never talked about it, and he'd had no reason to ask. As it turned out, her father had been a senator for the state of South Carolina. The seat he himself now held. That weekend had been a defining point in his life, although he certainly hadn't realized it then. He'd encouraged Savannah to make amends with her family, and he supposed that was what had made her father take note of him when he had apparently been dismissive of the other boyfriends she'd brought home.

They'd actually nearly broken up over her father's approval of him. But in those early days, there had been something real and hard to find between them. And for the first few years of their marriage, they had stayed hungry for each other. They'd moved back to her hometown of Greenville, opened a law practice with her family's support and approval. And for a good long while, life had mostly been everything he'd once dreamed about.

He wonders, not for the first time, what would have happened if he'd never gone to work for her father, never agreed to run for the senator's seat when he'd been forced to retire because of his health. Would he and Savannah have stayed in love? Would he be less tarnished in her eyes?

Maybe.

How many times during his early years in Washington had she accused him of letting it change him? And how many times had he denied it?

She'd been right, of course.

It had changed him.

Power does that.

He'd resisted at first. Tried not to be influenced by the doors that continued to open for him, doors behind which he found things offered to him that he'd never thought to imagine. Temptations he'd proved too weak to resist. Savannah was no fool. She recognized the changes in him. He denied them at first, but eventually, there was no point in denying it. He didn't want to go back. Not even for her.

He opens the top drawer of his desk, reaches to the back and pulls a cell phone from a hidden compartment at the back. He turns it on, hits Contacts, scrolls down to Hotel California and opens it. He stares at the number, his finger itching to tap the screen. A late-night visit would certainly even the score. But the proprietor frowns on impulsive appointments, prefers a certain restraint in her clients.

And he likes being at the top of her preferred client list. She believes in rewarding those who go by the rules, and the bonuses are worth the good behavior.

So, no, not tonight. Let Savannah have her fun. He'll make sure the guy doesn't get a repeat performance.

Mia

*"Intuition comes very close to clairvoyance; it appears to
be the extrasensory perception of reality."*
—Alexis Carrel

YOU KNOW THAT little voice that pings inside you
when something doesn't feel quite right? The signal that
goes off deep in your gut like a smoke detector just before
you smell the smoke?

Mia had that feeling.

It was the second time she'd seen the Range Rover circle
the street right beyond the festival limits. Maybe it was
noticeable because there was so little traffic. Most people
were still inside the cordoned-off area, dancing and eating
cotton candy, buying T-shirts and bumper stickers.

Grace had eaten too many of her favorite things and
didn't feel well. She wanted to head home. And they had
a standing rule that they stayed together when they went
places.

It was something Emory had made her promise she
would always do, and Grace's parents had been equally
pleading in their insistence that she do the same.

Mia and Grace, even though they'd arrived at their
county elementary school without ever having met, had
an amazing amount in common where their families were
concerned. Emory had raised Mia, but no parents could
ever out-parent Emory when it came to Mia's well-being,
and the rules she thought necessary to keep it first and
foremost.

23

As much as Mia hated those rules, she made a decent effort to stick to them because Emory had no problem taking her phone away when she crossed lines or neglected to remember some piece of safety advice that her sister had drilled into her.

And she mostly did remember. Except for the Range Rover and the little voice that made her wonder about it.

She saw it again as she and Grace left the festival and walked in the direction of the parking lot, a temporarily converted field. They could have avoided it by veering off to the right and walking through the crowd.

But they didn't.

Grace was talking about a boy from school she liked and had seen in line at the concession stand. She couldn't decide whether he liked her back and wanted Mia's opinion. Part of Mia's brain focused on her question, but another part was assessing their proximity to the car and how many steps they would have to make in getting past it. A dozen. She picked up her pace. Grace followed her lead, still talking.

Just then, the back of the car popped open in a single instant, the way light floods a room at the flick of a switch. A man appeared out of nowhere, pointing a gun at them, his expression blank in a way she'd never witnessed in another human being. It was as if he didn't see them as human beings at all, his eyes flat and lifeless, like maybe he'd been dead once and forced back to existence through no choice of his own.

"Get in," he said in a low, flat voice, moving the gun to the center of her forehead. "Get in now, or I will shoot you both and leave you here to bleed out."

That was their mistake, of course.

Getting in.

Because in the end, it would have been far better to die

there. At a place where they'd had a good time. Where life was familiar. And the choice of living or dying was still theirs to make.

Sergio

*"Good loses. Good always loses because good has to play
by the rules. Evil doesn't."*
—Henry Mills

IT'S A HIGH like no other he's experienced in this life.

Getting away with something does that. Makes him feel
like he's cracked a secret code or been given the keys to the
kingdom.

And he's become something of an expert at flying under
the radar of societal rules. Take, for instance, the fact that
he lives a very affluent life in the United States, but where
citizenship is concerned, he's a ghost. He doesn't exist.
And he has every intention of keeping it that way.

He takes certain precautions in his everyday life. Wears
a baseball cap whenever he's in public. Sunglasses outside.
Fake eyeglasses when he's not. One thing about America is
true. Nothing is private anymore. Cameras are tucked into
every mall entrance. Every traffic light observes your stop
and go. Every ATM notes your deposits and withdrawals.

It takes some effort to go unobserved in this country.

But it's worth the challenge. He has no social media
footprint. No Facebook page. No Snapchat account. No
Twitter feed. No email address. No credit cards. He uses a
disposable cell phone. And he doesn't visibly break laws.
He comes to a full stop at stop signs. Never runs yellow
lights. Leaves good tips at restaurants but not extraordinary
ones because he doesn't want to be remembered. He never
goes to the same hairdresser to get his hair cut.

He's good at what he does. But he's not smug about it. Smugness creates overconfidence. And overconfidence creates mistakes. And mistakes, well, that's death.

Taking two girls tonight could be considered overconfident. But he'd watched them a full three hours at the music festival before making his move. They'd been so comfortable with their safety. Oblivious to any thought of risk. The world was their Garden of Eden. Not a serpent in sight.

Or so they'd thought.

He comes to a full stop at the light ahead, listens for any sound from the back. Not a peep. The injections are doing their job. They'd be out for at least another forty-five minutes. Plenty of time to get them where he needed to take them. Tuck them away in their private conversion chambers. The room where they will either concede to a completely new and different life. Or no life at all.

The proprietor will be pleased.

And if she is pleased, life goes smoothly on. As he needs it to do. And then one day, when he decides it is time, he'll step away from all this, take what he'd earned in the selling of his soul and disappear to yet another land in which he will be his own king with a woman of his own who will be with him because there is no other place she would rather be.

Not a woman he's had to steal.

Emory

"Life changes fast. Life changes in the instant. You sit down to dinner and life as you know it ends."
—Joan Didion

I COME AWAKE with a start.

At first, I'm not sure where I am, sleep a heavy veil between my brain and consciousness. I sit up on one elbow, realizing I've left the lamp on, and that I'm on the couch in the living room and not in my bed.

I bolt upright, glancing at the watch on my wrist. One a.m. How had I fallen asleep? I'd sat down on the couch at just before midnight to eat the sandwich I made after getting in from work, expecting Mia home at any minute. I glance at the end table next to the sofa, spot my sandwich sitting on its plate and realize I never even ate it.

A meow sounds from behind my head, a tentative paw taps my shoulder. I turn to see Pounce, Mia's twenty-pound cat, balancing the beam of the sofa back. Mia. Had she not woken me up when she came in? Or was I so out of it that I don't remember?

She always tells me when she's home though. Maybe she hadn't wanted to wake me, thinking I needed the sleep. I pick up Pounce and walk the short hallway to her bedroom. The door is closed. I knock once, then turn the knob.

But she isn't there. Her bed is neatly made, the stuffed animals lined up in front of the pillows in the soldier-like order demanded by Mia's OCD.

After our parents' deaths, Mia's teenager-typical room

29

had become as neat and ordered as any museum. The counselor had explained to me that this was a way Mia could impose order on her suddenly chaos-filled life, and that I shouldn't question her need to return to the room half a dozen times before school to double-check that she had turned off the light.

"Mia?" I call out for her, thinking she might be in the bathroom across the hall. The door is closed. I knock, only to turn the knob and find the light off.

I put Pounce down. He bounds into the bedroom and onto Mia's bed where he knows he's supposed to already be at this time of night.

I walk quickly to the kitchen. Lights off there too. I check the front hallway, glancing in the bowl where Mia always drops her car keys. The bowl is empty.

A flutter of panic assaults my chest. I squash it back, certain there is some explanation for Mia's not being home yet. They could have had a flat tire. Or run out of gas. But she would have called. I pick up my cell and check recent calls. Maybe she's spending the night with Grace. Had she mentioned this to me, and I've just forgotten, or maybe I didn't hear her in the rush of getting out the door this morning?

My sleep-groggy brain grapples for accurate memory of Mia's plans tonight. "Is midnight okay?" I recall the question from our earlier call.

Again, panic renews its attempt at a foothold in my chest. I draw in a deep breath, hurrying to the living room where I've left my cell phone. I pick it up, scroll Contacts for Grace's mom's number, wait for her to pick up.

When she does, the voice on the other end is groggy, raspy with sleep.

"Mrs. Marshall, it's Emory Benson. Sorry to wake you. Did Mia come home with Grace tonight?"

"What?" she asks, as if trying to get her bearings.

"Mia. She hasn't come home tonight. Is she spending the night with Grace?"

"No. I assumed Grace was at Mia's. She said she was spending the night with her after the festival."

"Neither of them is here."

"What time is it?"

"After one."

"The festival ended at eleven. They wouldn't still be out," Mrs. Marshall says, her voice clearer now, as if sleep has released its grip.

"Yes, I know," I say.

"There has to be some explanation," she says. "Could they have stayed with another friend?"

"Mia wouldn't have done so without letting me know."

"Of course," Mrs. Marshall says. "Grace lost her phone yesterday but asked me to call Mia's if I needed to get in touch with her."

And then I remember the Find My iPhone app and Mia's agreement to keep it on. "I'm going to check Mia's laptop and see if I can locate her phone. I'll call you back in a couple of minutes, Mrs. Marshall."

"Okay," she says, a tremor in her voice.

I hurry to Mia's room, flipping on the light and then finding the laptop on her desk by the window. I open the lid and login to her Apple account. I had used the account one other time when Mia lost her phone, and we were able to figure out that she had left it at school.

I can feel my heart bumping as I scroll through the menus, finally finding the Find My iPhone option and clicking on it. I stand waiting, impatient as the satellite screen opens up and a circle at the center flashes for a minute or so before pinpointing the phone. The address pops up: 1219 Rosemary Avenue, Washington, DC. That's the site of the festival Mia and Grace had gone to.

She's still there.

Sweat beads across my forehead, and I force a breath of calm.

Maybe it had gone on longer than expected. Still. Why hadn't Mia texted? Why wasn't she answering my calls?

Pounce yowls from the bed next to the desk. He's curled up against the pillows, looking at me as if asking where Mia is.

I grab my purse from the cabinet near the front door and pluck my car keys from the nearby bowl I always leave them in. "I'll find her," I say.

~

THE DRIVE TO the festival location would take twenty-three minutes from our house in McLean. I drive too fast the entire way, a speeding ticket the least of my worries right now.

It's nearly one-thirty. The highway is virtually deserted. I pass one car with its lights on bright. The driver weaves into my lane and then overcorrects, running off the white line on the other side of the lane.

Just the thought of Mia still being out when the only other people on the road are likely to be drunk drivers makes my stomach drop.

The festival had been held in a large field adjacent to a city park, temporarily transformed by enormous white tents and a stage.

I spot some cars still parked at the far end of the tents and drive my way down one of the makeshift lanes, looking for Mia's car, the old Land Cruiser that had belonged to our dad.

I see it at the far end of the parking area, my heart

beating now with relief and then worry for the fact that it is still here.

Had she and Grace fallen asleep in the vehicle? Had she turned off the ringer to her phone? Was that why she wasn't hearing my calls?

I whip my car in beside the Land Cruiser, leaving it running as I quickly jump out and run to the driver's side door, peering through the glass to see if the girls are inside.

My heart drops as I realize the vehicle is empty.

Just to make sure, I run to the back, looking through the glass there, only to find it empty also.

Panic breaks across me in a cold sweat. Find My iPhone indicates she's here on the festival grounds. Or at least her phone is.

I fumble for my own phone in the back of my jeans pocket, pull up a browser and log in to Mia's account. I wait for the search icon to again locate the phone.

Another minute, and it still shows the phone is at this address.

I turn off my car, but leave the lights on, then start dialing Mia's number. From my end, I can hear it ringing, but see nothing in the darkness.

I start walking toward what had been the main entrance of the festival, listening to the phone ring, ending the call as soon as her voice mail picks up and then dialing again.

I walk a full circle around the outline of white tents, still not hearing the phone in the dark night.

I start walking alongside the street I had driven in on, following the flashlight on my phone.

A hundred yards or so away from the festival entrance, I decide to turn back, when, ahead of me, I hear the familiar ringtone of Mia's phone. Luke Bryan. Sweat breaks across my forehead. I am at once clammy and burning up.

I shine the flashlight in the direction of the ringtone.

When it shuts off into silence, I frantically redial the number. The phone begins to ring again, and it suddenly occurs to me that I might not only find Mia's phone here.

Mia could actually be here in the undergrowth on the other side of the ditch.

I plunge forward through the weeds, not caring now that I can't see where I'm going or what I'm standing on. Luke Bryan's voice is closer now. I drop to my knees, grappling in the tall grass in every direction, cutting my hand on a sharp rock. I keep crawling toward the sound until I spot the soft glow of the phone screen.

It's lying on its face, the light barely visible. But I reach for it, picking it up to see my own number flashing back, "Mia!" I scream her name over and over again. But there is no answer.

I've found her phone on the side of the road, far enough away from the festival that I can only imagine how it got here.

My stomach tumbles on a wave of nausea. A series of horrifying scenarios begin to flip through my mind like a collage of scenes from horrible movies I've seen at some point in my life.

"Mia!" I call out again, her name breaking in half across the sob rising out of my throat.

I get up and walk back to the pavement, staring down at the two phones. I realize I have no choice but to call the police.

~

I HEAR THE SIREN's wail long before headlights shine on the stretch of street before me.

I stand on the pavement directly across from where I found Mia's phone, afraid to move in case I might not be able to show them if I have to find it again.

As the vehicle finally approaches, I wave my arms. A

squad car slows to a stop. The policeman in the driver's seat cuts the siren, but leaves the blue lights on top of his car flashing.

He gets out, shining his flashlight directly at my face. "Are you Emory Benson?"

"Yes, I made the call about my sister. She's missing."

"Tell me why you thinks she's missing, Ms. Benson. When did you last see her?"

"This morning when she left for school," I say. "I spoke with her about seven-thirty this evening. She was going to the festival here with a friend tonight and planned to be home by midnight. I fell asleep on the couch and when I woke up at one o'clock, she hadn't gotten home yet. She's not at her friend Grace's house. Neither one of them has come home. I drove here and found her phone in the grass over there," I say, pointing behind me. "But no sign of Mia."

The officer shines his very bright light up and down the tall grass at the edge of the woods.

"How old is your sister, Ms. Benson?"

"Seventeen," I say. "She's seventeen."

"Has she ever not come home before?"

"No. Never. She wouldn't do that without letting me know."

"Ms. Benson," he says in a voice that indicates he's heard it all before, "at that age, there's a first time for everything."

"I know. But you don't know Mia. She wouldn't—"

"You're right, ma'am. I don't know your sister. I do know teenage behavior though. But because you found her phone in such an out-of-the-way spot, let me get some backup, and we'll search around here."

I nod, grateful that he's taking me seriously, and, at the same time, wondering what it is he thinks they might come up with. The thought of Mia being found somewhere in those woods is more than I can process.

"Whatever information you need," I say, "please just ask."

He walks back to the door of the car, ducks inside and speaks into the microphone on his shirt pocket. He's back in a minute.

"I'll take a walk farther into the park. Why don't you wait in the car?"

"I'm fine here," I say, wishing for something to do, anything other than stand and wait helplessly.

In ten minutes, two more police cars pull in behind the first. Three officers in total get out and walk over to Officer Duncan. They speak in low tones, and I'm assuming he's briefing them on what I've already told him.

One of the policemen walks over and introduces himself. "I'm Officer Adams," he says.

He's young, but his eyes are serious and concerned. I realize it is only them taking me seriously that will allow for the possibility of Mia being found quickly.

"Her car is parked in the field over there?" he asks, pointing in the direction of the festival tents.

"Yes."

"Would you mind letting me take a look in the vehicle?"

"I don't have the keys to open it."

"I can open it. Not a problem. You can ride with me and show me where she parked."

"Okay," I say, walking around the front of the car to slide in the passenger side.

I am instantly sobered by the wire divider between the front and back seats, and the official-looking computer attached to the dashboard.

He starts the car and pulls onto the road. I tell him where to turn and then point to the Land Cruiser at the end of the grassy field, my own car still sitting next to it with the lights on.

"Wait here," he says, getting out and walking toward the four-wheel drive. He shines the flashlight under the vehicle and then inside each passenger window, until he reaches the back. He walks to the trunk of his car, opens it and pulls out a tool which he uses to slide between the window and door lock.

The door opens easily, and he again uses the flashlight to search the inside of the car.

My phone rings, and I glance at the screen. Grace's mom. I answer with an uneven hello.

"Any word from the girls?" she asks, her voice no longer sleep-roughened, but laced with panic. "I've been calling everyone I can think of. We've driven anywhere I can imagine she might have gone, but there's no sign of them."

"I'm at the festival grounds," I say. "I found Mia's phone on the side of the road and called the police."

There's a moment of stunned silence. "We'll come there," she says and hangs up.

Unable to stand the confines of the car any longer, I get out and walk over to Officer Adams. "Anything?" I ask.

"Just a purse on the passenger seat."

He hands it to me. "Is this Mia's?"

"Yes," I say. I open it, glancing inside to see the pink canister of mace I had pleaded with her to carry when she was out at night.

As if he's read my thoughts, Officer Adams says, "I know it's hard not to panic, but usually these things end up with a simple explanation."

I know he could be right. Could she have left the festival with other friends? Maybe on a first ever night of inevitable rebellion?

But I can't believe that even for a second because I know

my sister, and it's not something she would do. I know this because of everything we've been through together. When you've shared the kind of loss we've shared, put the shattered pieces of your family life back together again so that it at least resembles something of what it once was, you know each other in ways you never would have otherwise. And while I want more than anything in the world to believe him, I don't.

I don't.

Emory

"The mind is its own place and in itself, can make a Heaven of Hell, a Hell of Heaven."
—John Milton

GRACE'S PARENTS ARRIVE, parking behind Mia's Land Cruiser.

Mrs. Marshall gets out of the car and runs to me, wrapping me in the kind of hug mothers give when comfort is desperately needed. I would like to shrug it off, assure her that I don't need it, but I would be completely unconvincing, so I accept it with the awareness that it has been a very long time since anyone comforted me.

When Mrs. Marshall steps back, she smooths my hair from my face, and, with notable reluctance, acknowledges Officer Adams now standing next to us. I introduce him to the Marshalls and explain that their daughter was with Mia at the festival.

"And she hasn't come home either?" he asks.

"No," Mrs. Marshall says with a crack in her voice, looking at me. "Mia's phone. Where did you find it?"

I point to the area where the other two police cruisers are parked, lights flashing. "Off the road there. In the weeds."

The look on Mrs. Marshall's face tells me she knows, as I do, that this is not good news. "I've tried Grace's phone a hundred times, but her voice mail just picks up. What do we do? Tears run down her face, and Mr. Marshall puts his arm around her, pulling her close.

"Officer Adams," he says. "Please. What can we do?"

39

~

THE ANSWER ISN'T a satisfying one.

Officer Adams leads us to the station. The Marshalls and I follow him in our own cars into downtown DC, the traffic nearly nonexistent at this hour of the night.

Once we arrive at the station, Officer Adams leaves us with two representatives of the Family Services Division. Both young women look barely older than I am. One says she'll be working with the Marshalls, and the other one leads me into a small room so newly painted that the chemicals burn my nose as she closes the door behind us.

"I'm Ashley Middleton," she says, offering me a chair. "I'm really sorry to be meeting you this way, but hopefully, this will all be some kind of misunderstanding."

I know she's trying to make me feel better, but by now, I'm growing weary of the pacifying. It's four o'clock in the morning. There can be no good explanation for why Mia hasn't come home.

Ms. Middleton takes the chair across the table from me, pulls a sheaf of papers from a brown leather notebook and pops the top from a BIC pen. "Can you give me your sister's full name and her birthday and social security number?"

"Mia Angle Benson. June 15, 2000." I recite the social, noting her surprise that I know it by heart. "I'm her guardian," I say, explaining. "Our parents were killed when Mia was eight."

"Ah," she says, sympathy lighting her blue eyes. "I'm so sorry."

"Thank you."

"Can you tell me exactly what your sister was wearing when you last saw her?"

I describe the jeans with the holes in the knees, the sleeveless top with its hippy flair that Mia had been so taken with during a shopping expedition we'd made to downtown D.C. at the end of last summer. I mention too the hoop earrings Grace had given her for Christmas.

"Do you have a current picture of her?"

"Yes," I say, opening my phone and clicking on Photos. I scroll up a few to the ones I'd taken last weekend when we'd both run in a 5K to raise money for victims of domestic abuse. I'd actually been surprised when she asked me to run with her. She and Grace normally ran together after school, and I realized then that maybe I had been a little jealous of Grace somewhat replacing me as Mia's confidante and companion.

I tap on the best shot of Mia. She's smiling, a water bottle held high in her left hand, her tank top wet with sweat. Her smile is the most beautiful thing about her. It always has been. She's one of those people who can change someone's day by simply smiling at them.

"What a pretty girl," Ms. Middleton says. "It's clear that you're sisters."

"Thanks," I say, refusing the urge to tell her that Mia is far prettier.

She asks me a series of more detailed questions then, about Mia's daily habits, whether she has a boyfriend, could she be pregnant, would she tell me if she were, has she ever disappeared before, even as a young child?

This question brings me up short, even as I start to say that she never had.

But there was that one time.

Mia had just turned nine. Mom and Dad had been gone less than a year, and Mia still cried for them every night. At nineteen, I had struggled with how to explain our loss to Mia. I'd been truthful with her, told her about the drunk driver, and when she'd asked where they had gone after leaving earth, I'd told her they went on to Heaven.

She'd told me many times that she wanted to go there too. That she didn't want to stay on earth without them anymore. Most of these declarations had ended with me holding her until she cried herself to sleep. And then, one day, she just quit asking.

One afternoon after my classes, I returned to the house to meet Mia when she got off the school bus, as I always did. But she wasn't on the bus. I actually chased it to the next stop a few houses down and insisted that the driver let me look for her in the rows of seats filled with children staring up at me with curious eyes, certain I would find her there asleep.

But she wasn't there.

I ran back to the house to call her school, but as soon as I walked through the door, the phone rang.

It was Pastor Dennis from the church we'd gone to with Mom and Dad, the church I still tried to attend on a semi-regular basis, more for Mia than for myself. The voice on the other end was sympathetic and familiar, and I felt instantly guilty for not being more faithful in my attendance.

"Emory," Pastor Dennis said with sympathy in his voice. "Mia is here with me. I know you must be frantic."

Without answering, I started to cry, dropping to the floor on my knees, the phone in my hand. I'd barely figured out that Mia wasn't where she was supposed to be, and my body was shaking with fear. Because it was then that I realized how alone I would be in the world without her. "Oh, Pastor Dennis, thank you. What happened?"

"She knocked at the front door of the church. She had come to see me."

"But why?" I asked and then hoped the question didn't sound disrespectful.

He was silent for a moment. "She wanted to know if I

could tell her how to get to Heaven. She said she wanted to go there to be with your parents."

The sob broke free from my throat so instantly and with such force that I couldn't hold back the torrent of tears that followed. It was a full minute before I could bring myself to speak. "Oh, no."

"It's not your fault, Emory. You've been an exemplary sister, taken care of her as only someone who truly loves her could. She's just missing them."

"I know," I said, my voice breaking again. "I don't know what to do. I can't replace them."

"Of course not. And you wouldn't want to."

"What do I do?" I asked, feeling as helpless as I had ever felt in my life.

"You just keep loving her. And maybe let her know how much you miss them too."

"I've been afraid to tell her that."

"Because you don't want her to think you're not strong enough to take care of her?"

"Maybe."

"It's okay to let her see your grief, Emory. It will make hers seem a little less enormous if it is something she shares with you."

I realized instantly that he was right. I'd kept my sorrow from her because I didn't want to add to hers, but I could see that wasn't the right thing to do. "I wish she'd asked me," I said.

"How to get to Heaven?" he asked.

"Yes."

"She says that she doesn't think you believe Heaven is a real place. She asked me how it could not be real if that's where her mom and dad are."

"It's not that I don't believe," I said. "I'm just—"

"Angry," he said softly. "How could you not be?"

"Have you ever been angry at God?"

"Of course," he said. "We've all been angry at our parents at some point in our lives. He is my eternal father, but that doesn't mean I always agree with or understand the things that happen in this world."

His answer surprised me. "You don't think I'm horrible then?"

"That is the very last thing anyone would think about you, Emory."

But I found that very hard to believe.

He didn't know that I'd let my parents leave this world thinking I didn't love them.

How much more horrible could horrible be?

The Proprietor

"Destroy the seed of evil, or it will grow up to your ruin."
—**Aesop**

SHE HAS THE sleep habits of a vampire.

Sleep is for the weak. She's always thought as much, even as a teenager when most of the girls she'd gone to school with at The Spence School in Manhattan had coveted an extra hour of sleeping in as if it were the key to the success they assumed was their rightful inheritance.

While they slept, she plotted her future. She supposed that was the difference between someone who was born with her future already mapped out and a girl who'd been granted a scholarship to Spence. A girl with a genius IQ that elevated the school's quotable stats in a way that made her a public relations bargain.

She certainly hadn't cared that they'd used her to enhance the school's reputation. Mutual use was an undeniable tenet of life on planet Earth. Success was determined by an individual's ability to spot the need in another human being and then to fill that need in a way that satisfied both parties. It was a roadmap she not only understood but had become an expert at implementing in every professional relationship that mattered.

She had her father to thank for that education. He had taken her hunting with him when she'd been a little girl. He liked to trap and then shoot, explaining to her that it was too much trouble to try to hit a moving target. He wasn't particular about what kind of animal he trapped, although his preference was deer. They could eat deer.

One morning, when she'd been seven or eight years old, he'd gotten her up early and asked her to walk with him through the woods behind their small house to check the traps. She had been happy to be asked and dressed quickly in snow bibs and boots. The New York winter bit at her cheeks as they walked through the trees, following the path her dad knew so well.

The first trap was empty. He added bait, and they walked on anther thousand yards or so before they saw the second one.

A young deer, probably born the summer before judging from her size, leapt up from the snow as they approached. The ragged iron jaw of the trap held her right front leg hostage. She bucked and reared against it, but the leg only began to bleed more, a bright red puddle forming on the snow beside her.

She'd had no idea deer could scream. But this young doe made a sound of terror that played through her head like glass against glass. The sound made her more curious than empathetic. How long had the deer been here like this, trapped by a fate she'd never thought to expect?

She noticed then the adult doe watching them from a short distance away. Even in the early morning light, she could see the fear and worry in the doe's eyes. She wanted to charge at them, make them leave her baby alone, but it was clear that she knew she could not. Somehow, that mama deer knew she had no power over them.

Her father held his gun out and said, "It's time for you to learn about follow through."

She looked at him, unable to hide her surprise. "You want me to shoot her?"

"There's no other choice now. Even when you're the captor, there comes a time to show mercy."

"What if I miss?"

"You won't," he said. "Aim the way I taught you, and it'll be over quick."

She lifted the rifle, the butt resting on her shoulder as she pointed it at the young deer. The deer was calm by now, staring back at her as if there was no longer any point in questioning her fate. Even so, she took her time, realizing the importance of not missing. Using another life for your own gain was one thing, suffering another.

For a moment, her fixed look slipped to the mother, meeting the deer's head on. Was there pleading there, or was it simply her imagination? For a single, emblazoned second, that pleading registered deep inside her, ignited recognition of something she would later value in life. That moment when both parties involved in a negotiation realize that one holds the winning card.

Pity swayed her for a brief, flickering second, but she understood somewhere deep inside her that losing wasn't an option. She moved her focus back to the young deer, bolting backwards now against the jaw of the trap, as if aware that death was imminent, that fighting back was her only option.

She found a spot on the deer's chest, let her finger find the resistance in the trigger and then pulled. The blast rocked the silence of the woods around them. The deer went down, and its stillness now seemed to her, merciful.

She lowered the gun, looked at her father. He smiled at her, pride in his voice when he said, "That's my girl."

The words echo in her mind as she picks up the piece of paper from Sergio on her desk.

Two deer in trap. 17 or 18.

She pictures their new captives as they must look now, terrified, trying to decide when is the right time to fight to free themselves. Little do they know, there will be no right time. That moment disappeared when Sergio gave them the option of getting in the cargo area of his Range Rover or being shot.

Freedom from the current trap will only occur when they agree to put themselves in the final and ultimate trap.

And make no mistake, it will only happen with their agreement. Of course, when their options are laid out for proper consideration, entertaining some of the wealthiest, most powerful men in the world will seem like a privilege, one they will welcome.

She figured out long ago that human beings relish choice. They like knowing they have options. Even teenage girls.

She pulls open the center drawer of her desk, removes a lighter, and ignites the end of the note, holding it over her metal trash can and then dropping it just as the flame engulfs the paper and turns it to ash.

Her insistence on leaving behind no evidence whatsoever is her greatest strength. She's been called anal, obsessive, controlling. But then she's never been caught.

Most everyone within her circle of influence, businessmen, senators, congressmen, live their lives on their phones, their laptops, their iPads. She wonders if they ever really considered the digital picture they've painted of themselves with every call, every text, every Google search. She'd asked a few along the way why they were so willing to trust in the privacy supposedly afforded them by such devices. Most answers involved some blustery rejection of suspicion. "The best minds in the world are working on cybersecurity. And what do I possibly have to hide?"

Quite a lot, actually, in most cases.

Her glance lands on the oil painting gracing the wall across from her desk. Behind it is a safe. Inside the safe is enough dirt to bury every single customer to walk through the doors of the Hotel California.

She often wonders what her father would say about her enterprise if he were still living. If he would approve of the direction she had taken with his desire to pass along his love of the hunt.

Maybe. Maybe not.

In all fairness, she considered her version a more compassionate take on it. At least there was some enjoyment to be had on the part of the victim. Blasting a hole through the heart of a deer was hardly a comparison.

She does enjoy meeting the newly trapped though. Witnessing the hope in their eyes when they see that she is a woman, certain that she's there to free them. She likes to toy with them a bit, enlarge that hope so that when it finally comes crashing down, she can actually feel its explosion, like the mushroom cloud after a nuclear blast.

The money is nice, but this single facet of her business would not have been enough to justify its continuing existence. It is like reliving that morning with her father over and over again, pulling the trigger, watching the surprise drown in the wake of instant death.

And too, there is the satisfaction found in the luring of men so powerful they think they are insulated from accountability. Now and then, she enjoys proving them wrong. Setting another kind of trap when one of them starts to outgrow his usefulness. And if they visit Hotel California often enough, it eventually happens, that sense of entitlement, refusal to continue paying the admittedly exorbitant price of spending an evening there.

Most retreat with a warning, a glimpse of one or two items from the wall safe behind the oil painting. More than once, she has witnessed, via hidden camera, the shock on their faces when they pull the photographs from their envelope. It is as if they are looking at someone they don't know.

A stranger.

Only it isn't a stranger.

It is that side of themselves they only let out of the cage under the most guarded of circumstances. So infrequently, perhaps, that between outings they let themselves believe it hadn't really happened, or at most, was a one-time thing, never to be repeated.

Of course, she provides them with proof to the contrary. So far, they have all stepped back in line with the warning.

But then what other choice is there?

Exposure would not only decimate their worlds, but also that of their wives and children as well. And their public image, that most of all, they would go to any lengths to protect.

All in all, the system works for everyone. In some ways, those who visit Hotel California need to be protected from themselves, whether they realize it or not. She sees her role not only as that of proprietor, but protector also. Letting some of the country's most powerful indulge their deepest fantasies without handing them rope to hang themselves.

How many people would be capable of maintaining such a delicate balance?

Few.

And that is what makes her unique. One of a kind. Omnipotent, even. Yes, that is the word. All-powerful. The proprietor.

Mia

"Those who want peace should prepare for war and be strong."
—Avigdor Lieberman

Three Years Ago

SOMETIMES, IT WAS no picnic, being raised by your sister.

Mia had often wondered how her childhood would have been different had her parents been the ones to teach her the things they thought she needed to know.

Would they have been as overprotective as Emory? Would they have insisted on this stupid self-defense class that was currently taking up the Saturday morning she would have preferred spending with Grace at her lake house?

She didn't think so.

For one thing, Mia remembered how much her father had enjoyed letting her have her way. As the youngest child in the family, she knew her parents had a tendency to spoil her. But who the heck didn't like being spoiled?

If there was one thing Emory was never going to emulate in their parents, it was their tendency to overindulge their youngest daughter. No, if anything, Emory was determined to make Mia grow up as fast as possible by stuffing her full of all the protective wisdom she could manage to glean from books and the internet. She took her job as guardian as the role of her life.

Mia stands with her arms folded across her chest now

in mute rebellion. The class instructor studies each participant, his confident gaze assessing, concluding.

"I know each of you has your own personal reasons for being here this morning, some of you obviously willing, others of you not so much. But however you arrived here, let's make the most of our three hours together. What you get from this today could save your life down the road. Or not."

Mia feels Emory's glance and its unconcealed frustration for her attitude. "Mia, please," she says.

"Can anyone tell me what a predator looks for in a victim?" the instructor asks, his piercing eyes landing on Mia as if he's identified her as the participant most likely to know the answer. She doesn't. And indicates so with a shrug.

He dismisses her response, and asks another girl around her age. She doesn't know either.

"Any of you moms have a guess?"

"Body language?" Emory throws out on a question.

"You're not a mother," Mia says under her breath.

"Good," he says with a nod at Emory who stiffens at Mia's jab.

"Did you know," he continues, "that for every victim who actually gets attacked, many, many are dismissed as not worth the risk by the predator?"

The group gives a collective no.

"So what differentiates a good victim," he says, putting the two words in air quotes, "from a not-worth-it victim?"

Again, in air quotes.

No one answers.

He trains his gaze directly on Mia. She glances away, even as he goes on, "In seconds, a predator figures out who is a worthy target and who isn't. A predator wants his conquest to be easy. He's looking for a woman or girl who won't fight back. Who has an air of submissiveness. He doesn't want someone who's going to put up resistance. That increases the risk of someone noticing or of him actually getting hurt. He wants someone he can control. Can any of you give me some ideas on what might make you look like someone he could control?"

"Walking with your shoulders hunched." The answer comes from the thirteen-year old girl who still thinks her mom hung the moon. Mia noticed it earlier, the way she rested her chin on her mother's shoulder, smiled whenever she looked at her and said something. She recognized her own jealousy. Knew it made her a not very nice person.

"Excellent, Addison," the instructor said.

"Someone give me another example."

"Looking like you don't know where you're going," Mia said.

"Good, Mia," he said, giving her a look of approval. "Confidence in your walk. How about awareness of your surroundings?"

Several murmurs of agreement went up.

"All right then, are we starting to see that there's an entire picture here that we need to affect? I'm going to teach you some lifesaving moves here today. But I'm hoping the most important thing I teach you is how to take yourself out of the potential victim category altogether. Are you with me?"

It would prove to be the one lesson in her entire education of life that Mia would eventually wish she had paid better attention to.

Knox

"Ours not to reason why, ours but to do and die."
—Alfred Lord Tennyson

HE'D BEEN WARNED it was a hazard of the profession.

Apathy.

Burnout.

Indifference.

Watching the sun rise from the balcony of a downtown, D.C. condominium on his forty-first birthday, he recognizes himself as the cliché he is. Apathetic. Burned-out. Indifferent Metropolitan police detective.

Shirtless, he notes the chill in the early May air, but he isn't sure what happened to that particular item of clothing last night and doesn't relish the thought of groping around the darkened apartment looking for it. Then again, he can hardly leave without it.

The sliding glass door behind him slips open, and he looks over his shoulder to see Senator Tom Hagan's wife holding out his shirt with an indulgent smile on her face.

"Missing something?" she asks, walking over to join him at the rail.

He takes the shirt from her, slips it on, but before he can button it, she slides a hand up his chest and says, "Or I could just warm you up."

He studies her almost too-perfect face for a moment,

searching for an answer that won't offend. "Gotta get to work," he says with a deliberate infusion of regret.

"But it's your birthday," she says, slipping her hands around his neck and pressing her silk-covered breasts against him.

Had he told her as much last night? He supposes so because there's no other way she could know. "Still have to work," he says.

She tips her head to the side, a pout replacing her smile. "Can't you be late?"

"Duty calls."

She gives him a long look, as if considering whether he's being truthful or not. "I actually knew who you were before we met last night," she says.

"Yeah?"

"There was an event a few months ago. That dinner at Senator Donovan's. You were working security. I wanted to know who you were. So I asked."

He raises an eyebrow. "Did you ask your husband?"

She laughs a short laugh. "Hardly. Senator Donovan's wife, Alicia, gave me the lowdown. Let's see if I can recall. Born to parents who were both doctors. Friends in high school called you the 'caretaker' because you were always defending the underdogs. You went to VMI and originally intended to go to med school, but opted for SEAL mentoring sessions at the United States Merchant Marine Academy instead. Which led you to later take a commission in the Navy where you would head for California for SEAL training. And that's how you ended up in Afghanistan fighting in the Global War on Terrorism."

"Looks like you did your homework," he says with little effort to conceal the sarcasm underlining his next words. "All your lovers get such thorough vetting?"

"Is that what you are?" she asks softly, kissing the side of his mouth. "My lover?"

He regrets the words as he places his hands on her shoulders to gently but deliberately push her away. "That would indicate something lasting beyond this morning, and believe me, you don't want me past this morning."

She considers the assertion, and then says, "Well, then. At least let me give you your birthday present." She unties her robe and begins to slide it from her shoulders.

"Hey," he says, walking her backwards to the open door. "I don't think either one of us needs that kind of publicity."

"Maybe not," she says softly, one hand on either shirt lapel as she pulls him inside the condo's master bedroom. "But I do need you. One more time. Because I have a feeling once I let you out the door this morning, I'm never going to see you again."

He doesn't bother to deny it. What would be the point? Right now, what they'd done could be called a lapse in judgment. No point in moving it into the category of an actual mistake.

She drops the robe fully then, standing before him with the complete awareness that few men had it in them to turn her down. He did have it in him. He understood all the risks associated with making the decision to go home with a senator's wife.

But then when you'd watched people you cared about get blown into pieces too small to identify on their way out of country, well, risk became a relative term. And besides, any good plan of self-destruction required risk to end up even being worth the effort.

Emory

"Two roads diverged in a wood, and I ... I took the one less traveled by, and that has made all the difference."
—Robert Frost

HOW MANY TV shows have I watched where someone's loved one goes missing? How many books have I read about unsolved cases where a missing person is never found, or if they are eventually found, they have been dead for a long time?

Sitting here in the parking lot of Johns Hopkins Hospital, I feel as if the lightbulb of reality has been turned off, and I am now trying to function in a universe I have absolutely no understanding of.

How can I go in to work? Act as if all is normal when a trap door has opened in the center of my life and everything, *everything*, that matters has fallen right through.

Mia is all I have.

Both of our parents had been only children. Our grandparents all gone before them. Any relatives we have left are so distant that calling them would be the same as calling a stranger.

The utter unfairness of this hits me center in the chest, and a sob, painful and raw, tears from my throat. I lean forward, dropping my forehead against the steering wheel and cry as I have not cried since the night two policemen knocked at our front door and broke the news that our mother and father wouldn't be coming home, thanks to the drunk driver who had hit them head-on as they were exiting I-66 on the way back from a medical seminar.

Then, I'd had no idea how to go on, how I would possibly raise my sister who was ten years my junior. I had just started college and she was still in elementary school. My parents had left me financially capable of taking care of her, and it was that and only that, which allowed me to move back home, but still continue going to college.

There have been times, looking back on it, when I have no idea how I managed to raise her, finish college and go on to medical school. But the years passed, with her now a senior in high school, me a resident, and now, how do I go on, not knowing where she is, if she's safe, if I will ever see her again?

Rain pelts at my windshield, and I am grateful for its temporary curtain of protection against the curious glances of doctors and nurses heading in for their shifts.

"Go about your life, Dr. Benson," Detective Early had said when she left the station. "We'll contact you the moment we have anything at all promising."

Go about my life? How? I wonder now what he meant by promising. Does that mean they'll only call me if they think they've found her? What if they never do? What if they can't come up with a single lead? Will I spend the rest of my life waiting for my phone to ring?

Fresh tears slide down my face. I think of the people I see every day in the enormous hospital before me. Of the utter hopelessness many of them have expressed to me. And how I've acted as if I understood. As if I could put myself in their place and predict that things would eventually be better. Hope would bloom as predictably as the daffodils in the spring. Just hold on. Don't do anything rash. Time heals. It always does.

But does it?

Aren't there some wounds that will never have the capacity to heal?

Have I been lying to every single patient I've ever tried to help with comforting words?

It is raining harder now, as if the clouds have increased their tears for me.

I cannot make myself leave the car. Go about my life. Somehow, in doing so, I will be conceding to the fact that life must go on without Mia. It's not a concession I can make.

I have to do something. I have no idea what.

And then my phone rings.

Knox

WITHOUT QUESTION, he knows why this task has been assigned to him.

It isn't a task any of the other detectives want to take on. Questioning the sister of a teenage girl who has vanished with no apparent trace. Pretending to be sympathetic without letting her know she's under suspicion.

But he doesn't mind.

If she had anything to do with it, he is happy to help nail her.

They'd spoken on the phone for a minute or less, agreeing to meet at her house. He's waiting at the front door when she pulls into the driveway. The seen-better-days BMW sedan is a surprise given the neighborhood and the house.

He gets out of his black Jeep, noting the startled look on her face when she spots him. He pulls his badge from his shirt pocket, holding it up so that she can see it through the window of her car.

She gets out, relief etched in the lines of fatigue around her eyes.

He walks over and sticks out his hand. "Detective Helmer with the Metropolitan Police Department," he says. "I have a few more questions about your sister, if you don't mind."

"Yes," she says, "of course. Would you like to come inside?"

"Sure," he says, noting the white coat she's wearing, the scrubs beneath. "You're a doctor?"

She leads him toward the front door. "Second-year psych resident at Johns Hopkins," she says. "I tried to go into work this morning, but couldn't get any farther than the parking lot. I'm not sure how I'm supposed to go back to normal as if my sister isn't missing."

She unlocks the door, swings it open and waves him in. An enormous yellow cat greets them in the foyer, its meow tinged with outrage.

"That's Pounce," she says. "Mia's cat. He's upset that she hasn't come home." Her voice breaks on the last word, belying the casual way in which she has imparted the information.

"How do you know?" he asks.

She turns to him, a question in her eyes. "What?"

"That he's upset about it."

The question seems to surprise her, but she explains with, "Mia found him when he was a kitten. He's never been away from her. He sleeps with her every night. I just know."

He realizes she's measured her response, can see that it is difficult for her not to label him a complete idiot.

"You and your sister both like animals?" he asks, doing a quick assessment of the living room, noting the family photos, two large ones of possible parents on a far wall. The rest seem to be only of her and Mia.

"Yes," she says, studying him intently. "We both like animals. You don't?"

The enormous cat chooses that moment to demonstrate the logic behind his name, launching himself from the back of the nearby sofa to latch onto the front of Knox's right leg, nails hanging on his suit pants.

"Pounce!"

Emory Benson grabs for the cat, but he's latched on with no intention of letting go. She squats in front of him, doing her best to disengage the cat's claws from his leg. The nails give the cat leverage though, and he sinks them in, penetrating pants and skin.

"Pounce, let go!" she demands, and as if he knows he's crossed the line, the cat instantly releases himself.

She swoops him up in her arms, apologizing. "I'm so sorry. I don't know what's gotten in to him."

"That's okay," he says, reaching down to rub his leg.

"He's never done anything like that."

"Glad I could be the first."

This brings a half-smile to her mouth, and as if it has surprised her, she instantly sobers. "Maybe he thinks you can help find Mia."

He raises an eyebrow. "Or maybe he's just an ornery cat?"

The assessment clearly offends her. She pulls Pounce a little closer and says, "I believe animals have the ability to sense things that humans do not."

"Yeah?"

"Yes."

"I have no idea whether you're right or not, but do you think you could stick him in another room until we're done?"

She considers the question long enough that he's fairly sure she's going to tell him to go screw himself, but instead, she disappears from the living room, the cat staring back at him over her shoulder. He hears a door open and close down the hallway and then looks up as she walks back in the room without the cat.

He feels a short stab of guilt that she's conceded to booting the cat, realizing he's given her absolutely no reason to like him enough to answer any of his questions. "If you'd rather he hang out in here, it's fine."

"Why are you here, Detective Helmer?" she asks, ignoring the concession. Her arms are folded across her chest, her manner now all business.

"So you got through medical school while raising your kid sister?"

"I did."

"That ever feel like a burden?"

Her eyes go wide at the question, shock rippling across her face. "Is there a point to your question?"

He lifts his shoulders in a half-shrug, holding her gaze. "Should there be?"

Outrage flares now, and he can feel her desire to give him the verbal dress-down she thinks he deserves. "Are you implying I had something to do with my sister's disappearance?"

"Did you?"

It's a little direct, even for him, going for the jugular that way, but he's not in the mood for dancing around the real reason he's here. He's already made one significant error in judgment within the past twenty-four hours. He doesn't need to add another to the list.

She visibly struggles for control, her cheeks red with a rush of anger. "So is this what's happening with Mia's investigation? This is the best your department has got? Send over a detective with an obvious chip on his shoulder to grill the sister who must have a reason to want her dead?"

"No one said anything about dead," he says, his voice even.

"Are you trying to back me in a corner?"

He watches her rein in her disbelief. When she speaks again, her voice is the one he imagines she uses as a doctor with a patient she expects to disagree with her recommendations.

"My sister is my entire world. She is the only family I have. I am dying inside at the thought of her being hurt or—"

Her voice breaks there, and the regret that shoots through his chest is a surprise.

"Can we sit down?" he asks.

She leads the way to the sofa in the center of the room and sits at one corner without answering him.

He takes the other corner and makes the decision to try a different course, pulling a pen and notepad from his jacket pocket. "Tell me what Mia likes to do."

"I went over all of this at the station last night."

"Indulge me."

She glances out the window at the middle of the room. She's quiet for several long moments. When she finally speaks, it's as if she's been trying to filter all the fear from her voice so that she can paint him an accurate picture.

"She's a runner. She likes to run because of the way it makes her feel. It's natural to her. Like breathing. We do races together, but she always beats me. She likes animals. She wants to be a veterinarian."

"Smart girl?"

"Valedictorian of her class at this point."

He raises an eyebrow. "Run in the family?"

"That particular thing, yes."

"Does she have a boyfriend?"

"No."

"You're sure?"

"I'm sure," she says, again notably offended by the

implication that she might not know her sister as well as she thinks.

"She likes boys?"

"Yes, she likes boys," she says, emphasizing the last word. "She just prefers focusing on her studies right now. She received an academic scholarship to NC State for pre-vet undergraduate work."

"She's a hard-worker then?"

"Very."

"Was the scholarship mandatory for getting to go to college?"

"Our parents left us well-taken care of, if that's what you're asking. We both thought it made sense to get whatever scholarships we were able to get."

"Why psychiatry?"

The question is out of the blue, and he sees the sideswipe of surprise on her face. A few moments pass before she answers with, "I like figuring people out."

"Are you good at it?"

"I'm getting better."

"That's honest."

"Take you, for instance."

Now it's his turn to be surprised. He waits for her to go on without giving her permission to do so.

"You hate your job. Or maybe it's your entire life that you hate. I'm guessing ex-military. Specialty, I would presume judging by your fitness, the haircut. SEAL?"

Her accuracy is startling, but he refuses to let it show on his face. He keeps his expression neutral, expecting her to stop, but she goes on with, "This work must bore you by comparison. Having to spend your days asking ridiculous questions of regular people like me. You're probably used to blowing stuff up, invading places in the dark. Adrenaline-inducing assignments. You seem like someone who would become addicted to that. Find life bland without it."

She stops for a moment and then goes on with, "My guess is you've also got relationship issues. You're not one to put down roots or take the time to invest in anything real. Affairs are probably more your thing. Expectations are obvious up front. You don't have to pretend to want more. Both parties get what they came for."

She waits for his response, clearly confident that she has nailed him.

"You're good with the diversionary tactics," he says, pinning her with a silent command for her to stop. "But I'm supposed to be the one drawing the conclusions."

"And have you? Drawn any?"

"One."

"Enlighten me."

"Your sister is probably lucky to have you looking for her."

She doesn't expect this, and he watches her previous desire to decimate him dissolve and fade away. "Thanks," she says, her voice now barely audible. "But I have no idea what to do other than trust that you and your department will do everything possible to bring her home."

"Tell me about the friend. Grace?"

"Yes. They've known each other since elementary school. Mia is the leader in the friendship. Grace would like to get off track sometimes, but Mia has always been able to steer her back."

"What do you mean?"

"Wanting to try things. The normal teenage stuff. Drinking. Cigarettes."

"Is it possible she could have convinced Mia to run away?"

"From what? They both have very good lives with their

futures planned in the fall. They're going off to college. They don't do drugs. Why would they run away?"

"I don't always know why teenagers do some of the things they do. I just know they do them."

"Not these two. It would be out of character."

"So what do you think happened to them?"

The question is direct, again catching her off guard.

"If I knew, would I be sitting here taking this from you?"

"I simply mean, what does your gut tell you?"

Her response is instant. "That someone took them. I know my sister. That is the only possible explanation."

He'd come here today, hoping to see evidence of something else. Something that would make him conclude this was another case of two teenage girls who had taken off on an adventure and would eventually find their way back home.

But he doesn't. He believes Emory Benson. And in his gut, he thinks she's probably right.

Someone did take them.

Emory

*"I don't count my sit-ups; I only start counting when it
starts hurting because they're the only ones that count."*
—Muhammad Ali

I CAN SEE the moment Detective Helmer decides he
agrees with me.

The realization sends whatever hope had been fluttering
at the center of my chest, plummeting. Despair erupts from
its ashes, and I am mortified by the tears I cannot control.

I do not want his pity, but it's clear that he feels it,
whether he wants to or not. "Ms. Benson, Dr. Benson,"
he corrects, "we have some great cops working on your
sister's case. It's early hours yet. We're combing camera
feeds in areas around the festival. We're going door to
door within a one mile radius, asking for information from
anyone who might have seen anything at all suspicious. I
know the waiting is the unbearable part, but give us a little
time. We'll do everything we can to find them."

I want to believe him. I need to believe him. But I think
of all the horrible cases I've heard about—on television, in
books and movies—and terror is all I can manage to feel.

He must see this despite my effort to hide it because he
says, "The moment I learn anything at all, I will let you
know."

He stands then, adding, "Is there anything else you'd like
to tell me?"

"Only that I can't imagine my life without Mia. Please
find her. Please."

He pulls a card from his shirt pocket, walks closer to hand it to me. "My cell number is on there. If you think of anything else, call me at any time."

Our gazes hang for a moment. Something passes between us. I feel its current-like electricity, and I wonder if, under other circumstances, we might be drawn to each other. But then I recall my predictions about him, feel certain I'd been right, and I know he's not a man I could ever be drawn to. My search in life is for stability, predictability, the opposite of out-of-the-blue middle-of-the-night phone calls that wreck an entire existence.

My only hope for anything from Knox Helmer is that he will help bring back the only thing that can ensure that life will make sense again: my sister, Mia.

~

ONCE DETECTIVE HELMER leaves, I let Pounce out of Mia's room. He trots behind me into the kitchen, sitting like an observing statue in the doorway while I empty the dishwasher and wipe the countertops. Once that's done, I clean out the refrigerator, throwing away leftovers I should have thrown away weeks ago. I fill a trash bag, take it out to the can at the door off the side of the kitchen and then come back inside to find Pounce still staring at me.

He meows a protesting yowl and trots into the living room. I hear a clatter and leave the kitchen to find that he is standing on the keyboard of my desktop computer. His tail swishes in agitation, and I swear it's as if he is asking me to do something.

Whether it has anything to do with him or if the prompting is purely coincidental, I realize I cannot fill my hours with cleaning and rearranging. I take the chair in front of the computer, lifting Pounce from the keyboard and depositing him on my lap. I hit the space bar on the keyboard, the screen lighting up.

Pounce's tail stops swishing, and he folds himself into a comma, his chin resting on my left knee.

I have no idea where to start, so I offer the search engine the most obvious thing that comes to mind: missing girls Washington, DC.

The first results shock me. A screenshot of the Metropolitan Police Department Twitter feed reads: Critical Missing. Two Teenage Girls. Mia Benson. Age 17. Grace Marshall. Age 17. Last seen at Spring Jam Festival.

Their physical info is given, their photos displayed along with information on how to contact the Youth and Family Services Division or the Command Information Center with any possible leads.

I stare at my sister's smiling face. It's the profile photo she used for her Facebook page, and I realize they must have pulled it from there.

Tears well in my eyes, and her smiling face blurs before me. Grief explodes from my chest, and I put my head on the desk in front of me, sobbing until the sorrow begins to be replaced with rage.

Pounce puts his paws on my shoulder, kneading my shirt the way he does his favorite pillow. I hear him purring, turn around and swoop him up against me, squeezing him so tight against me that he lets out a protesting yelp.

I loosen my hold but don't let him go, and he doesn't want me to. He tucks his face against my neck, and we sit that way until my angry crying drains me into silence.

I tap the space bar on the keyboard and back out of the current page to my original search findings for missing girls Washington, DC.

Washington DC Police locate missing 12-year-old girl

Nov 11, 2015 – WASHINGTON, D.C. – Police were searching for a missing 12-year-old girl.

7 facts about missing children in the DMV | WUSA9.com

May 25, 2016 – 1. According to the National Center for Missing and Exploited Children, there are 140 missing children in the Washington, DC, Maryland; and ...

11-Year-Old DC Girl Missing Since Friday | TBV3 Washington

Dec 9, 2014 – An 11-year-old girl from Southeast D.C. has been missing since last Wednesday, police say.

I exit the screen, unable to read more.

Overwhelm hits me like a cascade of rocks, and I fall back against the chair, Pounce still clinging to me.

We sit there in the middle of our living room, shipwrecked passengers who have washed up on an island they have never seen before and have no idea how they will exist on.

But we have no choice other than to figure it out. We have to be here for Mia when she comes home. And she will come home. Anything else is unthinkable.

The Proprietor

THE ENTRANCE SIGN is discreet.

Hotel California

The two words are scripted across a heavy brass estate plaque mounted to a single stacked-stone column.

Her driver makes the turn onto the narrow asphalt drive, hits the remote for the iron gate. They wait for it to swing open, and, as always, she takes the moment to admire the setting before her.

Here, on this northern fringe of Virginia countryside, barely an hour beyond the power corridors of downtown Washington, DC, the Hotel California had once provided occasional escape to some of the country's most well-known political families. She had found guest books in the hotel vault dating back to the early 1900s with names like Roosevelt and Wilson gracing the pages.

It was a source of pride to know that she was the modern-day proprietor of such a place. Of course, when she'd first found the hotel in the real estate for sale listings of properties close enough to the city, it had looked nothing like it now looks. It had been a sad, drooping shadow of its former self.

And she, *she*, had been the one to spot the diamond in the rough, wave the magic wand and transform it.

Little had she known the extent of the bounty inside the treasure chest of the Hotel California.

No, that discovery hadn't made itself known until the contractor had discovered the secret elevator shaft.

Ahead, at the end of the long drive, just barely visible from the gate entrance, the hotel stands now like a reinstated beauty queen, the deep lines of fatigue blasted from her surface by one of the country's best architects with the same determined skill as a Beverly Hills plastic surgeon. Her brick walls had been cleaned with bleach and water, mildew and mold fleeing like no longer welcome guests from its surface.

The manicured lawn and accentuating boxwoods resemble the English country houses they'd originally been patterned after. Two enormous oak trees flank each side of the main building. The arborists told her it was extremely unusual that neither tree had ever been damaged by lightning, every single limb still strong and thriving.

She liked to think of the trees as protectors of the hotel, warding off encroaching dangers like storms and wind and ice. Much the same as she was the protector of the very precious guests and residents of the hotel.

The car glides down the long driveway, her heart beating a little faster as they near the main entrance.

The city holds some allure for her, its bright lights and pounding pulse appealing in their own right. But it is here, in this place she has resurrected from its own ashes, that she thrives. Recognizes her purpose in life. Knows the kind of control and power that make her wish for an extension on her probable number of years on this earth.

She thinks of the new residents awaiting her approval, wonders if their detox is working at its most effective or if they will require her more convincing measures.

This part is always exciting for her. Assessing whether the original trap creates a willing partnership or not.

It is the rare captive who does not respond to this first phase.

She has learned though that most people think they are strong. They've been convinced of this by the paper-thin walls of their lives, which they view as their security, their right to a safe existence. It takes so little, really, to throw them into chaos, confuse them as to what is up and what is down.

She realizes this could be considered cruelty, but it's really nothing more than a necessary part of the process. Human beings make decisions based on what they think is true, not what actually is. She has to show them what actually is so that they understand the importance of choosing correctly.

At the hotel's front entrance, her driver stops the car, sliding out to come around and open her door. "Welcome back, madam," he says.

"Thank you," she says, looking at the front door. "Although somehow, it doesn't feel as if I ever really leave."

Knox

"In my life, I have made the occasional catastrophic choice, and it's just a case of moving on and learning from it."
—**James Nesbitt**

THE CHIEF IS a woman.

But anyone foolish enough to mistake her gender as license for assuming softness almost certainly lives to regret it.

At least anyone associated with the Metropolitan Police Department.

Knox has never considered himself foolish, and he's the last person to underestimate Willa Parker. Or the reason she has called him to her office this afternoon.

He sits across from her desk, right ankle over left knee, aware from her expression that he has been called to the principal's office.

"A senator's wife?" she says in a former smoker's voice. "Seriously, Helmer?"

He chooses silence as the best option, keeps his expression blank, unwilling to give her any cards to play.

"You were sent to that party as a representative of this department. I chose you as one of only three detectives deserving of the recognition." She leans back in her chair, arms folded, giving him a long look. "Are you aware of your propensity for shooting yourself in the foot?"

"Was that what it was?" he asks.

"What the hell else could it be?"

79

"Sex, ma'am."

The words drop between them. Her eyes widen for the briefest second, and he takes a small degree of pleasure in having shocked her at least a little.

"I repeat," she says. "With a senator's wife?"

He shrugs. "I didn't feel it was my role to question her choices."

"What about her motivation? Did you question that?"

"I really think it was the same as mine."

Exasperation throws enough color in her Irish cheeks that her hair is a near reflection. "Well, I'm so pleased it was such an excellent match. Unfortunately, if Senator Hagan is made privy to the same surveillance video I was, you might need to rejoin the military."

"Why is that, ma'am?"

"Because I can't have that kind of heat in my department."

"No one got hurt. We were both consenting adults."

"No one got hurt *yet*."

He raises an eyebrow, starts to stand, a hand on either arm of the chair. "If that's all—"

"It's not. Sit down."

He eases back into the chair, reluctant, but he knows an order when he hears one.

"You know I had my reservations when I hired you, Helmer. My gut told me you were set on self-destruct. I was right, wasn't I?"

He meets her gaze, holding it for a moment before saying, "Not with the intention of taking anyone else down with me."

"Intention counts for shit. Stupid choices will get you there every time."

"What exactly do you want me to say, Chief?"

"That you value this job. That you're not going to make me regret hiring you."

"That's not my intention."

"That intention thing again. Here's what I see, Helmer. I know what your past looks like. My guess is you could have gotten yourself blown up in Afghanistan any day of the week. Living on that kind of tightrope would have to change your outlook on what a normal existence looks like. This job isn't that. Are you trying to make it that?"

"Not that I'm aware of."

"So maybe you need to be aware of it."

"Noted."

"And don't think I'm not aware of your ability to pacify."

"Pacify?"

"Say what you think I want to hear."

"Is it working?"

"No."

He blows out a rush of breath, concedes with, "It won't happen again."

"The senator's wife or the questionable judgment in general?"

"Both."

"I'd like to believe you."

"You can."

She makes a pretense of shuffling some of the papers on her desk, suddenly changes course with, "The missing girls case. You spoke to the sister of the Benson girl?"

"Earlier this afternoon."

"What's your gut?"

"About as devoted as a sibling could be. Parents died when the younger sister was eight. Oldest had just started college and moved back home to raise her sister. No other immediate family."

Chief Parker raises her eyebrows. "Damn."

"Yeah."

She glances out the window to the side of the desk. "I don't have a good feeling about this one."

"Me either," he admits.

"I'd like you on it full-time until further notice. Get with the uniforms and find out where they are with the door to door. And then you need to start looking under rocks. Get online with the pervs and see who knows something. Let's give it the gas. You know we don't have much time."

"I'm on it," he says, standing up and adding, "That it?"

"For now."

He's just reached the door when she says, "Helmer?"

"Ma'am?" he says, turning back with a neutral expression.

"It sure would be nice to see you reach your potential."

"I'll see what I can do." He turns the knob and walks out, wondering what she would say to the fact that he no longer thinks the word applies to him.

Emory

"You can't stay in your corner of the forest waiting for others to come to you. You have to go to them sometimes."

—A. A. Milne

I AM A DOER.

I have to do something.

I can't sit and wait for my phone to ring.

My next online search is "what to do when a person is missing."

WikiHow brings up **"How to Find a Missing Person."** I read through the thirteen suggestions, making a list on the notebook beside my keyboard.

I long ago figured out that lists are my friend when life feels out of control. Making a box to check off beside each task will at least give me the illusion of doing something that might make a difference.

I start writing.

_____ **Contacting the police and file reports**

_____ **Provide the police with information about the missing person**

_____ **Keep a record of the report.**

_____ **Contact the National Missing and Unidentified Persons System (NamUs).**

_____ **Contact the person's friends and acquaintances.**

_____ **Check with hospitals and coroners in the area.**

This one brings me up cold, a feeling of panic skittering along my skin. Call a coroner and ask if my sister is there? It is unthinkable. I leave this one for now and go on to the next one.

_____ **Check with your local county jail.**

_____ **Check social media sites.**

_____ **Put up fliers with a picture and description of the missing person.**

_____ **Ask people to spread the word.**

_____ **Alert the local media.**

_____ **Consider hiring a private investigator.**

Once I've written down all the suggestions, I stare at the list, a staggering despair washing over me. I push it aside though, relieved to have something to focus on, anything to take my thoughts off where Mia might be and all the awful possibilities for what might have happened to her.

I can't go there. I tell myself to complete the list, and it is very likely that someone will come forward with information that will lead to finding her. And so I go back to the top of the list. The first three I've done. I check the boxes. Number four. **Contact the National Missing and Unidentified Persons System (NamUs).**

I find the link and start entering the information.

~

IT TAKES THE entire remainder of the day to get the next-to-the-last box checked. I've personally contacted every friend and acquaintance I am aware of as someone Mia interacts with on a regular basis. I ask each of them to please let me know if they hear anything at all from her.

I've called every hospital in the DC and northern Virginia area. That was painful, but calling the coroner's offices within a fifty-mile radius, that was excruciating. It is only when I've hung up from the last call that I breathe a sigh of relief for the fact that neither office had anyone there who matched Mia's description.

I call every local jail within a fifty-mile radius. I cannot imagine Mia doing anything that would have landed her in any of them, but I'm following the list. There is no one in any of the jails who sounds like Mia.

I log on to her computer and check every social media site saved in her Bookmarks. I check the messages of each, find nothing relevant. Her posts are typical of what I would imagine her posting. Positive memes, funny animal videos, photos of Grace and her, several of Pounce.

Next, I write up a press release with as much detail about what has happened as I can come up with. I include one picture of Mia and another of her with Grace. I email it to sixty different editors of TV news stations, newspapers, and radio stations.

Once that's done, I make up a flyer and use my printer to print two hundred copies. I leave the house with the stack of flyers in my arms and drive to the location of the festival where I start posting them on every light pole within a mile of where I'd found her phone. I post the rest of them at local grocery stores, a fitness club, and the restaurants that allow me to leave one on a community bulletin board.

It's after ten o'clock when I get home. I'm so tired that I can barely drag myself back to the desk chair where Pounce has not moved since I left. I pick him up, arrange him on my lap, and stare at the to-do list I had spent the day completing.

There's one suggestion left.

Consider hiring a private detective.

The thought of pursuing this tonight is more than I can process. I will call Detective Helmer first thing in the morning and see if I can get a feel for whether or not he thinks they're making progress.

If not, I'll start researching private detectives.

Pounce meows, stands on my leg, his paws kneading back and forth, his nails pricking my skin. He hops down then and heads for Mia's bedroom, and I'm sure he expects her to be home in a bit. Why would he imagine anything different? This is the routine they follow every night.

I start to call him back, take him to my room with me. But I can't bring myself to do it, so I put one foot in front of the other until I reach my own bed where I fall face first onto the mattress.

I am asleep before my brain can again latch on to the fear that has kept me awake for the past forty-eight hours.

Knox

"Life is an unfoldment, and the further we travel the more truth we can comprehend. To understand the things that are at our door is the best preparation for understanding those that lie beyond."
—Hypatia

HE WAKES TO a strip of light through the crack in the black-out drapes of his bedroom.

He'd finally bought the curtains a few months ago in an effort to sleep more than a few hours each night. The difficulty was in getting to sleep in the first place, but once he did fall asleep, the blocking of sunlight sometimes prevented him from waking at the crack of dawn.

He'd once been a great sleeper. He could go to bed at ten and wake up at seven, feeling renewed, rejuvenated.

His deployment in Afghanistan had changed all of that.

Dr. Thomason, the psychiatrist he reluctantly sees once a week, tells him PTSD is responsible for his inability to go to sleep. Trauma rewires the brain, convinces it that it must always stay on guard. To lower awareness is to invite disaster. And if a person is asleep, how can he stay on guard?

He's tried the artificial versions of sleep inducement: Ambien, Halcion, and Restoril—the last of which was supposed to make him stay asleep in addition to falling asleep. They all work for a couple of hours. But his brain usually wins out. It yells and screams behind the artificial veil until inevitably, finally, he comes wide awake, often in a sweat, as if he's been running or waving his arms frantically trying to get his own attention.

It isn't as if his SEAL training hadn't prepared him for the horrors of war. In a six-month program that included its own Hell Week, where the dropout rate was as high as ninety percent, he'd withstood the tests of torture himself and knew that every man has an eventual breaking point. The key was holding out just short of it.

Among the methods used to teach him how to survive torture had been five nights of sleep deprivation and a handheld generator the size of a cell phone that when applied to his nipples made him lose control of all bodily functions.

So he'd arrived in the Middle East fully understanding the depths of depravity to which a human being could stoop in a quest to torture, demean, break.

And still, nothing really prepares you for its reality.

Eyes open, he stares up into the darkness of his bedroom, letting each word of the long memorized Code of Conduct for members of the US Armed Forces march through his mind.

I am an American, fighting in the forces which guard my country and our way of life. I am prepared to give my life in their defense.

I will never surrender of my own free will. If in command, I will never surrender the members of my command while they still have the means to resist.

If I am captured I will continue to resist by all means available. I will make every effort to escape and aid others to escape. I will accept neither parole nor special favors from the enemy.

If I become a prisoner of war, I will keep faith with my fellow prisoners. I will give no information nor take part in any action which might be harmful to my comrades. If I am senior, I will take command. If not, I will obey the lawful orders of those appointed over me and will back them up in every way.

When questioned, should I become a prisoner of war, I am required to give name, rank, service number and date of birth. I will evade answering further questions to the utmost of my ability. I will make no oral or written statements disloyal to my country and its allies or harmful to their cause.

I will never forget that I am an American, fighting for freedom, responsible for my actions, and dedicated to the principles which made my country free. I will trust in my God and in the United States of America.

During captivity, he had recited the code so many times that his brain had become programmed with each word, set on an endless cycle of repeat. It was the repetition of this code that saved his life. His determination to hang his will on every word.

He'd been one of four captured from his unit after a two-hour shootout on a blazing hot afternoon when they had finally surrendered in exchange for the life of another team member bleeding out in the center of it all. Their surrender had gotten him help, and he'd ended up in a German hospital recovering two days later while the four of them endured round after round of torture that made his SEAL training seem like child's play.

Each time they'd come for him, when his number had again risen in the line of order, Knox turned his mind to the code, hammering each word into his resistance like nails into a coffin. The words allowed him to make himself not present, to hang what was happening to him on a higher cause. He'd used it like anesthesia, so that his own screams had registered as if they were coming from far away, rising up out of someone else.

Lying here in the dark, those screams echo in his mind, and his eyes fly open. He doesn't want to see the memory on the back of his eyelids so he vaults out of bed, turns on the shower in the bathroom, and stands beneath the freezing spray until the screams are gone, and he can close his eyes without seeing himself in that torture room.

Only then does he get out of the shower, pull on some clothes, and head out of the apartment, hitting the sidewalk at a run. He doesn't stop until his watch beeps ten miles.

Mia

"A drowning man cannot be saved until he is utterly exhausted and ceases to make the slightest effort to save himself."
—Watchman Nee

IT WAS THE kind of perfect July day that made a person think life couldn't get much better.

At age ten, Mia was again beginning to believe that happiness wasn't something that had forever abandoned her and her sister. There had been plenty of days when she couldn't believe anything else. When it had felt as if not even the sunshine could penetrate the clouds of sadness that hung over them both.

But today, today, Mia had seen Emory smile at something Grace's mother said to her about a book she'd just finished reading. She really couldn't remember the last time she'd seen Emory smile out of the blue like that. Had it been before their parents were killed? She tried to think of when the last time would be, but all she could come up with were memories of when she was really little and Emory was a teenager. Maybe it had been the time she had let Mia try on her makeup, watching as she applied it herself and ended up looking more like a clown than the high-fashion model she'd been attempting to look like.

She decided then that it didn't matter when exactly. She was just glad to think that Emory might be happy again. Because if she could be happy, then maybe Mia could be too. Maybe that would make it all right not to feel guilty.

"Your sister's really pretty," Grace said from her spot beside Mia on the dock.

Mia dragged her toes through the warm lake water and said, "A lot prettier than I'll ever be."

"You're pretty too," Grace said.

"Thanks," Mia said. "But Emory looks like our mom. And she was beautiful."

"Do you miss her?"

"I miss her and my dad. But sometimes, I wonder if my memories about them are real. Or if they're just dreams I've had."

"I bet they're real," Grace said.

"It scares me that they'll all go away. And I won't have anything of them left."

Grace went quiet for a few moments, and then, "Maybe you could think of some special memories and go through them every now and then. Sort of like practicing the memories so they stay strong."

Mia glances at Grace and says, "You're really smart."

Grace shrugs. "I've thought about how hard it must be for you and Emory. Not to have your parents, I mean."

"Maybe it's been harder for Emory than for me," she said, glancing at her sister who is still talking with Grace's mom. "She kind of had to grow up overnight."

"She sure does love you," Grace said.

"Sometimes I wonder what would have happened to me if Emory hadn't been my sister."

"Well, she is, so you don't have to worry about that."

The two girls sat there in silence for a couple of minutes, glad for their friendship. At ten, Mia didn't take any of the people in her life for granted. She knew how one day everything seemed like it would last forever, and the next it could all go away.

"Wanna swim?" Grace asked, getting up from the dock and shucking off her jean shorts.

"Sure," Mia said, pulling off her coverup.

"One, two, three," Grace said. "Here I go!"

Mia watched as Grace dove headfirst into the water. She glanced at the life jackets a few feet away and then at Emory whose back was to her. She knew the rule was that she always had to wear a life jacket in the lake, but Grace hadn't, and just this once wouldn't hurt anything.

Wanting to jump in before Emory spotted her, Mia dove headfirst into the blue green water just out from the dock.

It felt amazing, cutting through the surface. She felt herself going down, down, down. She hadn't meant to dive so hard. Fear shot through her, and she wished she hadn't jumped off. Her head hit the bottom of the lake, and she opened her mouth in a scream, instantly choking on the water that started filling her lungs.

Disoriented, she tried to swim up but found herself hitting the dirt floor again.

Panic grabbed her by the throat, and the desire to breathe was almost more than she could resist. Her lungs felt like they had been pumped full of water, her chest so tight that she feared it would rip open beneath the pressure.

She began to flail with her arms and legs, her mind screaming with fear. She found the bottom of the lake with her feet and pushed off, reaching for the surface, for air.

She felt the hand grab her arm, and instead of latching on and letting it pull her to the top, she began to fight. Her lungs felt as if they were on fire. She kicked in an effort to break through the surface, grabbing onto the waist of the person trying to help her.

She opened her eyes and in the murky water could make out the pattern of Emory's bathing suit. It took a few seconds for Mia to realize she was preventing her sister from getting them to the top. She forced herself to quit fighting even though her brain screamed for her to climb over Emory.

They broke the surface then, and Mia could hear Emory coughing and gasping. And then she was coughing too, so hard that it felt as if her insides would come up through her throat.

She locked her arms around Emory's neck, holding on so tight that she pushed her sister beneath the surface.

Others were in the water now, Grace's mother, wearing a life jacket, and Grace, also wearing one. They each grabbed Mia's arms, pulling her away from Emory and dragging her toward the dock.

Mia was aware of Emory resurfacing, coughing and gasping. Every instinct screamed for her to continue fighting, but she was too exhausted. She let herself be dragged to the shore where Grace and her mom pulled her onto the sand. Grace's mom dove back into the water, swimming toward Emory and then helping her back to safety.

Once Emory was on the ground beside her, Grace's mom ran back to the dock, and Mia could hear her calling 911, pleading with the operator to send someone quickly.

Mia was so spent she could barely hold her eyes open. But she could see Emory's face through her squint, how pale she was and the way her chest heaved for air. Another kind of fear swept over her then, and she reached for her sister's hand, realizing that in addition to nearly drowning herself, she had almost drowned Emory.

"I'm sorry, Em," she said in a barely audible voice. "You saved me. I—"

"Shh," Emory soothed, linking their fingers together. "You're okay. We're okay."

Mia wanted to thank her, but she couldn't force another

word past her lips. She lay there, staring at her sister, imagining what would have happened if she had not come to her rescue, knowing she would now be on the bottom of the lake, staring straight up with her eyes open but unseeing.

~

IT'S THIS IMAGE that brings Mia upright from her position on the cold, stone floor. A scream is stuck in her throat, and she can't draw air into her lungs.

It was a dream. She'd been sleeping.

But the sensation of not being able to breathe is the same as the one she'd known drowning in that lake all those years ago. She opens her mouth and forces air in, grateful for the fact that she's not filling her lungs with water, but oxygen.

She presses her hands into the concrete, her back screaming now from her sleeping position on the hard floor. No blanket, no pillow, just the cold floor.

Tears well in her eyes, slide down her face, even as she hates herself for them. Something tells her this is what they want. They want her to break. To stop fighting. Accept whatever it is they have in store for her.

She wonders if Grace is nearby. Has she stopped fighting?

Is it inevitable? Can someone break your will simply by being determined to hold out longer than you?

She wonders how many days it has been since she's had food. The water comes through the window in the door at what seems like regular intervals. Just enough each time to keep her mouth from drying up to the point that she can't swallow.

She wonders if this tomb they have created for her is a slowed-down version of drowning. She thinks about the bottom of that lake, the terror she'd felt in imagining that she would find death there.

She feels the same terror now for the thought that she might find it here, in this dungeon-like room. She forces herself then to think of what Emory would do. Pictures her sister diving off the dock that July day to save her with no thought as to her own endangerment.

Is Emory looking for her now?

Of course she is.

Mia knows her sister. Knows how devoted she is.

Even if she doesn't deserve that devotion.

Mia feels a bone-deep shame for the way in which she's taken that devotion for granted. She vows then and there that if she makes it out of here alive, she will never again take Emory's love for granted.

Loneliness hits her like concrete being poured onto her chest. She starts to cry, even though she hates the undeniable evidence of her own weakness.

"Please don't give up on me, Emory," she says out loud. "Please keep looking. I don't want to die here. Please don't give up on me."

Laughter echoes from the other side of the door, sending a chill up Mia's spine. A woman's laugh. Amused. Indulgent?

Mia wraps her arms around her knees and covers her head with her arms. She will not cry. She will not. She. Will. Not.

The Proprietor

"There is no hunting like the hunting of man, and those who have hunted armed men long enough and liked it, never care for anything else thereafter."
—Ernest Hemingway

APPARENTLY, THE GIRL hasn't spotted the camera tucked behind the air vent in the ceiling.

She stands outside the door and listens to the silence the young girl has forced herself into. She studies her on the small screen attached to the door.

Tough, this one.

She doesn't mind that. In the long run, the girl will last far beyond those who give in early on. From an investment point of view, this is far preferable.

So much goes into the initial process. The breaking down of the will. Time being the most precious resource, of course. In these first days, the world is still looking for them, tracing every possible clue, connection, lead.

But she's seen the timeline often enough to know what begins to happen when the connections fall through, the leads don't pan out.

The girl is right to worry.

Whoever Emory is, whatever role she plays in the girl's life, her commitment to finding her will start to wilt like cut flowers in a glass vase. No matter how much you replenish the water, place them in a stream of sunlight, the flowers will die. Cut off from their life source, death is inevitable.

And so is the original charge of determination so

admirable in the families of the abducted. Hope is their life source, and when that begins to fade, the fire of their commitment reduces from flame to spark to cinder.

But the girl can't know that. And so she will continue counting on rescue. Holding onto her resistance, as if her family will be able to feel that, to know that she is waiting on them to come for her, that she will never give in to what is expected of her here.

There is a very different truth awaiting her though.

She walks to the end of the hall, stares at the monitor on the door and the very different picture provided to her here.

The other girl is eating from the plate of food brought to her this morning. Two large, glazed donuts and a tall glass of milk. Her expression is one of extreme gratitude, and she can see the girl has already begun the descent into submission.

Very good.

Soon enough, this one will be ready to release from the trap and introduce to her new world.

She glances down the hall at the other door. Her friend will take a bit longer. But she'll get there. Eventually, they always do.

Knox

"But I do nothing upon myself, and yet I am my own
executioner."
—John Donne

IT'S THE SECOND time he's been called into Chief Parker's office in as many days, and no one needs to tell him there's not going to be a positive outcome.

Knox takes a seat in front of the chief's desk. "You wanted to see me?"

"I tried," she says, giving him a long, assessing look. "There's video, apparently."

This gets his attention. "What do you mean?"

"There was a camera in the apartment. In the bedroom to be exact. Apparently, Senator Hagan was on to his wife's philandering."

He knows this should bother him, wonders why it doesn't. He weighs how to answer. "And?"

"I was told to fire you. From high enough up that I'm risking my own position to debate that decision."

"So why would you debate it?" he asks without letting his eyes waver from hers.

"I have no idea. But there's something I know about you, Helmer. I just don't know the why."

"What's that?"

"When you start getting a little too good at something, you hijack it with self-sabotage."

He tries not to roll his eyes. "Was a psych degree a prerequisite for your job, Chief?"

"No," she says evenly. "But I know what it takes to make it to the level you reached as a SEAL. Creative thinking and teamwork under ridiculously high-stress and high-risk situations. Most of the missions you were a part of probably made what you do here look like child's play. Are you bored, Helmer?"

"No, ma'am," he says quietly.

"You're up for a promotion."

"It wasn't my intention to mess that up."

"You sure about that?"

He starts to nod, then stops himself because, all of a sudden, he isn't sure at all. Does he really want this job? Is this where he'd imagined himself ending up?

He's been with the department for four years, seen most every twisted crime the city's been able to throw out and, until now, hasn't questioned whether this is where he belongs or not.

"I don't know," he says quietly.

"Well, maybe this is your chance to figure it out. Higher-ups have agreed to six weeks suspension without pay. That's the best I could do. Why don't you take the time to figure out whether or not you want to come back?"

"Guess there's no changing your mind," he says.

"It's not up to me," she answers.

He stands, pushing aside his own self-flagellation long enough to show appreciation. "Thanks, Chief. I don't deserve your loyalty."

"You could change that if you wanted to."

He doesn't share her optimism.

"Give John your notes on the Benson-Marshall case. I'll see you in six weeks."

At his desk, he opens drawers, pulling out anything that seems necessary to his surviving his time away. There isn't much, but he throws what there is into a leather backpack and heads for the elevator without letting himself meet eyes with anyone he'll have to offer an explanation to.

It's only after the doors slide closed that he slams a palm against the side wall.

The Senator

"Power does not corrupt. Fear corrupts. Perhaps the fear
of a loss of power."
—John Steinbeck

IT PAID TO have friends in law enforcement. Or at least people there who were a little afraid to cross him.

He could have gotten Helmer fired. But that was the kind of thing that created permanent enemies. He made a policy of avoiding that when possible. The suspension was good enough. He'd been right about the military background. Navy SEAL, in fact. The detective probably thought he deserved the suspension. Man of honor and all that.

At least he's not likely to have a second go-round with Savannah. And if he does, well, he can come up with something worse than getting fired. Anyway, he has bigger things on his plate to deal with right now.

A knock sounds at the office door. He closes the file he'd made on Helmer and slides it inside his desk drawer. "Come in."

The door opens, and Will Arrington steps into the room. He's dressed in a crisp Armani suit, his style as effortless as it is enviable. "You wanted to see me, Senator?"

"I did. Thanks for giving me a few minutes. Come in. Sit down."

At age thirty-one, Will Arrington is the youngest elected member of the Senate. He'd graduated at the top of his Harvard class and makes every decision put before him as if the survival of America depends on it. With his GQ good looks and Upper East Side enunciation, he's received more requests for appearances on MSNBC than most of the other senators combined. And he takes it all in stride, as if it is his birthright.

Tom pushes aside the unproductive resentment and says, "Will, I wanted to talk with you about the upcoming vote on that expedited DNA analysis."

Will takes a seat in the chair closest to the desk. He leans forward with his elbows on his knees, his expression one of deep concentration. "I read through the company presentation again. Have to say I still have some reservations."

Tom tries not to exhale the sigh threatening to rise up out of him. "What reservations?" he asks, keeping his voice as even and light as possible.

"The reliability of the results, actually. Previous methods proved their accuracy. And because DNA evidence can send a man or woman to prison or free them, our decision seems a critical one."

"I couldn't agree more," Tom says, leaning back in his chair and making a tent of his fingers. "That's why I met a third time with experts from DNA Answers. They are cutting edge. And I believe several steps ahead of the next company in line."

"I wish I could agree."

The two men meet eyes, and not for the first time, Tom wonders if all is as it appears with young Senator Arrington. If his agenda is as pure as it is presented to be. Somehow, some way, he's going to have to convince him to vote for this bill. He thinks of his last meeting with the founder of DNA Answers. Of the Cayman account in which he will find a transfer of funds, significant funds, if he can bring Arrington to a yes vote.

He'd like to think he has the time to bring him around

the old-fashioned way, some long conversations over a few lunches in the Senate dining room. But the vote is coming up, and he doesn't have that kind of time. No, he'll have to settle for another method of bringing Arrington around to his way of thinking.

Something simple, but tried and true.

Blackmail.

Emory

I WAKE TO the realization that it's Day Three since Mia disappeared.

Three days.

I reach for my cell phone on the nightstand by the bed, tap the screen to see if there had been any messages during the night.

No notifications. No texts. No calls.

I hurl the phone to the foot of the bed and stare at the ceiling, frustration churning in my stomach like acid.

How did this happen? How can I be lying here in my bed when Mia is . . . I don't know how to finish that.

Because I don't know where she is. How she is. If she's alive or . . .

I don't let myself finish that thought. I can't. It's too unbearable to even think.

Pounce meows from the open doorway. I pat the side of the bed, and he trots over and sails up beside me. He'd slept in Mia's room again last night.

I rub his soft back, and he arches against my leg, meowing softly.

"I'm sorry," I say, picking him up and wrapping my arms around him. Pounce is not a cat who likes to be hugged by anyone but Mia. This morning, though, he seems to know that I need it as much as he does. I press my forehead against his neck, and the sobs that rise up out of me will no longer be denied. I cry until I have no more tears to cry. God love him, Pounce tolerates my grief, and I rub my hand across his tear-drenched neck.

I have never in my life felt so helpless. I have no idea what to do. Who to turn to. How can I do nothing? Go in to work as if my life has not been upended and my baby sister will be home anytime?

I can't.

I know my residency is at stake, but I cannot return to life as normal.

I decide then that I will call Dr. Maverick as soon as I've had a decent cup of coffee and cleared the anguish from my voice.

What else? *What else* can I do?

I glance at the stack of papers I left on the nightstand the night before. I pick up the paper on top and glance down the list of recommended things to do when a loved one has gone missing. I've done all but the last one: hire a detective.

Is it time for that? What if the police find out I've hired someone? Will that lessen their efforts to find Mia?

My stomach drops at the thought. But I can't leave this box unchecked.

How do you find a private detective?

I have no idea.

My phone rings. I jump to a sitting position, grabbing it from the foot of the bed. Pounce yowls and leaps to the floor, prancing out of the room with his tail straight in the air.

I don't recognize the number and answer with a question in my voice. But I recognize the caller's voice immediately. "Detective Helmer."

"Sorry if I'm calling too early."

"No," I answer quickly, and then more frantic. "Have you found Mia?"

"Ah, no," he says. "I'm sorry. It's not that."

I release a sigh of incredible disappointment. "Do you have any leads?"

"As of yesterday, no. I didn't mean to upset you. I just wanted to let you know that another detective will be handling your case starting this morning."

"What? But why won't you be working the case?" I think of the time a new detective will need to get up to speed, and a fresh wave of despair floods through me.

"I'm going to be on leave for six weeks."

Something about this statement strikes me as odd. "Personal leave?"

"Of a sort."

I realize then it must not be voluntary. "Oh."

"I wanted to let you know." He hesitates. "I didn't want you to think I just walked off and left the case."

I try to process everything he's said. All that he knows about the details of the disappearance of Mia and Grace and how frustrating it is to think of throwing it out the window. And then I remember the private detective box I haven't yet checked. "Detective Helmer?"

"Yeah?"

"Since you have six weeks of free time on your hands, would you be willing to work for me? Privately?"

If his silence is any indication, I have shocked him. "I'm not licensed for private work, Dr. Benson."

"Would it have to be official?"

"I'm afraid so."

"But I found this list of things to do when someone you love goes missing, and I did all of them yesterday except the last one. Hire a private detective. When you called, I was just trying to figure out where to start, how to find someone. The phone rang, and it was you. Surely, that must mean something."

"Dr. Benson . . ."

"It's Emory. And please. Detective Helmer, you already know as much or more than anyone involved. To think of someone else starting over when she's already been missing . . . this is day three." I start to cry then. I don't want to. I want to plead with him from a point of strength, but my reserves are at rock bottom. I try to speak again, but a sob is stuck in my throat, and I make this awful choking sound.

"Hey," he says.

"I can pay you," I say quickly. "I still have some of the money our parents left us. They would want me to spend it on finding Mia."

Silence hangs from the other side of the phone, and I am wondering if he has hung up when he finally speaks. "I can't take money from you, Dr. Benson, Emory. I'll follow through on the leads I was working on my own. But I can't promise you anything. I would be doing you a disservice if I told you anything other than the truth."

"And that is?"

"We're going on seventy-two hours. And every hour that passes lessens the likelihood that your sister will be found."

Rage bubbles up inside me, and I want to scream that he doesn't know what he's talking about. But I know that he does. And so I force my voice into a neutral tone when I say, "Please. Can you start this morning? Now."

He's silent for another string of moments, and then he says, "I'll pick you up in thirty minutes."

This part surprises me. But I don't let him hear that in my voice when I say, "I'll be ready."

Knox

"One of the most important things you can do on this earth is to let people know they are not alone."
—Shannon L. Alder

HE NEEDS TO have his head examined.

This is what he's telling himself when he pulls into Emory Benson's driveway thirty minutes after their phone call. A near bark of laughter erupts from his chest, because he does have his head examined on a weekly basis with Dr. Thomason. What more proof does he need that those sessions are a complete waste of time?

He wipes the smile from his face under the realization that Dr. Benson's psychiatric experience could be used against him if he's sitting here smiling like a lunatic when she comes out.

She steps through the front door just then, locking it behind her and then walking to the Jeep, looking at it as if she's surprised not to see the department sedan he'd driven here before.

She opens the passenger door and climbs in, and suddenly, he's wondering if he should have gotten out and opened it for her. Okay, that's crossing the line for sure.

"Good morning," he says.

"Hi," she says. "So where are we going?"

She's brusque and to the point, and he pulls his thoughts back from the realization that she smells like some clean spa smell that fills the Jeep in a nice way. Her hair is wet and pulled back in a ponytail. She's wearing jeans and running shoes and a light-blue, collared shirt. She doesn't look anywhere near old enough to be a psychiatrist. Even one who's still a resident. "Ah, I wanted to take another look at the area where you found her phone. Let's start there with you showing me the exact spot."

"Why?" she asks. "Surely, the police have thoroughly covered that?"

"I'd like to make sure nothing was missed."

She stares out the window and then says, "I don't know whether to be hopeful or discouraged by the fact that you think it's a possibility."

He glances in the rearview mirror and reverses out of the driveway. He stays at the edge of the residential speed limit, keeping his view straight ahead. "Here's a fact about all investigations. They're conducted by human beings. And human beings make mistakes. Sometimes, it's the smallest clue that solves a case. I heard a football coach say once that you never know which play will win the game. So you play them all like they're the winning one. I tend to look at evidence the same way."

She visibly processes what he's said, then nods once in understanding.

They drive in silence until he reaches the Capital Beltway.

"You've had cases like this before?" she asks, her gaze leveled at the windshield.

"Yeah."

"How many?"

"Five."

"Were they all solved?"

He hears the hope at the end of the question and wishes for a moment that he didn't have to crush it. "Four of them."

She swings to him, and he already knows her focus is on the one they didn't find. "What happened?" she asks.

He settles over the memory for a moment, feeling his own reluctance to go there. "Thirteen-year-old girl waiting for the school bus. The little sister said two men in a black car pulled over and grabbed the older one. The younger sister ran back to the house to get help, but they were out of sight by the time the mother got to the bus stop."

He senses her stiffen beside him.

"Does anyone know . . . ?" She breaks off there.

"No," he says, shaking his head.

"How can someone just disappear?" she asks, her voice barely audible.

He has no answer that will do anything other than crush whatever hope she has left. "It depends on why they were taken."

"You mean whether the abductor continues to have a purpose for them or not?"

He nods.

"I keep thinking about those three girls in Cleveland who were missing for ten years. Can you imagine being the 911 person who took that call?"

"No. Some people might not have taken her seriously."

"After ten years, they still had enough fight left in them to take a chance to go for help."

"They never gave up," he says.

"But that long. How did their families survive?"

"I don't know."

"Do you think they believed they could still be alive?"

"Honestly?"

"Yes."

"No."

She draws in a quick breath, as if he's stabbed her with

something sharp. The truth can be like that. He should know. "I don't blame them," he says quietly.

"What do you mean?"

"Human beings need resolution to go on. It's the waiting, the not knowing what's going to happen that does us in."

He can feel her desire to reject what he's said.

She studies the blurred buildings outside the window as the Jeep rolls down the Beltway. He dips in and out of the traffic lanes, eager to get where they're going.

"What sets apart a survivor from someone who doesn't survive?" she asks in a low voice.

He considers the question, not wanting to give her a flip answer. "It's probably a lot of different factors."

"Indulge me."

"The most important thing is whether the victim is a fighter or not. Is she?"

"Yes," she says without hesitation. "She is. But I've always been her protector, and I hope I haven't—"

"Don't," he interrupts. "I'm sure you've taught her everything she would need to know."

"Maybe I've been there too much. Stepped in when I should have let her work it out."

"It's a delicate balance, that parenting thing."

"With an eighteen-year-old taking over the job, I have no doubt she got shorted."

"But you were there for her. What if you hadn't been?"

The shadow that crosses her face tells him it's something she's considered. "I can't imagine."

"I'm sure she couldn't either."

She glances at him, and he lets his eyes meet hers for a second before turning back to the road. In that brief flash of connection, he realizes she's let the veil down, her pain clearly visible. "Tell me about the friend," he says.

"Grace," she says, the name little more than a whisper.

"She's a follower. Mia is the leader in the friendship. But it seems to work for them."

"They'll separate them," he says. At Emory's stricken glance, he shakes his head. "Sorry. I have a bad habit of voicing my thoughts out loud."

Tears well in her eyes, and he could kick himself for the visual he's given her. "Emory—"

"It's okay. I want your honesty. I have nothing to gain from being told anything that isn't true."

Traffic starts to pool in front of the Jeep. He brakes, slowing the Jeep to a crawl. "Did Mia mention anyone unusual in the days before her disappearance?"

Emory bites her lower lip, and he sees her concentration, her desire not to give him an answer until she's considered the breadth of her memory. "The only new person in her life was a guy at school. She thought he was cute. A football player. She hasn't been too interested in dating so my ears perked up at that, but she never mentioned anything that would make me worry."

"Do you do that a lot?"

"What?" she asks, swinging her gaze to mine.

"Worry."

She shrugs. "More than Mia would like."

"Did . . . does she keep things from you because you worry?"

As if she realizes where he's going with this, she says, "I think she understands why I'm protective."

"But would she keep things from you if she thought you might worry about her if you knew?"

"Maybe," she concedes.

"So you can't be sure that what you know of her daily habits, routines, choices is definitely what you believe them to be?"

"Detective Helmer," she says, her voice iron-edged now,

"why is it starting to feel like I'm under investigation here?"

"You are," he says, following through on her desire for honesty. "Anyone I can find who has any connection to your sister is under investigation, as far as I'm concerned. I'm connecting dots here. And I'll follow whichever dot leads to the next one. That is the only chance of connecting them all so that we have any hope of ever seeing a complete picture."

"How did this happen?" she asks softly, shaking her head. "Is life really this random? Do any of the efforts we make to drive the speed limit, eat the right foods, pick the right guy, never run on the jogging path alone, does any of it matter at all? Or is the asteroid headed right toward us the whole time so that none of the things we do ever matter at all?"

He draws in a breath, blows it out slowly. He'd like to reassure her, tell her he believes those efforts do matter. But the truth is, he's seen too much evidence to the contrary.

"That's all right," she says, holding up a hand. "You don't need to say anything. I should know the answer to my own question. My parents were two of those people who tried to live within the lines. And one driver who decided to get under the wheel after a night partying with his buddies obliterated all of their efforts in a single moment."

"I'm sorry," he says, because what else is there to say?

"So maybe the truth is we're all living under this grand illusion that we're in charge of our lives and what happens to us. I'm working on another year of education in a field where I'm supposed to end up being someone who tells other people how they can regain control of their lives. How crazy is that?" She laughs a short laugh, and then the laughter flows up and out of her. She leans forward with her arms wrapped around her waist and tries to stop. But she can't.

He's debating what to say when the laughter instantly changes to a sob, and her shoulders begin to shake hard. And she's crying, as he's never heard anyone cry before.

He takes the next exit, staying to the right until he finds a parking lot to turn into. He pulls in a spot and cuts the engine, unhooking his seat belt and turning a knee toward her. He feels awkward and unsure what to do. "Has anyone hugged you since this happened?" he asks finally.

She looks up, tears still flowing. She shakes her head a little, as if the realization has just occurred to her.

He doesn't give himself or her time to think about it. He unsnaps her seat belt and reaches for her, pulling her up against him and locking his arms around her. She holds herself stiff, as if giving in to the comfort will label her incapable of dealing with what she's facing.

"It's okay," he says, resting his hand at the center of her back.

She holds out for another fifteen seconds or so, but when she breaks, it is instant, and she folds herself against him, burying her face against his shirt. The sobs are back, and he understands that she has absolutely no control over them. That all the pain she's been keeping behind the dam between her heart and reality has broken. He absorbs the pain, holding her as tight as she'll let him.

Birdsong drifts in through his lowered window, along with traffic sounds and the muted laughter of children somewhere nearby. He's reminded of how easily the world goes on, despite the pain and those times when people have no choice but to stop and release it.

Her grief is a tangible force inside the Jeep, and he feels the knot in his throat thicken. As her sobs soften, he becomes aware of the woman in his arms. The clean scent of her hair, the feel of her cheek against his chest. His body stirs, and he shoots himself with a mental cussword. He's the one who stiffens now, and she takes it as a signal to pull away, comfort session over.

She wipes her hands across her face and then reluctantly lets her gaze meet his. "You're kind," she says.

He turns in his seat, facing forward. "No, I'm not," he says. "Believe me."

"That's what you want the world to think."

"Hard to take off the psychiatrist hat, I guess," he says.

"I don't need to be a psychiatrist to figure that out."

"Look. That was inappropriate. I shouldn't have—"

"Thank you," she says. "It felt good to let another human being feel what I'm feeling."

He looks at her then, sees the earnestness in her blue eyes, and tells himself not to make a big deal out of this. So he's human. Maybe he'd forgotten.

They sit in silence for a string of awkward moments. Awkward for him, anyway. He tries to put this outing back in professional territory. "We should get going," he says, turning the key and starting the Jeep.

"Why are you on leave?" she asks.

The question surprises him, and apparently, he doesn't do a very good job of hiding it.

"Did you have a choice?" she adds.

"No," he says, shaking his head. "I didn't."

She stares at him, waiting for him to go on.

"I agreed to go home with the wrong wife of the wrong senator," he says, scrutinizing her face so that he doesn't miss the shock that flashes in her eyes.

"Oh," she says, looking away as if she realizes she's bitten off more than she knows what to do with. "Well, that's—"

"Not what you expected," he finishes.

"No. It isn't."

"What did you expect?"

She looks back at him, shrugs. "Defying an order from your superior? Late to work one too many times?"

He smiles a little at the sarcasm in her voice. It doesn't fit her. "They probably would have been better choices."

"Yeah. Why would you—" She breaks off there, holding a hand in the air. "Sorry. None of my business."

"She offered," he answers. "I like sex and beautiful women."

Her face suffuses with color. "You're very direct, aren't you?"

"What purpose would it serve to be otherwise?"

"I suppose I did ask the question."

"You did."

She leans against the door, studying him. "Have you ever been married?"

"Yes."

"Are you now?"

"No."

"Why?"

"She deserved better than me. I think we'll be better off sticking to Mia's case and leaving the personal stuff out of it."

"Fine," she says, folding her arms and staring straight through the windshield.

They drive the rest of the distance to the festival site in complete silence.

Emory

"You simply have to put one foot in front of the other and keep going. Put blinders on and plow right ahead."
—George Lucas

TO CALL THE remainder of the drive awkward would be as much of an understatement as I can come up with. I can still feel the heat in my cheeks, even as I realize how much Knox Helmer probably enjoyed putting it there.

The field where the festival had been held is now empty, flattened grass and a few bits of trash the only remaining evidence of its existence.

Detective Helmer pulls his Jeep off the road, cuts the engine, and says, "Can you show me the exact spot where you found her phone?"

"Yes," I say, getting out and scanning the area to make sure my memory does not mislead. I walk along the edge of the road for a hundred yards or so and then step into the tall grass and cover the steps to where two, small, blue flags mark the spot. "Here," I say.

"That's accurate?" he asks, glancing at the flags.

"Yes."

"Given that the phone was off in the weeds away from the road, it's not likely that she lost it here. Maybe someone ditched it after grabbing the girls."

The words send a chill straight through me. As if he realizes what he's just said, he looks at me and says, "Sorry. Thinking out loud again."

"You think out loud," I say.

"Surprised they didn't take the time to destroy it so that it couldn't be tracked."

"Why do you think they didn't?"

"Someone could have been coming. A car. A person walking by. And they needed to go or get caught."

A tight band stretches around my chest, squeezing out all the air. A fresh image of Mia and Grace, terrified, flashes through my mind, and I draw in a deep tear of air.

The detective drops to his knees, and runs his hands through the grass where I'd found the phone. I drop down a few yards away and start to feel along the ground too. "I assume we're looking for anything that might serve as a clue?" I ask.

"Sometimes, it's the tiniest imaginable hole that sinks the ship."

I search in one direction, while he takes the opposite. I feel at the base of the grass, digging my fingers into the dirt, feeling increasingly desperate to find something, anything, that might give a hint, some sort of direction to help find Mia.

By the time we circle back around to each other, I am sweating and clawing at the grass, tears of frustration wetting my cheeks.

"Hey," he says, reaching out to cover my right hand with his. "It's okay. I didn't expect that we'd find anything. But I had to look."

I lean back on my knees, wiping my hand across my eyes. "I feel hopeless. How can someone just be gone in an instant? With no evidence of what happened to them?"

He holds my gaze for a long moment. "Someone knows. There are clues. It's a matter of being persistent enough to keep looking until one of them surfaces."

"And what determines persistence?"

"Time and money."

"I'll spend everything I have to find her. But what if it's not enough?" I hear the panic in my own voice.

"Let's just take this one step at a time. Not think about anything except the one I'm currently exploring."

"So what's next?" I ask, pinching my left palm hard so I won't cry.

"The security footage for the night of the festival. I've seen it, but I'd like to get a copy so I can go through it frame by frame."

"How do we do that?"

"Fortunately, I've got friends in high places," he says.

~

HE MAKES A call, and I try not to listen while he talks with the person on the other end. There's some mention of him owing the person a cold one, and when he ends the call, he turns to me and says, "We'll need a computer to view the video."

"We can use my desktop at my house."

"I'll just need to access my email so I can download the file."

"No problem."

Back in the Jeep, I force my eyes away from the spot where I'd found Mia's phone, not wanting to see in my mind all the various scenarios I've imagined as to how it got there. I lean my head against the seat and close my eyes, thankful when music fills the interior, and I hang on each word of the Train song until calm descends enough that I can breathe.

We say nothing at all for the remainder of the drive, and he pulls up in front of the house. I get out, unlock the front door, and tell him to come in.

It's mid-afternoon by now, and the house has lost some of its light. I flick on lamps and show him to my office where the desktop is. Pounce saunters through, greeting us with a yowl of disappointment when he sees that we aren't Mia.

"I'm sorry," I say, bending down to rub behind his ears. I tap the computer keyboard, tap in my password, and the screen pops to life. And then to the detective, "Make yourself comfortable. Can I get you something to drink?"

"Water would be good."

"Be right back," I say.

I go into the kitchen, Pounce on my heels, and pull a bottle of water from the drawer of the refrigerator. I grab one for myself and walk back to the office. I hand the detective one of the bottles and open mine, taking a long sip. I watch as he opens the email, clicks on the Dropbox link, and waits for it to load. I can feel my heart pounding and wish for a moment that I could fast forward to the part where he finds something, sees someone who will have the answer.

The clock at the top of the recording indicates 5:38 p.m. I point to it. "Is that the day of the festival?"

"Yes, that's when they began the surveillance." He glances up at me. "This is going to take a while."

"I can help," I say.

"I'd like to go through it alone initially."

"Oh. Okay."

"I'll let you know if I have any questions."

"Sure," I say, backing up and then bending over to pick up Pounce. He lets out a meow of protest, but I tuck him under my arm and close the door behind us.

In the kitchen, I set him in front of his food bowl, reach for the jar where we keep his kibble, and fill it halfway. He concedes to my peace offering and crunches in semi-contentment. I stand at the sink, my hands clenching the tiled edge and stare out the window, where cars continue to pass on the street in front of the house, the postal worker continues to deliver the mail, and the grass continues to grow.

How can everything go on as if Mia has not disappeared, as if she will arrive home at any moment with some logical explanation for where she's been and why she's had me so worried?

I don't want to believe that the world is this indifferent, but how can I deny the evidence? I think of the patients I've worked with whose life no longer makes sense. Of how I've believed that it could make sense again, despite my own evidence to the contrary.

My cell buzzes on the countertop next to the sink. I glance at the screen. Not recognizing the number, a jolt of hope stabs through me, and I stab the answer button. "Hello?"

"Dr. Benson."

The voice startles me. "Dr. Maverick. Hello."

"I hope I'm not getting you at a bad time. I just got word of what's happened with your sister. I'm so sorry."

"Thank you," I say.

"I received your message about taking some time off. You do what you need to do. Your spot will be waiting."

This surprises me, I have to admit. "I appreciate that. I would understand if it wasn't possible."

"Don't worry about it, okay?"

Not knowing what else to say, I again manage, "Thank you."

"Would you like some company?"

The question surprises me, and I say, "I'm sorry?"

"I'm actually in your area. I have some time if you'd like to talk."

I'm not sure how to take the offer. A psychiatrist offering help to a colleague who's experiencing something horrible? Or maybe I hadn't imagined the spark in the coffee lounge the night Mia had disappeared? Regardless of the reason behind it, I don't want to sound unappreciative. "Dr. Maverick, you don't have to—"

"I'd like to," he says, and I can hear in his voice that he really would.

"Okay," I say, and then I realize I've forgotten about Detective Helmer. "When—"

"Be there in ten minutes," he says and clicks off.

I drop my head back and stare at the ceiling, trying to imagine myself in the living room having a session with Dr. Maverick while Detective Helmer inadvertently listens from behind the closed door of my office.

Pounce winds himself between my calves. I reach down and run a hand across his spine. "This should be interesting," I say.

I walk back to the office, stick my head inside and say, "Anything you need?"

Detective Helmer responds without looking up from the computer screen. "No. Thanks. All good."

I close the door and hope he'll remain this focused until Dr. Maverick leaves. I'm not even sure why, but the thought of the two of them meeting makes me uncomfortable.

The doorbell rings, redefining "ten minutes." I run a hand across my hair, remembering that I hadn't put on makeup this morning. Just as well. I would have already cried it all off by now anyway.

I open the door to find the very tall, very handsome Dr. Maverick looking down at me with sympathetic eyes. "Hello," he says.

"Hi." I step back, waving him inside. "You're kind to come."

I lead the way to the living room where we take opposite ends of the sofa. "Have you learned anything?"

"Nothing," I say, shaking my head. "She and her best friend Grace were supposed to come home after a music festival they went to. They've just disappeared."

My voice breaks on the last word, and, despite every intention I'd had of being strong, the tears start up again. All of a sudden, he's sliding across the sofa and pulling me into his arms. I know I should pull away, that a line is being crossed here. It's the second time today that I've been given comfort from a member of the opposite sex, and I'd like to say I'm above needing it, but I'm not.

He rubs a hand across the back of my hair and says in a low voice near my ear, "I realize my coming here was a questionable thing to do, but I understand what you're going through."

"You do?"

He nods, and then, in a slightly distant voice, "When I was nineteen, my younger brother came to Princeton to visit me one weekend. I took him out with some of my buddies for a night on the town. He was sixteen, and I was hoping he would apply to Princeton. My mom said he'd seemed kind of down for most of the school year and thought it might help to visit me. We went to a party, and he said he had a headache and wanted to go back to my dorm room. I didn't think anything of it and told him I'd be back in an hour or two."

My stomach drops as his voice lowers, and I somehow know that something horrible is coming. I want to stop him, but I can feel his need to go on.

"I found him. He hung himself on my bathroom door."

Shock rips through me, and I pull back, look into his face and see the deepest kind of grief there. "Oh, no. I'm so sorry."

He studies me for a few moments, and I cannot imagine how hard it must have been to share what he just told me.

"It's the greatest regret of my life. I would give anything to be able to redo that night. Have the chance to see it all differently."

I press my hand to his arm, squeeze once.

"In hindsight, the signs were there. He had talked to me a few times about things feeling hopeless. He said he felt like he was a burden to our mom who had raised us without my dad. I thought it was just normal teenage stuff. Problems with friends at school." He shakes his head a little. "I didn't see it."

"I know how hard it is not to blame yourself, but we both know that once someone has committed to the idea of taking their lives, they don't want anyone to stop them."

"Yes."

"Is that why you became a psychiatrist?"

He shrugs. "Clichéd as it sounds now, I thought I could help others avoid the pain my family went through."

"And I know you have. Countless others."

He gives me a long look, and I recognize in him my recent thoughts of whether we can ever really help people get through the worst that life has to offer. But neither of us says it. Maybe it is too painful an admission, given our line of work.

"Are the police making any headway?" he asks.

"To be honest, I don't know," I say. "I've done every recommended thing I could find to do when someone is missing. I've even hired a private detective."

"That's good," he says. "Smart to have one person dedicated to doing everything possible."

As if on cue, the door to the office opens, and Detective Helmer steps out. Instantly, I slide away from Dr. Maverick, noting his questioning gaze collide with the detective's.

"Ah," I say, standing, "Dr. Maverick, this is Detective Helmer."

Helmer walks across the room and sticks a hand out. They shake. Neither says anything right away, and I can see them sizing each other up.

"I work at Johns Hopkins with Dr. Benson," Dr. Maverick says, holding Helmer's gaze.

"Dr. Maverick is the head of the department," I say. "He came by about Mia." As soon as I say it, I wonder why I feel the need to explain his presence.

"Yes," he says, taking a step back. "I should get going. I don't want to interrupt your work on the case."

Helmer doesn't say anything, merely glances from Maverick to me and back again.

"Well," Dr. Maverick says, moving toward the door. "Take whatever time you need, Dr. Benson. Your job will be waiting for you."

I follow him out, thanking him again as we step outside onto the stoop. "It was incredibly nice of you to come by."

He glances over my shoulder, and I resist the urge to look back and see if Helmer is watching us.

Once he backs the black Mercedes out of the driveway, I step inside and close the door behind me.

"The doctor makes house calls?"

I force myself to meet his slightly mocking grin head-on and say, "Is that a problem?"

"He's a little old for you, isn't he?"

"He's my boss," I say, folding my arms across my chest and refusing to yield any ground. "But do you really feel qualified to be giving this lecture? All things considered, I mean."

He raises an eyebrow, and she sees the touché in his eyes and feels a ridiculous gratitude for the point in her column.

"There's something I want to show you," he says, and then turns and walks back to the office.

Knox

"The most confused you will ever get is when you try to convince your heart and spirit of something your mind knows is a lie."
—Shannon L. Alder

WHAT THE HELL?

Knox takes the chair in front of the computer and gives himself a silent berating.

Had he really just said that? What business was it of his if Emory Benson dated her boss?

None.

So what was up with the hair-trigger reaction?

He hears her footsteps behind him and decides he's not up for answering his own questions.

Without looking over his shoulder, he points at the computer screen and says, "There. That's your sister, right?"

She steps in close, leaning forward to stare at the screen, and then, with the breath catching in her throat, "Yes. Yes, it is."

Her voice is so low, he can barely hear the response. He glances at her face, sees that all color has drained from it. "I've been able to spot her and Grace in four different frames. I've also noticed the man in the gray baseball cap in three of those frames."

He can feel her stiffen beside him. "That's not a coincidence, is it?" she asks.

"Probably not," he says.

He clicks on the man's face, enlarges the screen. "His

features distort when I zoom in. The only thing I can make out is the logo on his hat."

"What is it?" she asks.

"Carlos Garcia."

"Is that a brand?"

I click over to the webpage where I've already found it online and read, "Streetwear brand Carlos Garcia offers the coolest everyday wear for kids looking to make a statement. T-shirts, jeans, backpacks make up a line of highly desirable clothing."

She visibly swallows and says, "Why would he be following them?"

"It could be a coincidence," he says.

"But you don't think so?"

He doesn't say anything for several seconds, and then, "Probably not."

"How can we find out who he is?" she asks, panic now edging her voice. "Is there some kind of facial recognition software—"

"Not with photos this blurred," he says, shaking his head.

"What then?" she pleads, pressing her hand to his shoulder.

He looks up at her, sees the warring emotions of hope and despair and struggles with which one to encourage her to latch on to. "I'll work on the hat label. I'll look into the DC stores that might carry it. Pay them a visit and see if anyone recognizes the guy in the photo."

Hope flares in her eyes, despite my unwillingness to build this into something more than it might end up being.

"Have you already looked up the stores?"

"I found three," he says. "All in downtown DC"

"Can we go now?" she asks.

"Maybe I should do this on my own."

"Please," she says. "I want to go. I'll go crazy if I stay here waiting to hear something."

"It could end up being nothing," he says.

"Detective Helmer. This is the first glimmer of even a hint at what might have happened to Mia and Grace. You don't need to protect me from hope. I realize how fragile it is."

He stares up at her, fully aware that he should refuse to let her go. There's something about her that interferes with his judgment, the way police radar scramblers mix a portion of the signal with background clutter, confusing the computer inside the radar gun. He's not sure if his own signals are strictly about the job at hand or something they shouldn't have anything at all to do with. But as strong as the voice telling him not to take her is, he finds himself saying, "Most of the leads we follow don't pan out. I need to know you understand that."

"I understand."

He picks up the images and addresses he's already printed out and says, "Then let's go."

Mia

"Life is about how much you can take and keep fighting, how much you can suffer and keep moving forward."
—Anderson Silva

SHE HASN'T EATEN since the night of the festival. What was it that she and Grace had eaten there and loved so much? They had told Emory about it when they'd FaceTimed.

It scares her that she can't remember now.

Mia presses her hand to her stomach, noticing that it is no longer growling in complaint, as if it has finally accepted that food is not coming, and it won't do any good to put out a request.

Her mouth is so dry she can barely swallow. It's the water she's missing most. The thought of food actually makes her nauseated. What she would give for a huge glass of cold water though.

But she won't let herself touch the one sitting by the door. They have been replacing it on a regular basis, ice cubes visible through the glass, as if they know she will eventually concede and down it.

So far, she has not. Something tells her that as soon as she gives in to accepting their food and water, she is theirs.

And that is something she will never willingly be. She would rather die first.

She's beginning to realize that might actually happen.

She tries to remember what day it is. How long she's

been here. But her brain can't seem to figure it out. Day three. Five? Or is it longer?

She's wearing the same clothes she'd arrived here in, and she hasn't had a shower. Her hair feels oily, and she shrinks from the smell of her own perspiration.

What was it the man standing guard outside her room had said? "It will be much easier for you once you start cooperating. Wouldn't you like for life to be nice again? A warm shower with lots of soap and shampoo. A hot meal of your favorite food. All you have to do is tell me what it is, and I will get it for you."

She hadn't given him the satisfaction of a response. Instead, had turned her head to the wall and refused to look at him.

She hears the door click and feels her stomach drop as it swings inward.

The same man who had abducted them stares at her from the opening. Her gaze goes to the logo on his baseball cap, recognizing the Carlos Garcia brand. She wonders if he grew up here or if he had made his way to this country with the life goal of kidnapping young girls. Or maybe the original plan hadn't worked out and this was the result?

"You must eat," he says, his strong voice startling her in the silence. She looks at him and shakes her head.

"Why should you make this much more difficult for you?"

I study him, noticing the line of frustration between his eyes. "You should have picked a pansy," she says.

"What is this pansy?"

"Someone who would give you what you want without a fight."

His eyes light up with amusement. "One of you has."

Rage erupts inside her, and something screams for her to

launch herself at him, claw his face into ribbons of blood. "I hate you."

He shrugs. "That is not problem. Is problem that you not eat. I will arrange for visit from doctor." He walks toward her, pulling a syringe from his back pocket. "First to prepare you for that visit though."

"What are you doing?" she screams, hating the fear propelling the question out of her.

He stands above her, the obvious awareness of his own power making her hate him even more. He jabs the needle in her thigh before she can raise a hand to stop him.

"You will sleep," he says. "When you wake, the good doctor will have filled you with many good nutrients."

"No," she says, her eyes growing heavy and her throat barely able to force the word out.

"It is much better to cooperate. You will learn this as you go along. Because eventually, the outcome can only be one. You will do what we ask you to do. Or we will get rid of you. You are much too young and beautiful to die. Surely, you agree with this?"

She tries to raise an arm to push him away, but her body will not respond. She understands in a way she never has before the desire to kill another human being. She would kill him if she could. But she can't. She can't. Her eyes slide closed, and he disappears.

~

SHE COMES TO in a snap, her eyes slamming open, the bright light above her blinding.

The light had gone out on the tail end of her screams, and she finds herself again screaming as she scrambles up, trying to remember what happened.

The man. He stabbed the needle in her leg. She feels there now, probing for the spot. She finds it, winces at the soreness, and then notices that her left arm is sore also.

She glances at the bend of her elbow, sees the telltale bruising of a needle mark. What had he done to her? She notices then that she's no longer thirsty. What had he given her?

A key sounds in the lock. The door swings in, and the man she has come to hate again steps inside, a wide smile on his face. "Feeling much better, yes?" he asks, a smirk in his voice.

"What did you do?" she bites out.

"The good doctor gave you nourishment. If you won't willingly eat or drink, we'll have to do it for you until you change your mind. We kept you out long enough to give you IVs of all the things your body needs. What is it they say? The miracles of modern medicine?"

Mia stares at him, an anger rising inside her that is like nothing she has ever felt. She feels as if the flames of it will completely melt everything in its path, her will, her resistance, the very essence of who she knows herself to be. "Why are you doing this?" she asks.

He studies her for a few long moments, and then, "It is not personal, beautiful. It is business. It's not that you and your friend did something wrong. You were simply the ones I came across that night as right for our operation. Do not waste time trying to figure out what you could have done differently. How you might have made another choice. There was no escaping it. This is your fate. Life is cruel that way."

She squeezes her arm at the place where the needle had gone in, as if she can remove the life-sustaining nutrients he had forced on her. "So you get to decide who is a victim and who isn't?"

"Yes," he says. "That is my job."

"You're despicable."

"Despicable?" he asks casually, as if she has called him something flattering.

"Scum of the earth." She struggles for other words strong enough to convey what she sees in him, but she can't find any. She spits at him, hitting him dead between the eyes.

She has never seen fury blaze to life the way it does on his face. He draws back a fist, and she closes her eyes and braces herself for the punch. But it doesn't come. Instead, he makes a sound that almost isn't human, both of his hands shoving her backward so that she slams into the wall and melts to the floor, the breath knocked from her lungs.

He's on top of her then, and she's trying so hard to pull in air that she can't scream, can't resist him.

"So, Miss Queen of Ice, I have never believed in waiting for you and the others like you to come willingly. Force works better anyway. Once I am done with you, you will be happy to receive the limp-dick senators who will be your customers."

He tears open the zipper of her jeans, yanking them off her with a loud ripping sound. The zipper catches the skin of her leg, tearing a scream from her throat. Her air is back, and she begins fighting, clawing at his face as she had wanted to earlier, knowing she will not give up until his blood covers her hands. He unzips his pants, and she feels his hardness against her leg. She struggles, writhing under him as she tries to remember something from the self-defense class Emory had made her take, and then the instructor's voice comes to her. "Go for the eyes. One finger is all it takes."

Mia jabs her thumb to the center of his eyeball. He turns his head in time to lessen the blow, but still howls, flinging himself off her, covering his eye with his hand.

She scrambles back to the wall, pulling her jeans up as

quickly as she can while she watches him roll in pain, his now limp penis flapping like a flag of surrender.

A key turns in the lock, and the door opens again. Mia looks up to find a woman staring at them both, her expression as blank as the wall behind her. She is tall and intimidating. Her black hair hangs from a center part and glances off her shoulders. She is wearing a dark-gray suit and a white blouse that seem as severe as the storm in her unnaturally green eyes.

"Sergio," she says evenly. "Leave us. Now."

Biting back a moan, he stumbles to his feet, pulling up his pants as he goes. Mia bites her lip at the sound of his zipper, resisting a suddenly hysterical urge to laugh.

Another glance at the woman's stone-faced expression kills the urge, and she pulls her knees up against her chest, holding her gaze on the instinctive knowledge that to look away would suggest weakness. Something tells her that would be a mistake.

"So you drove Sergio to cross a line he has never crossed before? This is interesting. That tells me a good bit about you."

"If you let us go," Mia says, forcing an even note in her voice, "I swear on my life that we'll never tell anyone what happened. We'll say we ran off for a few days. Just being teenagers."

The woman laughs, a low, throaty laugh that suggests she is very much used to being in control. "Oh, my dear, I am afraid it is much too late for that. We have plans for you. Guests for you to entertain. Your friend Grace is already well on her way. She's already grown tired of being hungry and thirsty. She very much enjoyed her shower and the luxurious massage and spa treatment we provided her. As we speak, she is trying on some of the clothes we bought her to wear tonight."

"You're lying."

"In fact, I'm not."

"What's tonight?"

"Tonight she will have the chance to become friends with one of our most valued clients. I believe she will impress him."

A twisting cyclone of fear and outrage torpedoes out of Mia. "You can't do that. Grace would never—"

"Actually, she would," the woman disagrees. "It's a matter of options, dear. She prefers this option to the others we have presented her with. Isn't that what all of life is? Choosing among options?"

"You're crazy!" Mia screams. "Please let us go! Our families will give you money—"

The woman laughs. "I am sure you have no idea what you are worth. But I doubt that your families could get anywhere near that."

Mia wants to argue, but she honestly has no idea how much money she and Emory have. And she knows that Grace's parents aren't wealthy. "Please. Don't do this. You have no idea what you've done to our—"

"They will go on," she says matter-of-factly. "It is a sad fact of life, but we do survive our tragedies. Your family will survive this one."

"Why are you doing this?" Mia asks, hating herself for the weakness in her voice.

"I have clientele to please. It is simple."

Mia stares at her, sensing that she is right when she says, "You enjoy this. The cat-and-mouse thing. You being the cat, of course."

"Of course," the woman says, smiling now. "Very perceptive of you."

"Were you born without the empathy chip or did someone create you?"

The woman's stare becomes a glare. But, as if she doesn't want Mia to think she has gotten to her, she smiles again and says, "Does it really matter?"

"I think it matters. If you were a victim, you should understand what it feels like to be one."

"A victim is someone with absolutely no choice in what happens to them. You have a choice."

"You call being a prostitute for you a choice?"

"Such a crass word, prostitute. What we do here can't really be equated with that."

"Sex for hire. Isn't that what it is?"

"We prefer to think of it as providing pleasure to those who can afford to pay for it. And who don't mind being generous when they get what they want."

"I won't do it."

The woman sighs. "I am afraid that if you don't soon come around to our way of thinking, I will be forced to have you spend some time with some of the less-desirable members of my team. And that will make your almost interlude with Sergio seem like an infinitely desirable thing. It would be a shame too because there would be mandatory recovery time for you. I've only had to play this card with a few of our girls, but it wasted valuable resources for us all. And if your situation required a hospital visit, well, you know we would simply have to end things there."

Mia's bravado wavers despite her attempt not to let it show.

"Once I make the decision to send you down that avenue, I will not change my mind. I'll give you one more night to come around to our way of thinking. I will check in with you tomorrow morning, and if you are still in this oppositional state of mind, you will be spending tomorrow night wishing you had. It is very simple really, this decision that is before you."

Mia swallows hard, despair replacing the blood in her veins so that she suddenly feels incapacitated by it. The fight leaves her, and she leans against the wall, sliding to the floor. She looks up at the woman, staring hard at her before she says, "Okay. I will do what you want. But only if you let Grace and me be together."

The woman folds her arms, studies Mia for a few long moments before saying, "I suppose that can be arranged. But first, my dear, you need a shower."

Knox

*"Beware that, when fighting monsters, you yourself do not
become a monster."*
—Barry Eisler

HE SHOULDN'T HAVE let her come along.

He doesn't need the distraction.

For the majority of the drive into downtown DC, he again uses music as an excuse for them not to talk. But at some point, she reaches over and turns it down. "What was it like being a SEAL?"

He glances at her, expecting to see casual interest on her face, but she is looking at him with serious eyes, and he resists the urge to be sarcastic. He considers the question and then says, "Every day is another opportunity to probe your weak points. SEAL candidates undergo six months of training by professionals whose mission is to find any weakness that might make you inferior when it comes to serving your country at the highest imaginable levels. They basically try to throw more challenges at you in six months than they believe a normal human being can handle."

"But you handled it?"

He shrugs. "Sometimes, that still surprises me. My class started with one hundred and forty-eight men. After six weeks, we were down to thirty-seven."

"And I'm assuming those are some of the country's most qualified young guys?"

"The competition is stiff."

"How did you survive it?"

He's quiet for a few moments, and then, "There have been accounts of soldiers who were shot multiple times, but weren't aware of it until the fight was over and the danger had passed. That's the power the brain has to adapt. You can train the brain to prepare for survival. The military calls it battle-proofing. Using the mind to visualize scenes of survival to produce psychological strength. It's sort of like meditation, I guess. Developing the ability to see in your mind a scene that you might have to live through. Like a firefight. You think of all the details you imagine you would experience. The sound of the gunfire. The smell of a nearby explosion. The screams of frightened women and children. The idea is that if the brain imagines something in extreme detail, it's as if you've lived through the experience, and if you have something similar happen to you, your brain has already conditioned itself to surviving it. So, during some of our make-or-break exercises, like riding out a night in shark-infested ocean waters, I had already lived through that night in my mind. I would lie in my bunk, imagining a shark brushing past my leg while I barely managed to stay afloat. I felt my heart thudding in my chest, prayed the shark wouldn't feel the pulse of fear. I made my brain accept that the fact that I would not move any more than I had to, to stay afloat. I wouldn't try to swim away or shove the shark away from me."

Emory studies him, shaking her head a little. "That's the opposite of what most of us humans do. We wait for the lightning bolt to strike before we understand what our response will be. So we are reliant on our most basic instincts. Fear, the irresistible urge to flee the danger rather than face it."

He nods, left hand on the steering wheel, his right thumb digging into the scar on his thigh where a bullet had once been lodged. "And you have to create a trigger."

"What kind of trigger?"

"Your ultimate reason for living. The thing you go to when giving up seems like a good option."

"What was yours?"

"In training, it was my parents. I knew how proud of me they would be if I made it as a SEAL. I would picture the look on my dad's face if I could tell him that I'd made it. I wanted them to be proud of me like that. And then later, when I actually got on a SEAL team and had to fight for my own life and the lives of my team, my trigger was the determination that we would all return home alive. I would envision each one of us greeting our families at the airport. I made myself see their smiles and happiness instead of flag-draped coffins and grief."

She nods once, looking out her window. "I wonder if Mia is envisioning coming home. Living for the moment when I open the door, and there she stands. When she can scoop Pounce up in her arms and hug him tight. What if she gives up? What if she can't imagine ever coming home?"

Tears break in her voice, and he looks across at her, wishing for a moment that he hadn't given her such a comparison to make. "If she's anything like you," he says quietly, "she's mentally tough."

Emory wipes a hand across her eyes, staring through the windshield. "I don't feel very mentally tough right now."

"Think about the things you've taught her, though, just by being who you are. How many eighteen-year-olds could take over the role of parent to an eight-year-old? She's absorbed strength with you as a role model."

"You're kind," she says in a barely audible voice.

"That's not something I often get accused of."

"What do you get accused of?" she asks, looking at him now.

"Getting the job done. Being efficient. Knowing what

the end goal is. But kindness isn't usually necessary to get those things done."

"You care about how I feel right now. That's kind."

He shifts in his seat, switches hands on the steering wheel. Continuing to declare the label as ill-fitting seems like drawing attention to something he'd rather not draw attention to, so he chooses silence as the best option.

"What was the hardest training mission? The one you thought you might not endure?"

"Hell week and staying awake for five days straight. I always took sleep for granted. I could grab three or four hours and be fine if I had an exam in college or stayed out half the night partying and had to get up for class the next morning. But you go that long without any, and reality takes on a new meaning. You're seeing stoplights in the middle of the ocean. Think you see a whale float by."

"Hallucinations?"

"Yeah. Your buddy next to you is seeing things too, so you resist the urge to feel like you're going crazy."

"How did you stay awake? Caffeine?"

"No. That stopped working on day two. Moving was the biggest thing. If you stood still, you would fall asleep instantly. Moving was the only thing that kept you awake."

"Why did they make you stay awake so long?"

"To make sure you can do it in a war zone. Seventy-two hours awake on a mission happens. You can't stop and sleep. You've got to be able to complete what you're there to do."

"Working as a detective must seem simple compared to that."

"Both jobs require you to deal with war. It's dressed up a little differently, but some of the things I've seen in domestic situations have been a lot harder to process than what I saw over there."

"How so?"

"In a war, you have a declared enemy, and, once identified, your job is to take them out. Here, when you get a call to a house where a husband has just shot and killed his wife and children, and he's sitting in his living room holding the gun he used, you don't get to finish the job and take out the enemy who just wiped out an entire family. You have to cuff him with restraint, read him his rights, and escort him to the legal system that might or might not fully hold him accountable."

"That's hard for you," she says in a voice that tells him she doesn't need him to agree. "Do you believe in vigilante justice?"

"The correct answer is no," he says.

"You don't believe there's ever any justification in a person taking the law into his own hands?"

"There shouldn't be."

"You think our legal system works perfectly and the guilty are always punished?"

"No."

She considers this for a moment. "I once read about a mother who worked late shifts as a policewoman. She let her daughter sleep over at her best friend's house when she had to work nights. When her daughter was twelve, she told her mother that the husband had molested her several times when she stayed there. The mother reported this to the police, but didn't get what she thought was a fast-enough response. She thought other children might be in danger. So she abducted the man and drove him to a wooded area where she made him take off his clothes and tell the truth about what he'd done. After he got cold enough, he confessed, and she drove him back to the police station so that he could confess there also. He was arrested for rape, but the mother was also arrested for kidnapping with intent to commit murder. She was facing five years in prison but ended up getting probation. He went to prison for four years. Do you think she should have gone to prison?"

"No," he says instantly.

"Me either."

"So we're both of the vigilante mindset, I guess," he says.

"I don't know that I want the label, but I do know that the world doesn't always work as it should. I do know that if I have the opportunity to punish whoever took my sister from me, I won't take it lightly."

He glances at her, sees the set of her jaw and realizes she might be even tougher than he's given her credit for.

Their exit comes up off the Capital Beltway, and he lets off the gas, rolling to a stop at the light, then pulling out behind the traffic. "We're almost there. Not sure it's a good idea for you to get out."

"I'd rather go with you than wait in the Jeep."

"Okay, but let me do the talking. I don't want to set off any unnecessary alarm bells."

"You're in charge," she says. "My lips are sealed."

He glances at her, notices the smile, and then comes the unsummoned thought that they are indeed nice lips.

Emory

"A man is known by the company he keeps."
—Aesop

THE STORE IS one of those hip retailers that feels more like a club than a clothing establishment.

I step through the door just behind Detective Helmer, noting several twenty-somethings assessing strategically hung blue jeans with enough rips in the legs to justify someone throwing them away instead of buying them. How many conversations have Mia and I had on the wisdom of paying ridiculous prices for clothing that has been deliberately destroyed?

"Emory, you're such a square," Mia had declared the last time I'd given in to buying her a pair.

A beautiful, young woman with straight, waist-length, blonde hair greets us from behind the register. The name tag on the left side of her blouse says Madison. "Is there something I can help you with?" she asks with a smile.

We walk to the register, and I notice the return smile Detective Helmer directs her way. And then I realize it's deliberate because Madison is already melting before our eyes. By the time he pulls out his phone and shows her a close-up picture of the hat we're looking to identify, she's completely committed to answering his question.

"We do carry the brand," she says, engaging in direct eye contact with him. "It's very popular. We can barely keep it in stock."

"Do you remember this exact hat?" he asks, leaning his right hip against the counter.

"Sure," she says. "We've reordered it a few times because it sold out. Haven't been able to get another shipment though."

"Do you remember selling it to anyone?"

"Yeah," Madison says. "A few guys."

"Do you think you could describe them to me?"

She leans back a bit, lets her gaze drift to me and then back to him again. "What's this about?" she asks, her eyes narrowing.

"We're investigating a missing girl."

"Are you a cop?"

"Not at the moment," he says evenly.

"What then?"

He gives her a long look, as if weighing the necessity of being truthful with her. "I'm working for the family of the missing girl."

"Is this your assistant?" Madison asks with a small, borderline flirtatious smile.

"The missing girl is my sister," I say, taking a bit of satisfaction in watching her sarcasm collapse like a balloon denied helium.

"Oh. I'm sorry," she says.

Detective Helmer taps the screen of his phone and hands it to the young woman. "The photo is blurred, but this is surveillance video of a guy following the two girls who are missing."

"Two?"

"Yes," he says, tipping his head toward me. "Emory's sister and her best friend."

"That's awful," she says, as if it's just occurred to her that horrible things like this really do happen.

Madison looks at the phone screen, then touches it and

presses both fingers outward to enlarge the picture. She doesn't say anything for a good bit, looking at the photo with a fixed expression. "It's hard to be sure," she says finally, "but I don't think I've seen him before." Madison glances at the camera above the door we came in through. "And anyway, I'm fairly sure I'm not supposed to be talking about customers. Like that's probably an invasion of privacy or something. I could get fired."

My stomach drops at the letdown.

Helmer folds his arms across his chest, and I notice his jaw clench. I realize in that moment that he's a man who's used to getting what he wants, when he wants it. Madison must notice too because she says, "Well, because it involves a missing girl, maybe it's okay. I think he's been in here before."

"Do you remember his name?" Helmer asks.

"No."

"Can you get us a last name? Look him up by his credit card?"

"He paid cash."

Helmer processes this, then says, "If you think of anything else about him, Madison, anything that might help us locate him, please call me." He pulls a card from his pocket and hands it to her.

She reads it. "I thought you said you were a private guy. This says MPD."

"I'm on hiatus," he says. "You can reach me at that number though. Call me from your phone now so I'll have yours."

"Okay," she says reluctantly, dialing the number on the card from her cell phone.

Helmer's phone rings. He answers it, then clicks off and types her name in the contact.

"I really hope you find her," Madison says.

"Thanks for your help," he says.

I follow Helmer out of the store, waiting until we're both in the Jeep before I say, "I don't know whether to be hopeful or flattened."

"It's a start," he says, one hand on the steering wheel, a set look on his face.

"What is it?" I ask, sensing he's holding something back.

"Something tells me she wasn't completely forthcoming."

"Why? What makes you think that?"

He glances back at the storefront. "Sixth sense, I guess."

"What would she be leaving out?"

"I don't know." He glances at his watch. "It's eight-thirty. The store closes at nine. Let's see what she does when she gets off work."

"You mean follow her?"

"Probably a dead end. Let's just make sure."

~

WE SIT IN silence for the next thirty minutes. Helmer has moved the Jeep farther down the street. We're hidden in the shadows, but we can see the storefront. At nine o'clock on the nose, the store lights shut down, and a last customer straggles out the door and walks down the street, bag in hand.

Just then, a Range Rover swings into a spot in front of the store. Madison walks out, looking right, then left, and quickly heads for the vehicle, climbing inside.

"Who do you think is picking her up?" I ask.

"I don't know. It could be her boyfriend. But let's follow anyway."

I buckle my seat belt and sit back as he pulls the Jeep onto the street and follows the Range Rover a few car lengths behind. It stays at the speed limit, makes complete stops at intersections. "Whoever it is," I say, "they seem law-abiding."

"Maybe a little too much so," Helmer agrees.

We drive a good ten minutes until we reach a neighborhood in Georgetown. The Range Rover pulls into an empty spot. We drive on by, and I resist the urge to look back and see if I can get a look at the driver. There aren't any spaces available farther down the street, so we have to circle the block. By the time we get back around, the lights are off, and the vehicle is empty.

"Damn," Helmer says.

"Now what?"

He aims his phone at the back of the Range Rover and takes several photos of the plate. "Let's see how long her visitor stays and what he or she looks like when they come back out."

"Or they could be planning to stay the night."

"I don't have anywhere else to be," he says, looking directly at me.

Neither do I.

~

I'M SETTLED DOWN in the seat, expecting that we'll be waiting a while, if the person even comes out at all. It's a little shocking then, when a door to one of the buildings opens and a man walks out and heads straight for the Range Rover.

"He's wearing the baseball cap," I say. "It's him."

"Stay cool," Helmer says, placing a hand on my arm. "We can't draw attention to ourselves. We'll follow him."

The vehicle starts and begins pulling out of the parking spot, just as Helmer's phone rings. He glances at the screen. From my seat, I can see it's Madison's number.

"Why would she be calling you?" I ask.

"I don't know, but here, answer it," he says, handing me the phone and pulling onto the street. "I'll follow this guy."

I slide the answer button on his screen. "Hello." There's no reply. I press the phone to my ear. "Hello."

"Help."

The word is so low I think I might have imagined it. "Madison?"

"Please. Help me."

"What is it?" Helmer asks, looking at me with a frown.

"She's asking for help," I say. "I think she's hurt. We have to go back."

"If we let him get away, we might not find him again," Helmer says.

From the other end of the phone, I hear Madison say, "I'm . . . dying. Please."

"We have to go back!"

Helmer hits the brakes and swings a U in the street. He guns it back to the apartment, pulling off the street without bothering to properly park. We both run for the building. I glance at the mailboxes just inside the front door, spot her last name and the number 208. We take the stairs two at a time.

"I'm calling 911," Helmer says. I hear him asking for an ambulance at this address just as we reach Madison's door. Helmer bangs hard on the knocker, but there's no answer. He turns the knob. It's locked. "Stand back," he says, and then rams the door with his left shoulder. It doesn't give the first time, so he moves farther back and then rushes the door again. This time, part of the frame breaks, and he reaches inside to turn the lock so that it swings open.

"Madison!" Helmer charges in, glancing left and right as he heads for the kitchen, calling her name again. I'm right behind him so that when he comes to a complete stop just short of the doorway, I barrel into him. He reaches back to steady me, and I step to the side, gasping at the sight before us.

Madison is lying on the floor in front of the stove, a gaping wound in her chest, blood staining her white blouse red. Helmer drops to his knees beside her, feeling for a pulse in her neck. Her lids flutter open, and she stares up at us both, her blue eyes welling with tears. "I . . . I should have told you I knew him."

"An ambulance is on the way, Madison. Hold on, okay? Who did this to you?"

"Ser-Sergio."

"Why?" Helmer asks, not hiding his shock.

"I . . . told him you were asking . . ."

"Shh," I say, dropping down beside her and taking her hand between mine. "Save your strength. They'll be here in a minute, and you're going to be fine."

Madison's gaze drops to the blood on her blouse, the blood pooled on the floor around us. I glance down to see that my jean-covered knees are now also red. When she looks up at me, her voice is barely audible when she says, "I didn't think he would do what you said. About your sister. He was good to me . . . gave me stuff." She stops there, her lungs audibly gasping for air.

"Don't," I say. "You can talk later."

"Madison," Helmer says, tipping her chin toward him. "I'll find him. He won't get away with this, but I need you to tell me everything you know. His last name? Where he lives?"

She stares up at him, and I cringe at the sound of her struggling to breathe.

"Detective," I say, "please . . ."

But he ignores me, imploring Madison to answer. "His last name, Madison."

"Sokolov," she manages to get out.

"Where does he live?" Helmer pushes.

"I don't know," she says on a whisper. "We always came here."

A siren wails in the distance and then the sound grows closer outside the building. "They're here, Madison," I say, squeezing her hand again, as if I can infuse my own life force into her. Her face blurs before mine, and I'm seeing Mia, watching the life fade from her. Is there someone there for her? Panic rises inside me, and I'm leaning over Madison, pleading with her to hold on. The girl's eyes flutter, and a gurgling noise sounds in her throat. Blood oozes from the left corner of her mouth.

I start to cry.

Helmer puts a hand on my shoulder, squeezes hard. "Emory," he says, and I latch onto the crazy question of whether this is the first time he's said my name.

Footsteps pound on the stairs outside Madison's broken door. Two paramedics rush through, calling out that they're here. But I look down at Madison's still body, her open blue eyes, and I can see that they are too late.

Knox

"I am both worse and better than you thought."
—Sylvia Plath

KNOX GIVES THE officers on the scene all the information he has about the driver of the Range Rover, the name he believes he goes by and the photo of the license plate.

Randall Macintosh, a uniformed officer he's known since joining the force, takes down everything Knox tells him. "What was your interest in Madison Willard?" he asks, his head swinging from Knox to Emory Benson.

Knox glances at Emory and then says, "I'm doing some private work for Dr. Benson. Her sister and her sister's best friend recently disappeared from the Spring Jam Festival. In reviewing the festival's security footage, I saw a man who appeared to be following them. I believe he might have bought the hat he was wearing at the store where Madison worked. We went there earlier tonight to ask her some questions. She indicated she didn't know who he was, but I had a feeling she wasn't telling us everything, so we waited for her to get off work. The suspect picked her up outside the store, and we followed them to her apartment. They had barely gotten inside the building before he was coming back out again, and my phone rang. She could hardly talk, but she was asking for help."

"You think she told him about your questions, and that's why he shot her?" Macintosh asks.

"I don't know what else to think."

159

The officer's phone rings. He answers, listens intently, before clicking off, and then says, "The plate on the Range Rover was stolen. Belongs to a woman in Maryland who reported it a couple of weeks ago."

"What about the vehicle?" Knox asks.

"Still working on that. We've got an APB out for the Range Rover. Chief Parker would like the two of you to come to the station and answer a few more questions."

Knox blows out a short breath, and says the only thing there is to say, "We'll head over now."

~

THEY'RE ON THE Beltway driving toward downtown before either of them speaks.

Strangely, they both start to say something at the same time.

"I should have . . ."

"How could we . . ."

They glance at each other, and Knox can see the horror of what they witnessed in her eyes. "I want to believe we could have prevented that," he says, his gaze now on the highway before them.

"But how?" she asks quietly. "Why did she lie to us?"

"She didn't think he could be capable of what we'd told her."

"But he is. And now he's back out there. What if he's already killed my sister and Grace?" She barely manages to choke out the last words, before her head is in her hands, and he can hear her quiet crying.

Without giving himself time to correct the impulse, he reaches out and puts a hand on her arm. "You can't think that. We don't have any reason to believe it at this point. The only way to get through this is to take each piece of information we have and follow it through to the best of our ability. Trusting only what's immediately in front of you is how you get to the next critical clue. Think of what we knew yesterday and what we know now. We have somewhere to go."

She presses her lips together, and he senses her struggling to bring her emotions under control. She nods once, her right elbow on the Jeep door, her hand running through her hair.

When they reach the station, Knox pulls into the parking spot it is his habit to park in. He's just getting ready to suggest she wait there for him when a text dings on his phone. It's the captain.

Bring the Benson girl in with you.

He doesn't bother texting her back, because an order is an order.

He looks at Emory and says, "The captain wants to speak with you too."

"I don't have a problem with that." She opens her door and slides out, then waits for him to walk around.

He leads the way inside the building, holding the door for her and then making his way to the captain's office. The door is closed. He raps once; opens it at her terse, "Come in."

He steps aside and waves Emory through before him.

"You must be Emory Benson," Chief Parker stands from the chair behind her desk, sticks out her hand.

"Yes," Emory says, shaking hands with her and keeping her gaze locked with the captain's. Knox takes note of the fact that she isn't intimidated.

Chief Parker looks at Knox, any residue of pleasantness leaving her expression. "You're on leave," she says matter-of-factly.

"Yes," he agrees.

"Would you like to tell me how you ended up in the middle of an investigation you were relieved from?"

"I hired him as a private detective," Emory answers before he can.

The captain's gaze swings to her. "I think Detective Helmer can answer that question."

"I didn't expect what happened tonight to happen, Captain," he says.

"I should hope not. But you have defied an order in continuing to work on this case."

"Chief Parker," Emory says, her voice suddenly a hard line of steel. "Has anyone you loved ever gone missing?"

The captain meets her questioning gaze, and it is clear she's surprised by her boldness. "No."

"But you have no doubt witnessed many families struggling with this reality?"

"I have," she says carefully.

"Then you must have some idea how unbearable it is to sit and wait for a phone call that might give you the smallest piece of information about the person you love? For three days, I have heard nothing. My seventeen-year-old sister, whom I have raised since she was eight years old, vanished. And while I know this police department will do everything within its power to find her, I also know it might not be enough. I can't stand by and do nothing. Detective Helmer agreed to help me because I all but begged him to. If anyone is going to get reprimanded for this, it should be me."

"You're not an officer of this department, Miss Benson."

"It's Dr. Benson," Emory says. "And no, I'm not. But tonight is the first lead I've been made aware of. The first piece of hope I have that my baby sister might be found. Only, I don't even know if I have that because the man who killed Madison Willard is a monster. And how do I know that he hasn't already killed Mia and Grace?"

Emory swallows once, as if trying to push back the emotion welling up inside her. "Can you find him, Captain?"

"We'll do our best," she says. "I can assure you of that."

"I believe you," Emory says. "But what if that's not enough? My sister is the only family I have left. I will never be able to live with myself if I don't do anything and everything I possibly can to help find her."

The captain glances from Emory to Knox. He holds her gaze, aware that, like his superiors in the Special Forces, to look away is to show weakness and lose her respect.

When she finally speaks, it is on the exhalation of a long sigh. "Detective Helmer, you will not in any way interfere with the ongoing investigation of this department. And if you develop the smallest of leads, you will notify Detective Carmichael, who is now the lead on this case. Am I understood?"

"Perfectly," Knox says, keeping his expression neutral.

"That will be all then. Maybe we could go home and try to get some sleep now."

"Goodnight, Captain," he says, opening the office door.

They're in the hallway when the captain calls out, "I'm really sorry about your sister and her friend, Dr. Benson. It is my fervent hope that they'll be found."

Sergio

"The power of the sin is in its secrecy."
—TemitOpe Ibrahim

HE'S HAD SECOND thoughts about keeping the Range Rover. He'll need to change the license plate again.

And he'll get a detail first thing in the morning to lose any traces of Madison having been in the Range Rover.

He lets his mind scan his own personal checklist for cleaning up potentially messy situations.

What had gone down tonight was more than potentially messy. It could end life as he knew it.

Inside the quiet walls of his Georgetown townhouse, Sergio pours himself a shot glass of tequila, downs it, and then pours another, waiting for the first to hit his bloodstream. He glances at the label on the bottle, Patrón en Lalique, and remembers the morning it had arrived by special courier on his doorstep. He remembers too the evening before that had prompted Senator Hagan to send it to him as a thank you.

At six thousand dollars a bottle, it was a gift not only meant to compensate for the favor Sergio had bestowed on the senator the night before, but also an implication of future expectations. Sergio wasn't stupid. He would concede to greed, but he knew that stupid and greedy would not allow for a lengthy lifespan.

Not where his employer was concerned.

He downs the second shot of tequila, aware of its nearly instantaneous ability to smooth the edges of his insecurity.

He'd taken care of the problem tonight. As soon as he realized there was one, he'd taken care of it. And wasn't that his job anyway? His employer had hired him to be a problem solver of the highest caliber. This was one problem she didn't need to know about, because it wasn't one any longer.

The proprietor did not suffer fools. And she would without doubt find him at fault for the fact that a cop was asking questions of a girl he was currently banging.

Growing up on the streets of Cartagena had taught him many things, but one of the most important lessons of all had been the fact that survivors never left loose ends. Above all, Sergio was a survivor. He had a second sense for knowing when it was time to cut losses.

Unfortunately, Madison was a loss he'd had no choice but to cut. Such a waste though. She'd been great in bed. Impressed by his willingness to drop five hundred dollars on a pair of jeans. Happy with the fact that he drove a Range and took her to dinner at places frequented by politicians she watched on cable news. She liked his accent and bragged to her friends that she was dating a "rich Colombian."

And he was, by any standard he'd ever imagined.

But then, he'd earned every penny of it.

He knew now exactly how far gone humankind was in the things people wanted in their secret lives. He knew too what those people were willing to pay for those things. Fortunately for him, there wasn't anything he'd yet been asked to do that he wasn't willing to do.

That made him invaluable. But it didn't make him irreplaceable. Where his employer was concerned, no one was irreplaceable.

Even in his street life as a kid, he had never met anyone

with the kind of ruthlessness his employer possessed. It was something they had in common.

It had been one of the coldest Januarys on record when he'd first arrived in the United States as a stowaway on a cargo ship that journeyed to Norfolk, Virginia. He'd hitchhiked his way to Washington, DC, and that winter had made him long for the climate of his birth. He had no money, no place to live, except for the nooks and crannies of the city where he saw other homeless people living.

One frigid Sunday morning, he'd slipped inside a church, taking a seat in a back pew, and listening to the man giving the sermon at the front of the sanctuary. He'd quoted a verse from the Bible during his message that had somehow branded itself onto Sergio's heart. "And if thy right hand offends thee, cut it off, and cast it from thee: for it is profitable for thee."

Nothing had ever made as much sense to him. He'd already accepted the fact that life had little rhyme or reason to it. Those words somehow gave him a vision for his future. A man had to take what was his, cull anything that didn't serve him. This had become his own life theme, and maybe it was this that his employer had seen in him when she'd walked down the center aisle of the church that morning, noticing him just before she shook the pastor's hand and thanked him for his sermon.

When he'd reluctantly left the warm sanctuary, turning up the collar of his thin coat and heading down the sidewalk with no destination in mind, she had been waiting for him. She'd asked if he might join her for lunch. There was a restaurant nearby that had a few Colombian items on the menu. He wondered, even as he nodded yes, how she'd known he was from Colombia. He hadn't yet spoken a word, but then it didn't take him long to figure out she knew things about people it didn't seem possible she could know.

At the restaurant, she'd ordered him ajiaco, a soup with chicken, potato, corn, capers, avocado, and sour cream. It made him so homesick, he couldn't speak, and she'd watched him inhale the food as if she were simply glad to have lent a helping hand to someone who needed it. And he'd had no reason to believe she was anything other than a nice Christian lady. She'd offered him a job that day, and he hadn't bothered to ask what he would be doing because he hadn't cared. She'd reached down and offered him a hand up, and he wasn't about to question any of it.

But then there was another lesson he'd learned on the streets of Cartagena. When something seems too good to be true, it usually is.

Of course, the proprietor had an ulterior motive in helping him. But he'd ended up with a life as a result of that day. And he liked to think he'd earned it by his willingness to do whatever needed to be done. That was all he'd done tonight after all. Cut off the right hand.

If he's learned anything from his employer, it is the necessary elimination of loose ends. First thing in the morning, he'll make sure he's tidied up each one. And everything will be fine. Life will go on.

He considers another tequila, but decides against it, recapping the bottle and putting it away. What he needs is sleep. And tomorrow, a fresh start.

Emory

"A cat has absolute emotional honesty: human beings, for one reason or another, may hide their feelings, but a cat does not."
—Ernest Hemingway

IT IS WHAT I want to believe.

With every fiber of my being, I will my own fear to the back of my brain. But it won't stay there and, like a ball of yarn whose end isn't firmly tucked to the center of the roll, continues to unravel.

"What's next?" I finally find the courage to ask when we are a couple of miles from my house.

"We'll hope to get a lead on the Rover," Helmer says, hitting the blinker for the exit.

"And what if there isn't one? Surely, he knows the police will be looking for the vehicle."

The detective is quiet for a few moments, as if weighing his response. "The thing about criminals is that eventually they mess up. I like to operate under the assumption that they'll do so sooner rather than later. I don't have the personal stake that you have, Emory. But I do want to find this guy. What happened tonight feels like it happened on my watch. Whether he had anything to do with your sister's disappearance, we don't know. But I want him for what he did to Madison. And I'm going to find him."

I hear the determination in his voice. Something about the strength I feel emanating from him rolls the ball of yarn back up again, and I put my focus on tomorrow, on another day that dawns with the opportunity to move forward.

~

WHEN WE REACH the house, he leaves the engine running, but gets out and walks me to the door.

"You don't have to," I say. "I'm good from here."

"I'd like to check the house out before I leave."

"Oh. Okay. Thank you."

I unlock the door, flick the porch light on, and step inside. He closes the door behind us. I turn on a lamp in the living room. Pounce saunters in from the hallway that leads to the bedrooms, his yowl expectedly offended.

"Mind if I look around?"

"No," I say, feeling a ping of unease for the first time. It's never occurred to me to fear for my own safety.

He goes from room to room, opening doors, closets, looking under the beds. The house is single level, so once he's done, he steps through the French doors off the living room and disappears into the backyard. I see the flashlight from his phone swoop from one end of the fenced lawn to the other.

When he comes back in, he says, "Do you have a gun?"

"No."

"You should. I'll bring one by in the morning."

"But I don't have a permit."

"We'll call it a loaner. Meanwhile, you should get one and apply for concealed carry."

"You're kind of scaring me."

He lets his eyes meet mine then, and the seriousness in his look further unnerves me.

"If this Sergio is involved in your sister's disappearance," he says, "and Madison told him that you were with me tonight asking questions, he might come looking for you."

Fear jolts through me. And right behind it, a stab of anger that my life, Mia's life, has been taken hostage by a likely psychopath so lacking in conscience that he had taken the life of a beautiful, young girl tonight. "Do I need to be afraid?"

He gives me a level look. "I have to be honest with you. I don't know."

I am suddenly frozen with the awareness that I do not feel safe in my own house.

"Is there someone else you could stay with for a while? A friend?"

"Yes, but then I would be putting her in danger too."

He blows out a sigh, and says, "You can stay at my place tonight. It's not much, but you'll be safe."

"Oh. Thank you. But I couldn't. You know, I'm probably overreacting. I'll be fine. If I hear anything at all, I'll dial 911."

He stares at me for several long seconds, glances at his watch, and says, "It's already one a.m. Why don't I just sleep on your sofa?"

Relief cascades through me. I can't summon any vestige of pride that might make me deny being afraid. I am afraid. "That would be . . . are you sure you don't mind?"

He shakes his head, and then with a half-smile adds, "As long as I don't have to sleep with Pounce."

~

I FIND BLANKETS and a pillow and make up the couch for him. I start to feel self-conscious when I realize he has no clothes except for the ones he's wearing. My brain does a quick flash of him sleeping under these blankets, and my imagination starts to run away with me.

I quickly finish tucking in the edges, fluff the pillow, and turn around to find him standing right behind me. My chest collides with his mid-section. My instant thought is abs of steel. I step back so quickly that my leg hits the edge of the couch, and I fall backward.

He stares down at me for a moment, then offers a hand to pull me up. I ignore the gesture, shooting up on my own and putting several yards of distance between us. "Would you . . . I have a new toothbrush and toothpaste. Can I get those for you?"

"Yeah," he says, his gaze still locked with mine. "I'd appreciate that."

"It's the least I can do. Is there anything else you need?"

I hear myself say the words, feel the undercurrent, and do not wait for him to answer. I head for my bathroom, opening the drawer and rummaging for the toothbrush and toothpaste. It is only when I'm about to head back out the door that I glance in the mirror and notice the flush in my cheeks.

Knox

"Grief does not change you. . .It reveals you."
—John Green

SHE DISAPPEARS INTO the bedroom, waiting for the overconfident cat to clear the doorsill before she firmly shuts the door behind her.

He flicks off the lamp before taking off his shirt and jeans and sliding under the blankets. The sofa is a good foot shorter than he is, so he tries several different positions before conceding to his feet hanging over the far arm.

He stares at the dark ceiling above him, wondering what made him offer to stay here tonight. He realizes it is definitely out of character for him, but then what had happened to Madison Willard was beyond anything he'd thought to expect.

Tomorrow, he'll make sure Emory has a gun for protection and knows how to use it. Then tomorrow night he'll be back in his own bed. Waking up to find out that something has happened to Emory Benson isn't a regret he wants to add to his list.

Because it's already a long list.

Sounds come from her bedroom, drawers opening, closing. He hears the soft tone of her voice, a meow from Pounce.

He closes his eyes, waiting for sleep. But the images that start to pan through his mind aren't exactly sleep-inducing.

Emory Benson isn't his type.

He doesn't go for serious, driven women who expect a relationship to have a purpose, a destination.

He'd made that mistake once in his life, even though he wasn't put-off by the realization going into it. But then the vows his wife had taken had not included any expectation of PTSD and all its accompanying demons. She hadn't known he would come home a different man. For that matter, neither had he.

~

Five Years Ago

WE DON'T GO into things expecting them to change us.

Knox certainly hadn't.

The end of his deployment should have been a cause for celebration.

The night before he had left to return to the states, he had Skyped with Mariah. She was so overjoyed that they would only be apart another twenty-four hours that she could not stop smiling. He'd sat inside the tent, sweat trickling down the back of his neck, his gaze glued to the screen, a smile he did not feel inside pasted on his face as he'd listened to her plans for what they would do when he got home from Afghanistan.

"I am going to devour you," she said, "as soon as we get through the door of this house. If I don't attack you in the car first, that is. And I might. It's been a year, Knox. Oh, my Lord, I have missed you so much, baby."

"I've missed you too," he said. And he had. But why couldn't he feel that? Why did he feel as if he had been soaked in some kind of numbing solution so that a real feeling seemed incapable of finding its way from his brain to his heart?

He stared at his wife's face on the laptop screen, noted with detachment that she might be even more beautiful now than she had been when he'd last seen her just over three hundred and sixty-five days ago.

To deal with their separation, she had made her already healthy fitness habit a near addiction, running six miles every single morning and teaching a spin class five days a week.

"I can't believe we're finally going to live like normal people," she said, leaning in to the camera and giving him a glimpse of the cleavage revealed by the neckline of her workout shirt. Her skin was still flushed from the class she'd finished teaching just before their call.

"I know," he said. "Me either."

And he couldn't. Because for the life of him, he didn't think he had any idea what that was any more.

But he had done his best to show excitement over the life they would be living together for the first time since they had gotten married.

The thing was, sitting there, listening to his happy wife, he didn't know how to tell her that he wasn't the same man she had married.

And he didn't know if he ever would be again.

~

IT DIDN'T TAKE long for Mariah to start to realize this.

In fact, awareness began to happen their very first night home together.

They had finally fallen asleep in each other's arms sometime after two a.m. Mariah had made good on her promise, bringing his tired body to life twice before exhaustion had claimed them both.

The nightmare came at its usual time, two hours or so after falling asleep. He woke Mariah before the dream woke him. She shook him gently, saying his name over and over again until he rose from the depths of the nightmare, tears streaming down his face.

"Baby," she said, fear in her voice. "What is it? You're having a dream. I'm right here." She slipped her arms behind him and pulled him to her, cradling his head against her chest. She began to cry. "Tell me. What happened?"

It was a long time before he could speak. When he finally did, his voice did not sound familiar to him. More like that of a man he might have met a few times but didn't really know.

"In one year, our unit found more than six thousand IEDs. Over two hundred men injured. Thirty-six killed. Five of them died right beside me." Once he started talking, he couldn't stop. "And every time, I watched a life combust before my eyes. Not just the life of that soldier, but the lives of all the people who loved him. And every time, I did what I had to do. Get him to safety as fast as we could. Even if it was too late, it seemed like we owed that soldier whatever dignity we could give him. And then we had to go back to being the soldiers we'd been trained to be, blanking out what we'd seen, telling ourselves it couldn't happen again, that it was a fluke. But it wasn't, and it did. Over and over again."

She wrapped her arms around his shoulders, hugged him as tight as she could, as if she could bring him back, hold him together. And he let her. He wanted the comfort, needed the solace, desperately craved feeling normal again. Feeling something. Anything. But the only time he didn't feel numb was in the dreams. And what he felt there was terror.

"It's not human," she said next to his ear. "You were sent there to make a difference for our country, for our world. And you were tested to every extreme limit imaginable to make sure you could handle it, that you would be able to face those situations and do what needed to be done. And I know you did. But what about what happens afterwards?

Does anyone prepare you for what it's like to see that kind of horror? For how it will change you?"

She leaned back and looked at him, her voice rising when she added, "My God. What can I do? How can I help?"

He leaned against the headboard of the bed, pulled her into the curve of his arm, maybe to offer her comfort, maybe to prevent her from seeing in his face what he was struggling to hide. Because she was right. He wasn't handling it. He felt as if someone had planted him in quicksand, and his boots were getting heavier and heavier, sucking him down inch by inch, pressing the air from his lungs.

He kissed his wife's hair, wished he could tell her everything would be all right. But for the first time in his life, a life he had defined by his own ability to fight his way forward regardless of the obstacles thrown in front of him, he wasn't sure that it would be.

~

THEY BOTH TRIED.

But the man Mariah had married was not the same man who came home to her from Afghanistan.

With every passing day, Knox watched the growing awareness of this reflected in his wife's eyes. He saw her joy in having him home fade to alarm over the fact that for the first time since she had known him, he was sleeping in. Getting up at eleven or later when he'd always been up with the sun, getting a run in before breakfast. But he wasn't able to go to sleep at night because he dreaded the dreams waiting for him there, and so he couldn't fall asleep until exhaustion pulled him under, even without his acquiescence.

Mariah planned things she thought he would like doing,

things they had once enjoyed doing together. Hikes. Long bike rides. Movies.

But he felt like a voyeur in his own life, like his soul had been removed, and he could only view the life going on around him as a bystander.

Mariah's patience knew no boundaries. And so he hated himself all the more for his growing resentment of her attempts to pull him back into their marriage, their life together. Fair or not, her insistence on making him happy again made him realize she would never understand what it was he'd witnessed in Afghanistan or how it had changed him.

How could she?

It wasn't fair to expect that she ever could. He knew now that he had deliberately set fire to his marriage, presented his wife with a reality that she couldn't possibly choose to live with.

When she left him, it wasn't a surprise.

But it was a relief.

Because then, he no longer had to try at all. He moved to an apartment and shut the door on everything that had once made him get up in the mornings. And for months, he barely left the place, only going out to get food when he remembered to eat.

One afternoon, he was sitting in front of his TV, staring at a talking head on CNN questioning America's role in the Middle East. He wondered if this was how it was for the men who returned from Vietnam to discover that the country that had sent them to fight a battle it declared worthy of so many lives had changed its mind somewhere along the way. Those soldiers had not returned home as heroes but as villains, as if they were somehow suddenly to blame for the tragedy of Vietnam.

His phone pinged. He glanced at the screen and saw the

group text from Ace Conrad, a former SEAL team member. He picked up the phone and read the message.

Hey, guys. Really sorry for letting you all down. The only easy day was yesterday.

Knox read the words again, his heart dropping to his stomach.

Instantly, he knew what they meant. He dialed the number, listened to it ring and ring. As soon as voicemail picked up, he dialed again. Over and over, but there was no answer. And he knew it was too late.

He sat there on his sofa, staring at the phone screen, suddenly aware of the pull inside him, the awareness that he could take the same out. He didn't even blame Ace. He knew the why. The pain in his head that never stopped, no matter what medicine or alcohol he threw at it.

He understood what Ace had just freed himself from.

He got up from the sofa, went into the bedroom, and pulled his Glock from the nightstand drawer. He went back to the living room and sat down, holding the gun on his lap, one finger on the trigger.

He had every reason to put the gun in his mouth. Just end it all. The black hole of peace in front of him held the answer he'd been looking for. He wanted out. Wanted the images in his head to stop their carousel rotation. Wanted the numbness that had trapped his heart and refused to let it feel anything let him go.

But the phone rang. Tanner Billings' name flashed on the screen. Another team member. He considered not answering, but something made his finger hit the button. He listened as one of the men he'd fought and nearly died with too many times to count raged against the decision Ace had just made.

Knox listened, and when Tanner finally went silent, all he could say was, "But I understand why he did."

Tanner started to cry. Knox listened to his quiet sobbing, picturing the enormous warrior who had saved his ass more than once. And he knew that the fact that Tanner could cry meant he would be okay.

Knox wanted to cry. But the tears were frozen inside him.

"You better not, man," Tanner said, the words barely audible. "Tell me you're not going to let that shithole we survived end up being the winner. Because I swear if you do . . ."

"I don't want to," Knox said softly. "I just can't picture anything else making sense."

"I'm getting on a plane, Knox," Tanner said. "The next one I can get a seat on. Give me your address. We'll figure this out together."

~

IRONICALLY, IT WAS Ace's suicide that ended up bringing Knox back to life again. But if it hadn't been for Tanner, Knox knew without question that he would have followed Ace's way out the afternoon he'd received that text.

Tanner arrived at his apartment late that same night, got their airline tickets lined up for Ace's funeral two days later. The two of them sat on Knox's sofa and shared their best memories of Ace and the close calls they'd all pulled through together.

Before the funeral, Tanner made some discreet phone calls and found a psychiatrist who specialized in PTSD and was able to book an emergency session the very next day. He drove Knox to the appointment and sat in the waiting room while Dr. Thomason began a slow drilling into the abscess that had become Knox's soul.

With his probing questions, Dr. Thomason released enough of the pressure that day that Knox considered the possibility that he might be able to climb his way out of the darkness.

And on the day that he and Tanner stood by their SEAL brother's grave, absorbed the sobbing of his wife and three children, and felt the bottomless well of their grief, he felt the first flare of anger for what had been taken from them all.

That in trying to serve his country, Ace had made a choice that had repercussions he didn't know to expect.

In trying to save the lives of innocents, he had ended up sacrificing his own.

That afternoon, with a cold October wind at his back, Knox wondered what it would take to write himself a different ending.

~

THE STORY WASN'T pretty.

And there were times when it just didn't seem worth it.

After learning that he was getting help, Mariah put a halt to her petition for divorce. Called him one afternoon and told him she wanted to try again.

But he couldn't let her. He wasn't the same. And no matter how much therapy he subjected himself to, that was never going to change.

"You deserve far better, Mariah, than I am ever going to be able to give you."

"Knox, I love you," she said, crying softly. "I married you because I wanted to spend my life with you. If I'd had any idea I was going to be giving up my husband, I never would have agreed to you going to Afghanistan!"

"I signed on for every bit of it."

"But it's not fair," she said, barely able to get the words

through her tears. "It wasn't supposed to mean that we sacrificed our life together for it."

"I know," he said, wishing he had more to offer her. But he didn't. He simply didn't.

Emory

"You need to spend time crawling alone through shadows to truly appreciate what it is to stand in the sun."
—Shaun Hick

I CAN'T SLEEP.

After a revolving effort of staring at the ceiling, restacking my pillows, and rolling from one side of the bed to the other, I finally give up and vault off the mattress to head for the kitchen.

I open the bedroom door quietly, hoping the click of the lock doesn't wake the detective sleeping on my couch. I close the door behind me so that Pounce doesn't come out, and then tiptoe my way through the living room and into the kitchen.

I crack the refrigerator so that the light doesn't shine into the living room.

I'm about to reach for a yogurt when I hear, "Not much of a night for sleeping, huh?"

I jerk up, cracking my head on the top of the refrigerator. "Ow!"

The yowl that comes out of me surprises me as much as it does him.

He steps forward and presses two fingers to the place on my scalp. "That's gonna be a goose egg."

His touch surprises me, stuns me, actually. I take a step back, reaching my own hand up to press the sore spot. "Yeah."

He picks up a dishtowel from the kitchen counter and

then opens the freezer and pulls out some ice, wrapping the towel around it. He walks over and holds it up in question.

I nod, wincing a little as he tentatively presses the ice to the knot. "Sorry. I didn't mean to scare you."

"I was trying not to wake you."

"I wasn't doing much sleeping." Something in his voice makes me look up. "Bad dreams?"

He shrugs. "I'm used to it. I have something at home that I take most nights."

"Can you sleep without it?"

"Not very well."

"That's miserable."

He shrugs. "One of the things I brought back from Afghanistan."

"PTSD?"

He studies me for a moment, as if weighing how to answer. "That's what they say."

I consider this before answering with, "I've worked with some soldiers who are dealing with it. It's way more common than anyone would think."

"Apparently."

"I've wondered why that is."

"That soldiers come back with it or people are surprised by it?"

"Both, I guess." I realize that I must sound as if I am taking the realities of war lightly. "That didn't come out right."

He stares at me for a few long seconds, glancing off when he finally says, "Maybe it used to be that soldiers didn't survive the horrible stuff as much as they do now. Or maybe they came home and put it away better than we modern soldiers seem to be able to."

"Your training—"

"Prepares you for the battle. Just not the aftermath."

I lean against the kitchen counter, weighing my next question. "Do you ever regret being a soldier?"

He shrugs, holding my gaze. "If we pull a thread from the person we've always been, how do we know what we'll be when we finish unraveling?"

"We don't."

"So I guess I'd have to answer that with, 'It's who I am.' I don't know how to be anyone else."

"Was it what you thought it would be?"

"Yes and no."

"Like most things in life."

"Yeah. You're young to have figured that out."

We're looking directly at each other, and even in the dimly lit room, I feel like I really see him and that he really sees me. It's the most unsettling thing I've felt in a long time, but I don't want to look away. I want to see him, want him to see me. "I don't think it's age as much as it is experience."

"Life's a steamroller. It gets around to all of us eventually. Some sooner than others."

"You're strong. Or you never would have made it as a SEAL."

"I always thought of myself that way."

"You don't anymore?"

"I never thought I had a breaking point. Now I know I do. Even steel has a breaking point."

I see him hesitate, wait for him to go on.

"A tensile test finds out what happens when steel is stretched," he says. "You can place a steel bar in a device that pulls one end away from the other fixed end. The tensile strength is the maximum amount of stress the bar can handle before it breaks. If I had to describe what it was like to be in Afghanistan, that would be it."

He glances away, and there is another stretch of silence,

before he adds, "We like to think some things are just indestructible. Certain people. Certain places. Maybe that's how we convince ourselves things are safe enough for us to do. Who would ever have thought two skyscrapers in the middle of New York City could be brought down with airplanes?"

"It was unthinkable."

"And yet they were. All that steel and concrete couldn't withstand the impact of a commercial airliner turned into a kamikaze."

The remembered image is a sobering one. "There really aren't any words, are there?"

He shakes his head. "I don't think we're made to handle the kamikazes in life."

I think about Mia, the true horror of what has happened in the past few days, and tears fill my eyes. I bite my lip and glance away, reluctant to let him see.

He takes the ridiculous ice pack from my hand and sets it on the counter. We stare at each other in the dim light, and I feel somehow as if I'm really being seen for the first time in a very long time. Maybe because my own mother and father could look at me and know exactly what I was feeling. The thought brings tears to my eyes, and I am instantly mortified that this man whom I barely know continues to see glimpses of my bare soul.

I turn away, but his hand is on my shoulder, turning me back.

We don't say anything, watching each other, absorbing the silence and all the unspoken things shooting through the air around us. I have never before felt this kind of awareness of another person's effect on me. The obvious reasons are obvious enough. He is a beautiful man in every way I have ever thought counted. I've never felt the physical pull of attraction to be so undeniable. But it is.

Undeniable. I think of the reason our paths have crossed—my missing sister—and my emotions are in a sudden jumble again.

He wants to kiss me. I know this as surely as I have ever known anything. I feel the pull of it in the air between us, an electric current with its own charge.

He wants to.

But he doesn't.

His restraint impresses me even as I am disappointed.

Knox

"Some seek the comfort of their therapist's office, others head to the corner pub and dive into a pint, but I chose running as my therapy."
—Dean Karnazes

THE SUN THROWS a strip of light through the narrow break in the living room curtains. Knox opens his eyes to the glint, turning over on the leather couch and wincing at the stiffness in his neck. He tries to stretch out, but the sofa's length prevents it.

He glances at his watch. Barely six a.m. He considers going back to sleep, but his brain is already playing back the events of last night. He thinks about the girl who'd been murdered and wonders again if he might have done something to prevent it. Picked up on some hint of what was to come. But then he didn't think the girl herself had feared the guy or had any premonition of her fate.

He runs a hand through his hair and stares at the ceiling, a familiar sick feeling settling in the pit of his stomach. It was the same feeling he'd known too many times in Afghanistan, the result of guilt and blame, constant companions of the battlefield, whether he'd deserved it or not.

He vaults off the couch, heads for the half-bath near the kitchen and uses the toothbrush and toothpaste Emory had given him last night. He splashes water on his face, makes an attempt to tame his sleep-crazy hair, and then decides a

189

run is the only thing that will subdue the tangle of anger inside him.

He lets himself out the front door, trying to be quiet enough not to wake Emory. From the back of his Jeep, he grabs a duffel bag in which he keeps a change of clothes and running shorts and a shirt.

Inside the house, he quickly changes and lets himself back outside into the crisp spring morning. He takes off at a brisk pace, intent on blanking his mind for the next forty-five minutes.

The McLean neighborhood is exclusive. Judges, senators, old money, each house he passes as impressive as the last.

He picks up his pace, his breathing increasing with the effort. He tries to concentrate on the sound of his shoes hitting the asphalt, but the questions won't leave him alone.

The guy in the Range Rover. Sergio. Was he just some pervert who might have snatched Mia and Grace on a whim? A guy who otherwise lived a normal life, dating normal girls like Madison? Or was that part of his cover?

What would have made him think he had no choice but to kill her? It seemed an extreme choice given that the most she could have told him was that a cop was asking questions about him. And it wasn't as if she had given them any information at all.

Had she told him that? Had he not believed her? Had she known something he wasn't willing to risk her divulging at some point? Possibly. Likely. Why else would he have killed her?

He kicks the pace up again, sweat running down the sides of his face. He wipes it away with the bottom of his shirt, glances at his watch to see how far he's gone. Three miles. He crosses the street and heads back the way he came.

And now he's thinking about last night, about the awareness between him and the woman who's supposed to be his client and nothing more. Had he imagined it? He didn't think so. Not that his own judgment where women were concerned was anything resembling reliable. Relationships weren't an option. He'd sacrificed his marriage to his own need to sabotage whatever good might be left in his life.

As for the senator's wife, he'd be the first to admit his judgment was severely lacking. But she was a woman who'd expected nothing more from him than what she'd asked for.

Emory Benson was a different thing altogether.

And he wasn't going there.

Maybe he wasn't a complete lost cause.

~

HE'D LOCKED THE front door when he left the house, so he has no choice but to knock when he gets back just before seven-thirty.

Emory opens it, peering around the edge of the door and then opening it wider when she sees that it's him. "Good morning," she says, running a hand through the ponytail at the nape of her neck. He's noticed she does this when she's uncertain about something.

"Morning," he says, stepping inside. "I hope I didn't wake you when I left."

"No," she says. "I set the alarm. But good for you, getting a run in this early."

"It's how I face the day," he says, trying to insert a light note in his voice. "How did you sleep?"

"Not much, actually. My brain doesn't want to turn off. I think exhaustion finally got the better of me."

"Yeah," he says, suddenly aware of his sweaty clothes

and the fact that he's probably smelled better. "You mind if I get a quick shower?"

"No," she says. "You can use the one in my room. There are towels on the rack by the tub."

"Thank you," he says.

"Thank you for staying last night. I went to bed thinking about that guy, and I don't think I would have slept at all if you hadn't."

"No problem."

"Do you like eggs?"

"Yes. That sounds good."

A few beats of silence hang between them, and then he heads for her bedroom while she turns toward the kitchen.

In the bathroom, he turns on the shower, pulling off his sweaty shirt. There's a rap at the door. He opens it, and Emory hands him a white mug of steaming coffee. "That looks great. Thanks," he says.

She stares at his bare chest, her eyes snagged there just long enough to allow the return of that same awareness he'd felt last night. She looks up, meeting his eyes with an uncertainty that makes him wonder about that doctor from the hospital and whether he makes her this uncomfortable.

"I thought you might like a cup," she says, her voice low now and a little uneven.

They stand there, locked in a moment that could have been a second long or a hundred. All he knows is that the pull of temptation is as hot as the coffee she's just brought him. "I won't be long," he says. He takes a deliberate step back and then closes the door.

Mia

"I guess humans like to watch a little destruction. Sand castles, houses of cards, that's where they begin. Their great skill is their capacity to escalate."
—Markus Zusak

ONCE WHEN SHE and Emory took a vacation to Saint Martin for her sixteenth birthday, they spent an afternoon in the hotel spa that overlooked the ocean. They'd had facials and massages, gotten themselves caked in a full-body clay detox thing that caused their skin to tingle and then glow afterwards.

The spa room there had looked much like this one—low, soft lighting, white walls with a special bed in the middle made to look inviting with its white sheets and soft white blankets. It had smelled like this one too. Eucalyptus and mint and citrus layered together.

But despite the similar appearance, this place wasn't actually anything at all like Saint Martin. In this room, she is lying flat on her back, staring at the ceiling, her wrists and ankles anchored to the bed with some kind of special clasp to prevent her from getting up.

She'd tried. So many times now that she knows there will be rubs on her skin. She doesn't care though. If she thought it would do any good, she would jerk at the bindings until she freed herself, not even caring whether she left behind a part of herself in the trap.

The heavy door at the side of the room opens. A woman enters. She's dressed like a doctor, white lab coat over white pants. Serious, black-frame glasses on her face. She walks over to the sink and washes her hands.

"Hi," Mia says, staring at her back.

She doesn't answer so Mia repeats, "Hi."

The woman turns, still without answering, and walks over to pull the sheet and blanket off Mia, exposing her nakedness beneath. She studies her dispassionately, up and down, as if she's observing a new car she's considering buying.

Crimson heat stains Mia's face. "What are you doing?" she asks.

"I am Helga. I will need to shower you," she says in a thick German accent, not meeting Mia's gaze. "Can you do this without my assistant, or will I need to call him?"

Mia knows who the assistant is. The same hulking man who had escorted her from the other room to this one. The one who had ordered her to undress and refused to turn his back while she did. The one who let his eyes take their fill of her as he strapped on the restraints. The thought of him watching her be showered made her instantly nauseous.

"No," she says. "He doesn't need to be here."

"Good. I have a remote in my pocket. Should I push the button on it, he will be inside the room within fifteen seconds. I believe you have already been warned as to what will happen should his powers of persuasion be necessary."

Mia nods. She doesn't trust herself to speak because the scream at the back of her throat will no doubt bring about exactly what the woman has warned her about.

"Excellent," the woman says, removing a key from her white lab coat and unlocking each cuff. "Stand up and walk to the shower, please."

Mia does so, trying not to think about her nakedness, realizing modesty is a long-gone luxury.

The woman opens the shower door, beckons her inside

with one hand. Mia stands with her back to her, closing her eyes on the futile hope that she can block out what is happening to her, somehow lessen its impact.

The water turns on, runs for a few seconds, and Mia feels it hit the center of her spine. She draws in a sharp breath. The woman rinses her entire back and legs, orders her to bend over and aims the spray between her legs. Tears well in Mia's eyes, but she bites her lip to hold them back. The woman turns her around and does the same to her front side. When she finally turns off the water, she picks up a bottle on the wall shelf and proceeds to squirt Mia from head to toe body with its contents. The smell is a familiar antiseptic smell, and she realizes she is being sterilized.

Humiliation threatens to choke her.

Next, the woman pours soap onto a white washcloth, and then cleans every inch of her with that. She works as if she is preparing an operating room for surgery and every inch must be impeccably sanitary.

Anger again burns through the humiliation, but there is no place for it to go. One misstep on her part will bring that monster of a man into the room, and so she is left with the choice of the lesser evil. But she doesn't bother to hold back the tears now. They stream down her face, mixing with the soap and antiseptic.

When the woman has finished cleaning her with the washcloth, she picks up the spray nozzle and blasts the soap away. She looks up at Mia's face, notices the tears there and then raises the spray to wash those away also.

When she's done, she hands Mia an enormous white towel and says, "Dry yourself, please, and then return to the table."

Mia takes her time, somehow knowing she does not want to go back to that table.

Noticing her reluctance, the woman reaches in her

pocket and pulls out the remote, her finger resting on the button. Mia instantly drops the towel and goes to the table, refusing to meet the woman's eyes.

Once she lies back down, the woman places her wrists and ankles back in the restraints. She opens a cabinet, removes something and places it in the nearby microwave. A beep sounds and then the microwave turns on. The woman pulls a phone from her pocket, taps the screen, and then studies it for the sixty seconds until the machine beeps and stops.

She pulls a bowl from inside and takes a wooden spreader from a drawer. She dips it in the bowl and stirs. Mia realizes it is a bowl of wax. The woman tests its heat with her finger, and apparently satisfied, begins spreading it on Mia's leg. "You have been waxed before?" she asks.

Mia shakes her head, refusing to look at her.

"I will do your legs and a Brazilian. You know what this is?"

Mia turns her head to the wall, a fresh wave of humiliation hitting her. How can this really be happening to her?

"I see that you do know. I won't lie. It's unpleasant. But it will be over quickly. And I have a special cream that will take away the sting."

She rips the first strip of wax from Mia's leg, and Mia bites her lip to keep from crying out.

For the rest of the time during which the woman spreads more wax, waits for it to cool, and then rips it away, Mia keeps her eyes closed. She tries to make herself believe that she is somewhere else, that she is *someone* else, that she will wake up and find this is all a nightmare. That none of it ever happened.

But the woman unhooks the ankle restraints and says, "Spread your legs, please."

Mia refuses to do so.

"Shall I call Hugo and ask him to spread them for you?"

Pure rage burns in the back of Mia's throat as she does as she's been asked.

The woman laughs a short laugh. "I suggest you get used to the idea. The doctor will come in to fit you with an IUD once I'm done. All guests are asked to wear protection, but accidents do happen."

At that moment, if she could have gotten her hands on a knife, a cyanide pill, a gun, she would have killed herself.

No question at all.

The Proprietor

*"Know your enemy and know yourself and you can fight a
hundred battles without disaster."*
—**Sun Tzu**

THE TEXT SIMPLY read:

**Please schedule a meeting for account 98. Would like
to bring guest.**

The message had arrived on the phone she used for her
most exclusive accounts—98 was Senator Hagan. Odd that
he was asking to bring someone with him. Discreet was
Hagan's middle name, and he'd never made such a request
before.

She types a reply.

Will need more info on guest.

The reply is nearly immediate.

100% reliable.

Did he really believe that?
She certainly didn't.

**Not possible.
Wouldn't ask if it weren't necessary.**

Necessary? Seriously?

Irritation needles her, but she pushes it away. Senator Hagan is the perfect client. Pays in cash. Takes care with the girls. No power plays or kinky crap.

But this is a big ask.

Will need dossier.
Already prepared it. Will send it by courier this afternoon.
If dossier pans out, when would account 98 like a meeting?
Tonight, if possible.
Booked.
Tomorrow night then.
I will let you know.
Look forward to hearing from you.

She does not like being strong-armed, but resists the urge to wage a power play. Hagan has brought her a number of good clients, but none with such short notice. Something about it raises her defense hackles. She'll look at the dossier, but the intuition she has always prided herself on tells her this one will warrant extra scrutiny.

One cannot be too selective or too careful.

Emory

WE'RE ON THE way to the store where Madison had worked. Knox wants to ask some questions of other employees there. He's already warned me we'll have to wait if there's any sign of other cops or detectives doing the same. Clearly, he's trying to avoid another entanglement with his chief.

We're sitting in traffic on I-66 when he looks over, one hand draped on the steering wheel. "What happened to your parents?" he asks, his eyes intent on mine.

I glance out the window of the Jeep, not sure how to voice the real answer. I could give him the one believed to be true by the rest of the world, the one that didn't make me look like the awful person I know myself to be.

The silence expands to fill the vehicle with a heavy expectation. He says nothing further, just looks straight ahead, driving. When I finally speak, my voice is laced with the heavy, bitter price of regret. "I'm fairly sure I killed them."

He swings a glance my way, and I can feel the question in his eyes. "What does that mean, Emory?"

"That people can die from hurt."

"How did you hurt them?"

I'm quiet for a stretch, weighing the words. "By rejecting them. Rebelling against who they were."

He's quiet for a good bit, and then, "Do you think you're unique in that?"

I shake my head, still refusing to look at him. "No. I'm sure I'm not. But that doesn't make it any easier to live with."

"I looked it up. Head-on with a drunk driver."

I do look at him then, surprise underscoring the single word question. "Why?" And then I realize the answer. "Because I'm a suspect."

"In the beginning, we have to consider all angles."

I shrug. "Yeah."

"Did you have a fight with your parents before that night?"

"Yes."

"Said things you wish you could take back?"

"Yes."

"We all have, Emory."

I look down at my hands, see the places on my palm where I've dug my nails in. "But some of us get the chance to apologize. Ask for forgiveness."

"True. But they loved you, right?"

"Yes. Although from here, I can't imagine why."

"Do you think they would want you to live with guilt over their deaths?"

"No. That doesn't mean I shouldn't."

"My guess is you've devoted your life to your sister in an effort to make up for that guilt."

"I love my sister. There wasn't anyone else."

"Not every eighteen-year-old would be willing to grow up overnight to raise a sibling."

I consider this, but cannot imagine having made any other choice.

"Life took a horrible turn, and you made the most of it. Give yourself credit for that."

"What kind of person would I have been to do anything other than what I did?"

"The kind I meet every day in my job. The kind who takes their shattered dreams out on their kid so they end up in the foster system. The kind who beats their dog because they had a bad day. The kind who dumps their old dad at the nursing home and never gets around to going to see him. A lot of people operate from the origin point of self first. So, yeah, you could have made some very different choices given your age and how much essentially becoming a parent was going to change your life."

I let the words sink in, and, on some level, I do know that I've tried to do right by Mia, to make up in whatever way I could for the ragged ending of my relationship with my parents. "One of the things I find myself telling patients most often is the need to figure out how to forgive themselves for the things they can't seem to let go of. And yet, I can't do it myself. That doesn't make me much of a psychiatrist, does it?"

"It's a tall order," he says, his voice dipping under a note of what sounds like empathy. "Believe me, I know."

I want to ask how he knows, but I'm not sure either one of us needs to go there.

The Proprietor

"All cruelty springs from weakness."
—Seneca

SHE COULDN'T FIND a speck of public dirt on Senator Will Arrington. She'd run him through her standard check process, and it was rigorous.

So she contacted the next rung on her ladder, a former FBI agent who'd been released from his position when he'd been caught selling information to a foreign government. Ten years in prison had honed his already admirable willingness to go to whatever lengths necessary to meet a client's expectations.

He'd hand-delivered a dossier to her with nuggets of useful feedback she knew weren't available on the regular person's internet. But then she wanted the stuff that wasn't readily available elsewhere. Those things that exposed a person's true vulnerabilities. Made it impossible for him to choose owning up to conscience as an option.

The ex-agent had found her a juicy piece of leverage that provided her with ample confidence that letting him visit Hotel California with Senator Hagan would not be an unwise move.

The senator had asked for two appointments this evening. He would be bringing the younger senator for dinner with dessert scheduled at ten p.m. She thought it would be a good idea to serve up her newest project for the younger senator's first time.

Based on the ex-agent's revelations, the delectable Mia

should still be in the age range of what suited his well-hidden tastes. In fact, they would make her appear younger for the occasion. A little less makeup, a dress with some lace here and there, and they would make the senator extra happy. So happy, that she had no doubt he would be a return customer. Trapped, like all the others, by the need to feed his own desires.

No matter the cost.

Knox

"How ridiculous and how strange to be surprised at anything which happens in life."
—Marcus Aurelius

HE RECOGNIZES DAWSON Healy's unmarked car sitting in front of the retail store. He considers circling the block and waiting for them to leave. Healy won't be a problem. But his partner will. Nonetheless, he'll get information out of Healy he won't be able to get elsewhere, so it's worth the risk. And there's the fact that Healy will probably talk his partner down from the ledge of reporting back to the chief.

He's just cut the engine to the Jeep when Healy and Detective Marsha Rutgers walk out of the store, headed for his black sedan. "Stay here, okay?" he says to Emory and gets out, calling, "Hey, Healy."

The detective turns, a smile accompanying his look of surprise when he spots Knox. "What are you doing here?" he asks, covering the sidewalk between them in a few long strides. He claps Knox's shoulder with a wide-palmed hand. "That's just shit about your disciplinary leave, man."

"I'm calling it unpaid vacation."

"The unpaid part sucks."

"Thought I might head down to the Bahamas for some sun and fun."

"You? Yeah, right."

"Not convincing, huh?"

207

"Not in the least. So what are you doing here? I heard you're temping for the sister of that missing girl."

Knox shrugs. "Yeah. I assume you're here on the murder last night?"

Healy nods. "Didn't get anything promising in there though. What were you doing here last night? Some connection between the missing teenagers and this girl?"

"Maybe. She was seeing a Colombian guy who bought clothes here. I think he might be the same guy I spotted on security footage at the music festival the two girls attended the night they disappeared."

"And he offed her for talking to you?"

"Looks that way."

"Damn. Any leads on the guy?"

Marsha Rutgers saunters over, nailing Knox with a you-know-better glare. She's five-five and bench presses three hundred and twenty-five. It's a well-known fact around the department that Detective Rutgers will chase a perp down like a German-trained dog given the Fass! command. "What are you doing here, Healy?" she asks, even though it's clear she already knows.

"Shopping. You?"

"Like hell you are. You're on leave. Or did you forget?"

"I haven't forgotten. Need some new clothes for my unexpected vacation."

"You wouldn't be in that particular boat if you hadn't been dicking around with a senator's wife."

"Language, Rutgers," Healy admonishes, folding his arms across his chest. "Helmer has a right to shop wherever he wants. I noticed they're having a good sale."

She leans back and gives him a silencing stare. "Do I look like I just fell off the turnip truck?"

"Actually, you're looking pretty hot today, Rutgers," Healy says, grinning. "If you'd like to practice that bench press, I'm pushing three hundred these days. I'll volunteer my body."

"You want me to get you written up too?" she asks without cracking a smile.

"No, ma'am," Healy says.

"Afraid I'll have to let the chief know about your shopping excursion, Helmer."

"Sure thing," he says. "Might want to let her know about the sale too."

Rutgers turns around and strides back to the black sedan.

"You see the smoke coming out of her ears?" Healy asks with a grin.

"Yeah. She can't stand me."

"I think she has a crush on you, actually."

"Right. I think she has a crush on the chief."

"No way."

"Way."

"I didn't see that one coming."

"What are you, blind?"

Healy shakes his head. "I'll see if I can get her to cut you a break."

"Would appreciate it. You learn anything at all in there?"

"Seriously, no. No one knew anything about the guy except he was a rich Colombian who paid in cash."

"Mind if I give it a try?"

"Not if you share what you get."

"Will do."

"Hey."

Knox turns to find Emory standing beside him. "Hey," he says. "Emory Benson, Detective Dawson Healy."

"Nice to meet you," she says, sticking out her hand.

Healy gives her a look that Knox recognizes. "You too," he says. "All right then, better get going. Already got an irate partner."

"Later," Knox says, taking Emory's elbow and heading toward the store. They're at the door when his phone dings with a text notification. He glances at the screen and sees the one word message from Healy.

Snack.

He shoves the phone in his pocket and opens the door, waiting for Emory to step inside.

"Something wrong?" she asks, giving him a look of concern.

He wonders what she would say about Healy's assessment even as he knows he would never tell her. Something about it doesn't sit right with him, even though it is typical of something Healy would have said to him about other women they've encountered.

Besides, that's not what he needs to be thinking about right now anyway.

"No," he says, heading for the register. "Everything's fine."

A very tall, very thin, twenty-something man stands behind the counter, piercings in an array on both ears, each nostril, and his lower lip. His name badge reads Jason. He gives Knox a once over and says, "Can I be of assistance? We have a very cool, gray leather jacket just in that I am imagining would look fabulous on you."

He feels Emory's smile but determines to focus on why they're here. "Thanks," he says, meeting the sales guy's hopeful stare with a look that immediately squashes any visible hope of a sale. "I'd like to ask you a few questions, if you don't mind."

"Are you with the police?" he asks, fingering the loop in his lip and looking suddenly suspicious. "I told the two who were just in here what I knew, which is nothing really."

"I'm not officially with the police," Knox says, putting

a hand on Emory's shoulder to bring her into the conversation. "I'm doing some private work for Dr. Benson here. Her sister and a friend were abducted. I believe the man who murdered Madison Willard might have had something to do with their disappearance."

"Well, that sucks, clearly," Jason says, looking a little more sympathetic. "But after what he did to Madison, do you think it seems like a good idea for me to rat on the guy?"

"Did you ever meet him?" Knox asks.

"Once."

"Here in the store?"

"Yes."

"What was your impression of him?"

"Honestly?"

"Yeah."

"Ice, man."

"What do you mean?"

"Something in those eyes. Like there was nobody home."

"So what did Madison see in him?"

"She liked the flash, I guess. She said he would take her out to dinner and pay for a three hundred dollar meal with cash."

"She didn't find that suspicious?"

He shrugs a narrow-shouldered shrug. "Not as much as she found it appealing, I guess."

"She tell you what he does for a living?"

"She didn't know. I said, girl, you don't think he's with the mob, do you?" He angles Knox a wide-eyed look. "I mean, is there a Colombian mob in our country? He certainly fit the make."

Knox ignores the assessment, saying, "Did she tell you

anything about where he lives? A place he might have taken her."

"She said he only wanted to go to her place. She was curious about what kind of place he might have, but she said he kept putting her off when she'd ask to see it."

"Can you think of anything she might have told you that could help us find him?"

He's silent for a few seconds, then slowly shakes his head. "I wish I could. But no. Nothing."

Emory has been standing next to him the entire time, silent. She steps forward, her voice low and urgent when she says, "Jason, my sister and her friend are seventeen years old. I am praying they are still alive. To think otherwise is unbearable. I will take any lead, no matter how small it might seem, if it gives us even the slightest hope of finding them. Please. Can you go over the times you saw him in the store just one more time. Anything that stood out about him? Anything at all?"

Knox stays quiet, letting Emory's plea stand on its own.

Jason studies her for a long moment, taps the stud in his left nostril with his index finger. And Knox can see there is something Jason is weighing the wisdom of divulging. It's a risk. Knox won't lie to him and say it isn't. The guy they're looking for is clearly a psychopath and intent on cleaning up loose ends. Knox can't blame Jason for not wanting to be one.

But decency wins out. Knox can see the moment the decision to reveal what he knows crosses Jason's face. Knox keeps silent, waiting for him to leap the chasm of reluctance on his own.

"There is one thing," he says in a soft voice, as if the Colombian might be hiding in the dressing room behind them. Knox and Emory both wait, even as he knows her patience is as thin as his own.

"Madison said he talked in his sleep. Some crazy stuff, mumbling about beatings, maybe when he was a kid. Or maybe not. I don't know. But there was a place he talked about."

"What was it?"

"Some place he called the hotel."

"What kind of hotel?" Knox asks.

"No idea." He hesitates and then pulls a phone from his back pocket. "She sent me a video one night of him talking in his sleep. She thought it was funny. We were fairly open with each other about our love lives, its quirks and whatnot."

Knox feels his heart kick up a beat. "Could we see it, please?"

His hesitation is only a flicker of a second, as if he realizes he's come too far to turn back now. He taps the screen, opens the text app, scrolls down, and clicks once, handing the phone to Knox.

Knox taps the play button and holds the phone closer to Emory. She's so still, he wonders if she's holding her breath. The video starts, the headboard of a bed is the first shot on the screen. There's no sound. The camera moves to a man, sleeping, flat on his back, one arm thrown up above his head. Even in the dimness, Knox can tell it's the same guy on the festival footage, the same guy who ran out of Madison's apartment last night.

A few seconds of silence pass, and then he mumbles something that isn't a recognizable word. His head moves side to side. The camera remains still on him. *Hotel California. Back to Hotel California.*

A low giggle follows. Madison's giggle. "You want to go to Hotel California? That's kind of a long way." And then the camera turns off.

Knox looks up at Jason. "Will you send this to me?"

"Keep my name out of it?" Jason asks.

"Will do."

Knox gives him his number and waits for him to send the video, before saying, "Thank you. I understand not wanting to be involved, but you're a stand-up guy."

Jason smiles, and it's clear that the compliment means something to him. "Thanks, man. I hope you find him. Madison was a good friend to me. She shouldn't have died like that. No one should die like that."

"No," Emory says. "No one should. Thank you, Jason."

They leave the store then, and it isn't until they're back in the Jeep that Knox plays the video again. They watch it five times, back to back before Knox looks at Emory and says, "Next on our list. Figure out where the heck Hotel California is."

Mia

"Nobody can hurt me without my permission."
—Mahatma Gandhi

THEY'D LIED, of course.

She and Grace were not together.

Following her sanitization, Mia had been taken to a different room from the one she'd been held in before. This room was like a place where she would be living. Alone. There was a bed. A sofa. A bathroom. A closet with clothes in it that looked nothing like anything she would ever wear. There was a small kitchen with a refrigerator and food in it.

There was a door, locked from the outside. And there were no windows.

There was a TV with a remote. Flicking through, she noticed there were no news channels. Only channels featuring old shows, most of which she'd never heard of.

Mia sat on the edge of the bed, fighting an overwhelming feeling of claustrophobia, panic clawing at her throat.

She felt paralyzed with a choking combination of fear and fury. How could this have happened to her? To them? Where was Grace? Was she hurt? Was she even alive? Was that why they weren't letting her see her? Had they already killed her?

Sobs rise in her throat, tears flooding from her eyes in a sudden rush. She's trapped. The absoluteness of this hits her as it has not until this very moment. She has no way out. No way to fight back. No way to free herself.

She can only sit here, waiting for her fate to come, and

she knows it isn't going to be a good one, given everything that awful woman did to her over the past couple of hours.

Panic grips her like a vice around her throat. She knows without doubt that she wants to die. She will not sit and wait for whatever they have planned for her to come.

She leaps from the bed, running to the small kitchen with its row of drawers. She yanks each one open, praying there is a knife inside, anything sharp enough to slice her wrists, allow the blood to flow out of her body, releasing the life they are going to take anyway.

But the drawers are empty, and she collapses onto the floor, sobbing so hard she cannot breathe.

The door clicks, and there is the sound of keys turning multiple locks before it swings open, and the hulk of a man who had brought her to this room steps inside, a syringe in his hand. "Proprietor says you are to have this. You have an appointment this evening, and you cannot greet your first customer with a face ruined by crying. You will sleep until you are needed."

"No," Mia screams, jumping to her feet and running to the far side of the bed.

He doesn't bother to chase her, merely pulls a gun from his coat pocket and points it at her. "I am allowed to use this as a last resort. Do you want last resort or syringe?"

Mia stares at the gun, wanting so badly to tell him to shoot her. But she won't. That would be leaving on their terms. She'll leave on her own.

She sits down on the side of the bed, her shoulders slumping, and waits for the needle to do its work.

Emory

"That which does not kill us makes us stronger."
—Friedrich Nietzsche

WE AGREE TO start online. This time at Knox's apartment.

We'd been closer to his place than my house when we'd left the store after our talk with Jason. Knox had asked if I would mind if he changed clothes and said we could use his laptop.

And so I find myself standing in the center of his living room, trying not to listen to the sounds coming from his bedroom that indicate he might be in a state of undress.

I focus on my surroundings, noting the fact that the walls are bare, the furniture is minimal, and it really does look like the kind of place a person would do nothing more than eat, sleep, and shower in. A place where a person has not chosen to create a life but rather an existence.

I circle behind the sofa to the lone table backed up against it. A single photo sits in the center in a silver frame. I pick it up, recognize Knox—a younger, obviously happier Knox. He's wearing a tuxedo, and the woman on his arm, a wedding dress.

They're both smiling, looking into each other's eyes. She's utterly beautiful. She's holding a bouquet of roses, and they look as if they can't wait to start the life ahead of them.

And yet, there was no ring on Knox's finger now. Yes, I'd noticed. No white telltale imprint to indicate he'd

217

recently removed it to hide the fact that he was married. This definitely wasn't an apartment made to look like a home by a loving wife.

The bedroom door opens. I attempt to place the frame back on the table, but set it down too quickly and it turns over, glass down.

I glance up to find Knox staring at me. "I'm so sorry," I say. "I shouldn't have—"

"It's okay," he says, walking over to right the frame.

The silence that follows is awkward, and yet I find myself saying, "She's beautiful."

"Yes," he agrees. "She is."

I want to ask, but I don't. It's none of my business, but I'm surprised when he says, "She deserved far better than what I ended up being able to give her."

"You look so happy in the photo."

"We were."

"What happened?" The question is out before I realize I am asking it.

He runs a finger along the top of the frame, his voice regretful when he says, "I guess I wasn't able to be two people. The man you see in this picture. And the one who came back from Afghanistan. That wasn't the same man she married."

"I'm sorry," I say, and I really am. It seems so unfair that two people could begin a life together, certain of what they had, only to find it all torn apart by something as horrible as war.

"So am I. But she's happy again. Remarried. And that's good."

"Do you mean that?" I ask, my psychiatrist's curiosity surprised that he could want something for her that he clearly no longer had.

"I actually do. She never wanted me to be in the military.

That was my dream. It blew up in my face and ended up damaging us both."

There should be something for me to say. I've spent years of my life studying how to help people with trauma, people whose lives have been upended by things they never saw coming. And yet, I can find nothing that seems appropriate. Maybe it's my own trauma, my own current inability to believe what has happened to Mia that has left me empty of anything resembling professional empathy.

Knox turns then, waves me toward the sofa and says, "Let me grab the laptop, and we'll get started."

I sit at one end while he disappears into the bedroom, returning a few moments later with a rather beaten-up computer. He sits down next to me, and I realize then we'll have to sit close for me to be able to see. A table with chairs might have solved that, but there isn't one, so I try not to think about the fact that our arms are touching. Is it my imagination that I can feel the heat of his body emanating like a force field colliding with my own?

"It looks bad," he says, "but still works." He opens the lid, waits for the screen to pop up, then moves the cursor to the top to engage the wireless network.

Once it has, he opens a new screen, cursors up to the search engine bar and types in *hotel california*.

I look over his shoulder at the first offering, a video for the song by the Eagles. Next, Wikipedia lists the song, declaring it the title track from the 1977 Eagles' album.

The next listing is the Hotel California in Todos Santos, Mexico.

"Could that be it?" I ask, pointing at the listing.

"It could be, but why Mexico? Let's see what else we can find." He traces his finger down the screen, past more references to the Eagles' song and then clicks over to the next page. It's halfway down the second page that his finger stops on Hotel California, Loudoun County, Virginia.

He clicks. The webpage features a beautiful old brick mansion, southern in architecture with enormous white columns on the front. A small discreet sign at the entrance gate reads, Hotel California. The heading at the top of the page says: "Known as a getaway destination for senators and Washington, DC, influentials."

"That's a lot closer," I say. "Maybe he had a rendezvous out there?"

Knox cocks his head, throws me a look. "Did you just say rendezvous?"

My face seeps crimson. "Hookup then. Is that modern enough?"

"I guess it's all the same," he says, trying not to smile. "Maybe someone out there would remember him. We'll show his picture around, see if anyone recognizes him."

We both read the description, noting the fact that it's on the National Register of Historic Places.

"It's about an hour away," I say.

"Probably a goose chase," he says, "but it's worth a shot."

"Agreed," I say, wishing I felt more hopeful about it.

He closes the lid on the laptop, starts to get up from the sofa just as I do. Our legs bump, and it's as if we've both been zapped with a jolt of stunning electricity. He looks at me. I look at him. And the air around us is charged with things I've never felt before. I want to touch him so bad that I actually can't even think beyond that single thought. My hand moves of its own accord, as if it doesn't need my permission to do what it wants. I touch his face, feel the stubble that is evidence of the shave he'd skipped this morning.

Again, feeling jolts through me, hot and searing.

"Emory," he says on a low, husky note of sanity, the awareness there telling me he knows this is a path we shouldn't take. And I know it too.

But still, my hand turns so that my knuckles smooth across his jawline. I hear his sharp intake of breath and know a wave of power I've never felt with anyone. When it comes to physical relationships, I am all but a novice. I've yet to have a single experience that convinced me the hype about sex was anywhere near accurate.

But here, in this moment, touching this man, I realize he's the one who could show me why I've been wrong. What I've been missing out on.

"Why you?" I ask softly, as if he knows what I've been thinking.

Judging from the look in his eyes, I think he does. How, I don't know. Maybe he feels it, but I can see that he wants me as much as I want him.

I lean in, so close that our lips are almost touching. We hang there between the urge to give in and the realization that it is a line that once crossed might permanently change our ability to go forward with the reason we are together in the first place.

Mia.

Her name flashes through my brain, and I sit back, suddenly ashamed of even this momentary lapse into my own needs.

"Mia," I say out loud, my voice breaking across her name. "What kind of sister am I?"

This time, it is Knox who runs his hand across my hair, one finger tipping my chin up so that I have to look at him. "A human one," he says quietly. "It's normal to want comfort from someone who understands. There's nothing wrong with that."

My psychiatrist mind knows he is right. But there's more

that I want from him. That's the part that makes me wonder how that could possibly be when the vast majority of me is in the worst kind of mourning for what has happened and the unbearable question of how it will end.

"Here's something I know," he says, no longer touching me, as if he doesn't trust himself. "Human beings aren't one dimensional. Life isn't one dimensional. Even when we're experiencing something we don't even know how to process, we need to feel alive, be reminded all is not completely insane."

"Was it like that for you in Afghanistan?"

"Yes. We somehow had to compartmentalize. Head out on a mission where we might end up losing civilians who weren't supposed to be in the line of fire. And then play cards that night before bed and try not to be shocked by our own laughter. Life is never all good or all bad. On a daily basis, it's a never-ending switching back and forth between the two. Somehow the blend is bearable most of the time."

"But the two of us right now . . ."

He gives me a long, layering look. "You know what I really want to do right now?"

I hesitate, not sure I need to hear what he's going to say. But I can't help it. I want to hear it. "What?" I ask, the word barely audible.

"Pick you up. Carry you into my room and make you forget about everything going on in your life right now except the fact that I am inside you. Make you certain with every move of my body that I don't want to be anywhere else."

A sharp intake of breath tells us both I have just visualized him doing exactly that.

And then he says, "But I'm afraid that's a recipe for regret on your part. And I've caused enough regret in my life."

I get up from the sofa then, walk to the door on shaky legs, turn the knob. Without looking back at him, I say, "I'll wait for you outside."

It isn't until I reach the Jeep that I allow myself a deep breath and the reluctant admission that I am in way over my head.

Emory

"To perceive is to suffer."
—Aristotle

I FEEL LIKE this is going to take us nowhere.

What is the likelihood that something the Colombian guy mumbled in his sleep is even real? Maybe it's a place where he grew up, or who knows what?

We're about to take the exit off I-66 for Route 29 when I spot a truck ahead, loaded with chickens in wire crates. Feathers are flying out of the truck and floating onto our windshield.

I let out a long sigh, and Knox looks at me, eyebrows raised.

"I hate those trucks," I say.

Knox lets off the gas, but the truck has slowed down too, and we're close enough that I can see the poor things flattened inside the crates, unable to stand. Tears spring to my eyes and start down my cheeks. I wipe them away, looking out my window to avoid seeing the picture ahead of us. But it's emblazoned on my eyes already, and I can't hold back the sudden urge to sob. Nor can I stop the scream that rips from my throat. "I . . . hate . . . this . . . world," I say, crying so hard now that I can barely get the words out. "Everywhere you look . . . there's cruelty."

"Hey," he says, putting a hand on my shoulder and squeezing softly. "They'll be out of sight in a minute."

"Does that change what's going to happen to them? Does my not seeing it mean they won't be slaughtered?"

225

"Do you want me to pull over?"

"No," I say, shaking my head. "We need to get to the next place. What if Mia is in a cage somewhere? What if someone is planning to do something awful to her?" I am outright sobbing now, and there's nothing I can do to stop it. It's as if a hole inside me has been ripped open, and all the pain I feel over Mia's disappearance, all the empathy I've ever felt for people and animals not in control of their own fate, comes pouring out of me, a tidal wave of emotion that flattens me.

"Oh, shit!"

I look up just in time to see one of the crates flying off the back of the truck. It bounces in the center of the lane in front of us. Knox slams on the brakes, and I just know we're going to hit it. Somehow, though, it's airbound again, landing in the pull-over lane and skidding across the asphalt into the grass at the edge of the pavement.

Knox whips the Jeep off the road and comes to a tire-smoking stop. Without saying a word, we're both out and running back to the spot where the crate is tipped up on one corner.

"Oh, my gosh!" I say. "Are they okay?"

"I don't know," Knox says, leaning in to get a better look at the chickens. "There are two in there."

He pulls the corner of the crate forward, leveling it on the grass. But just then the latch at the top pops open, and the two chickens fly upward like a phoenix rising from the ashes. They flap onto the grass just beyond the crate and land, only to fall over. They get up and try to walk and fly at the same time.

"You get the one on the left," Knox says, taking off after them. "I'll get the other one."

And that's how we end up on the side of I-66, chasing

after two chickens whose destiny has somehow just taken a one-eighty turn. It takes us five minutes or more, and I can't even imagine what the cars driving by must think. I catch mine first, but only after all but throwing myself on top of the chicken, her outraged clucks making me laugh even as I hold on tight to her, turning over to lie on my back and stare at the sky that is now bright blue again.

"Got her!" Knox yells out. He is laughing too, and a minute later, he's standing beside me holding that chicken as if it's the prize at the end of a battle that has overthrown a rogue dictatorship.

He drops down beside me, holding his chicken on his chest. We both drag in deep breaths until we can talk again without gasping. The chickens cluck softly now, no longer fighting us, and I have to think they somehow know what they've escaped.

"For a psychiatrist," Knox says, "you're not the sanest person I've ever met."

I start to laugh again. "Coming from you, I'm going to take that as a compliment."

The Senator

*"I've come to know that what we want in life is the
greatest indication of who we really are."*
—Richard Paul Evans

HE'D EXPECTED PUSHBACK from the younger
senator. From everything he'd heard, the guy was a
straight-up arrow. Driving all the way out to Loudon
County for dinner might interfere with the eight hours of
sleep he publicly declares necessary for his well-being.
Arrogant little shit.

Hagan knows he sounds like a pissy old fart, but
sometimes the arrogance of his underlings was more than
a little hard to take. They thought they knew everything.
Had it all figured out. Riding high on their ideals and the
certainty that they were the sole mediums for all solutions
to human problems sent to them via the universe.

Will Arrington wasn't the first upstart he'd had to shape
into a new way of thinking. There had been others before
him. With the right inducement and the appropriate
compromising position soundly documented via today's
technology, there had yet to be a resister.

He actually looks forward to these virgin initiations.
There's the power aspect for sure, but something innately
satisfying about bringing the proud to a slightly more
acceptable position of humility.

He gets up from his desk, pulls a key from beneath the
middle drawer, and walks over to the filing cabinet in the
corner of the office. He opens the drawer, then pulls it

out altogether. He reaches inside and uses a second key to open the door carved into the actual wall. It's small, six inches by six inches, but large enough to hold the small boxes of Rohypnol. The oval, greenish-gray pills are hard to get these days. He uses four layers of purchasing to get to the actual dealer so that he's as removed as possible. These newer versions of the drug make clear liquids turn bright blue and dark drinks cloudy. He'll need to make sure Arrington orders red wine or a dark soft drink. As a last resort, coffee at the end of the meal will do.

Also known as roofies or the forget pill, it's his favorite inducement because most people don't remember what happens when they are under its influence. He knows from personal experience that the Proprietor records what goes on in the rooms at the Hotel California. Which is where Sergio comes in. He has agreed to get him a copy of the video. He knows it's risky. The proprietor would do away with Sergio in a heartbeat if she knew of their agreement. Not that Sergio is going to tell her. He's got his own motivation, admitting once that he is saving up for a new life on an island somewhere. Hagan just hopes it's not anytime soon. But then, given the way the guy likes to spend money, probably not.

He places one of the small pill boxes in the pocket of his suit jacket, makes sure it's securely hidden.

Tonight's the night, to quote an old Rod Stewart favorite. And then everything'll be all right.

Knox

"I did not become a vegetarian for my health, I did it for the health of the chickens."
—Isaac Bashevis Singer

THEY ARRIVE AT the entrance to Hotel California just before four o'clock. Knox makes the right turn onto the long, paved drive that leads to the hotel.

The chickens are sitting side by side in the middle of the back seat, their heads tucked close to each other.

"I can't believe they're just sitting there like that," he says, glancing at Emory.

She reaches back to rub each of them, and, amazingly, they seem to like it. "They know they're safe," she says.

"I've never spent any time around chickens, but they seem content."

"Wow. It's beautiful," Emory says, as the hotel comes into sight.

"Yeah. Explains why it's a getaway for the wealthiest of the wealthy."

Knox turns the Jeep into the parking lot to the right of one of the enormous oaks on the front lawn. A half dozen cars are lined up in the individual spots, all Mercedes or better. He notices a couple have Washington, DC, plates.

He pulls in at the end of the row, cuts the engine to the Jeep.

"Should we both go in?" Emory asks.

"Why don't I go in first?" Knox asks. "Get the lay of the land."

231

"Okay. I'll stay here with the chickens."

Knox shakes his head as he walks across the parking lot and up the wide stairs at the front of the hotel. What the heck are they going to do with two chickens?

The lobby is impressive—gleaming, old, hardwood floors, walnut maybe? Enormous, ornate gold mirrors line the wall of a winding staircase centered in the middle of the entrance. To the right is the check-in desk.

The man standing at the center looks up to greet him with a subdued smile. He's wearing a stern navy suit, starched white shirt, and muted pink tie. His bald head gleams beneath the crystal chandelier hanging above him. "May I help you, sir?" he asks in a voice that sounds as if he's spent a good deal of time reading classic novels. Somewhere between Charles Dickens and F. Scott Fitzgerald.

Knox steps up to the counter, rests a hand on the rolled edge of the heavy wood. He decides to use his MPD credentials on the hunch that he isn't going to get far with this guy without them. Hoping he doesn't ask for ID, Knox says, "I hope so. I'm with the DC Metropolitan Police Department. I'm looking for someone who might have visited your hotel or be connected in some way."

The man draws in a nearly invisible breath, makes an obvious effort to keep his smile in place. "Yes?"

"His name is Sergio."

The man considers this for a moment, raises an eyebrow. "Do you have a last name?"

"No. I don't." Knox keeps his voice even, as if he isn't aware of the other man's subtle condescension.

"Our guest records are confidential, of course, but I don't recall anyone by that name visiting the hotel in recent history. Nor am I aware of anyone by that name connected to the hotel."

Knox weighs the answer.

"Is there a manager I could speak to?"

The smile becomes more accommodating, even as he shakes his head. "I'm afraid she is not available at the present. If you would like to leave your name and number, I will ask her to call you."

He hands Knox a pen and a white notecard. Knox writes down his contact info, handing it back to him. He thanks the man and turns for the door, unable to shake the feeling that there's something going on under the surface of their communication.

His phone dings. He pulls it from his pocket, taps the text app, and sees that it's a message from Emory.

Just saw a dark Range Rover pull out from behind the hotel. Headed for the entrance gate.

Knox slips the phone back in his pocket and takes off running for the Jeep. He jumps under the wheel and says, "How long since you saw the vehicle?"

"He pulled out right after you went in the hotel. I texted you, but wasn't sure it went through. I only had one bar. I started to come in and get you, but I didn't want to give away anything."

"Let's just see if we can catch up. Luckily, this place is at the end of the state road, so he could only go one way."

He guns the Jeep out of the parking lot, one of the chickens clucking in protest.

"Did you get a good look at the driver?"

"I think it was a man. He was driving fast, and I wasn't expecting to see it. Did you find out anything inside?"

"No," he says, reaching the hotel's entrance gate and swinging right. He floors the Jeep, and they're at seventy on the two-lane road with no vehicles in sight ahead of them. "Can't put my finger on it, but something was up with the guy at the front desk. He was doing his best to not look bothered by my questions."

They drive over the speed limit for ten minutes before he finally lets up and says, "Afraid we aren't catching up with him."

He pulls into the parking lot of a small car garage. A mechanic standing in the entrance of one of the bays lifts a hand in greeting. Knox lifts a hand to let him know they're all good.

"What now?" Emory asks.

"Well, no idea if we're on to anything or not. Let's go back as customers though. We could have dinner at the restaurant. See what we see."

"Tonight?"

"Yeah."

"You do remember we have two chickens in the back seat?"

He glances over his shoulder. "You call and see if we can get a reservation, and we'll run back to the city, deposit the chickens at your house, and change clothes."

"I'll look up the number," she says, picking up her phone.

Emory

"Hope is the thing with feathers
That perches in the soul
And sings the tune without the words
And never stops at all."
—Emily Dickinson

THE RESTAURANT AT Hotel California has an eight o'clock reservation for two available. Knox drops me and the chickens off at my house and heads back to his apartment to get clothes, because a coat and tie are required attire.

I spend twenty minutes or so fixing a spot for the chickens in the laundry room. An extra litter box borrowed from Pounce filled with kitty litter seems to suit them fine for a potty, as they both make immediate use of it. I place a water bowl and food bowl next to a pillow, then look online to find out what to feed chickens, afraid to guess and be wrong.

At the top of the search request: "Many chickens also love food treats such as corn, bananas, tomatoes, or leafy greens. Healthy treats such as these make a nice supplement to a pelleted ration. Make sure to avoid feeding highly salted foods, chocolate, avocado, alcohol, or caffeine, as these foods can make your bird ill."

For now, spinach, tomato, and banana should suit them nicely.

Remembering that chickens like to roost, I place a broom between the washer and dryer, then pick up each

235

chicken and set them atop the broom stick. They each squawk at first, but then massage the stick with their feet, moving left then right until they find a spot they're happy with. Soft clucking indicates they're satisfied with my offering.

I leave the laundry room, closing the door firmly behind me. Introducing them to Pounce will have to come later.

In my room, I scan my closet for a dress that seems appropriate for the restaurant, finally deciding on a black sleeveless that fits nicely but falls short of sexy.

I jump in the shower, quickly pull my hair out of its ponytail and give it a quick shampoo, not taking time for conditioner. I run a razor over my legs and armpits, then towel off before grabbing the blow dryer from a cabinet drawer.

Pounce meows persistently, weaving back and forth between my ankles. I reach down and rub his back. "I miss her too. We just have to get her back. Neither one of us is going to give up hope."

Knox

*"Knowing someone isn't coming back
doesn't mean you ever stop waiting."*
—Toby Barlow

HE SHOULDN'T NOTICE how she looks.

He actually tries not to while she locks the front door of the house and walks quickly to the Jeep. He wonders if he should get out and open her door, then decides it will seem like this is something other than what it is.

She gets in, tugs down the skirt of her dress, before clicking her seat belt.

He backs out of the driveway, keeping his focus straight ahead. "Chickens settled in?"

"Actually, they seemed happy. I looked up what to feed them. Luckily, I had some spinach and bananas."

"Are you going to keep them?"

I think about it for a moment, and then, "Yeah, I think I am."

"What did Pounce think of them?"

"I decided to wait on that introduction."

He smiles, one wrist draped over the steering wheel. "I'm guessing that was a good idea."

"I think he'll come around."

"I'd bet against it." He looks at her then, a second too long, and the Jeep swerves a little. "Sorry."

She glances down at her hands, and he can feel her awareness of the fact that he was looking at her.

"You look nice," he says.

237

"Thank you. So do you."

They drive in silence for a mile or two while he searches for appropriate footing, a place to steer the conversation that is in line with the actual reason they are dressed up and headed back to Hotel California.

"What happens if we see him?" Emory asks, looking at the darkness speeding by outside her window.

"I'll call for backup. We already know he's willing to kill to keep his tracks covered."

"What if he's already killed her?"

"You can't think like that."

"I don't want to. I just can't bring myself to think about how she is, if she's hurt or hungry or—"

"Emory. Don't, okay? It won't help anything. And she needs you to keep pulling for her."

She looks at him then, and he lets himself glance at her face. The pain has unraveled, her eyes damp with tears. He's realized that most of the time she keeps it tightly wrapped, the edges pressed together one over the other, so that anyone who didn't know what was going on in her life would have been hard pressed to notice anything was wrong. Maybe it was the professional persona she'd had to develop with an impending career in psychiatry.

"How long do families wait?" she asks quietly. "Before they give up."

"Some never do. Others need to at some point. Have to have the closure to go on. We're not there yet, Emory. I'm not giving up."

She reaches across, covers his hand with hers. He can feel her gratitude in the pulse throbbing in her palm. And something else he's reluctant to name. It's nice though. He doesn't pull his hand away and feels a bit of a loss when she finally pulls her own back to her lap, and her view to the darkness out her window.

The Senator

"Knowing where the trap is—that's the first step in evading it."
—**Frank Herbert**

HE GIVES HIS driver Arrington's Georgetown address. When they pull up in front of the Beaux Arts townhouse on Massachusetts Avenue, he realizes the young senator is even more well-funded than his own research had indicated. The Embassy Row properties were hard to come by and would be valued at upward of seven million.

Nice to know though that he had chosen the appropriate form of persuasion with Arrington. Money wasn't likely to have much pull, when it was already in such apparent abundance.

He sends a text to let Arrington know they're out front. The driver leaves the engine running, and in less than a minute, the young senator appears at the door, turns to tap a code into the lock, and then strides down the stone walkway, his very posture indicative of his position in life, his confidence that he has it all nailed down and perfectly within his control.

The driver gets out to walk around to the back of the car, opening the door as the senator approaches. Hagan turns his head to the window, allows himself a smile of satisfaction. But when Arrington slides into the back seat, Hagan's greeting is just plain old South Carolina glad-you-could-come.

Mia

"Man is the cruelest animal."
—Friedrich Nietzsche

SHE COMES OUT of the fog with a start, opening her eyes to find a woman standing next to the bed, studying her.

Mia has never seen anyone with eyes like this. They make her think of a machine. Her eyes are more robot than human. Taking in what is in front of her without emotion, simply processing information and drawing a conclusion.

"You are awake," the woman says.

Mia bolts upright, the haze around her brain fully lifted. She doesn't bother answering, pulling the front of her robe closed and sliding back to the headboard of the bed.

"There is nowhere to go," the woman says matter-of-factly. "Surely you realize this by now."

The sudden urge to launch herself at this evil woman is nearly overwhelming. Mia's fingernails aren't long but she wonders if they would be sufficient to claw the woman's eyes out. She wants to. She wonders where the girl of a few days ago has gone. That girl would have been nauseated by the idea. Now, the thought is so exhilarating that she has to forcibly tamp it back down.

"Yes," she says, reaching deep for a note of meekness.

The woman smiles. "You might try whatever tricks you feel are worth your effort. But I must assure you that I am aware of them all. You are not the first to be here. You will not be the last. You see, once you are in the trap,

241

fighting will only expend your energy. There is no escape. The trap has been created to make certain of that. It has been perfected."

"You're sick," Mia says. "How does anyone become so evil?"

She stares at Mia long enough that Mia is certain she is reconsidering her fate. Maybe she will go ahead and kill her, end what is inevitable.

"I've always respected a worthy adversary. I can see I've found one in you. But you must know there have been others like you. And that I never lose. It is time for you to get dressed. Your clothes have been laid out for you." She points to the outfit at the foot of the bed. "Shall I have Helga come and help you?"

"No," Mia says quickly.

The woman laughs. "I thought not. And so I will share with you some information about your guest this evening. His taste apparently runs in the direction of younger . . . women. You will notice the outfit I have provided is more girlish than we will normally give you, but we try to make sure our guests get exactly what they wish for. The doctor has told me you're still a virgin so that will be a bonus, I'm sure."

Mia feels all the color drain from her face, as she realizes the doctor must have examined her while she was unconscious. Her face burns, as if hot pokers have been pressed to her cheeks. "I won't do it. You can't make me."

The woman sighs. "More theatrics? You will do this, my dear. There are cameras in the room, and if I do not see that you are giving our guest what he has paid to receive, I will send Sergio to your sister's house and instruct him to finish with her what he started with you. Before he kills her, that is."

Tears of pure fury well in Mia's eyes and stream down her cheeks. "I hate you."

Her laugh is lighter now. "Hatred is not a bad thing. It might just keep you alive."

Sergio

"The best laid schemes o' Mice an' Men..."
—Robert Burns

THE CHOP SHOP thrives in a hidden garage behind a well-known car dealership in downtown DC. New vehicles are sold on the front end, happy customers driving off with no idea that the real moneymaker at the place is the stolen car business on the back end. Some of the stolen vehicles are even sold as new.

Sergio pulls around to the rear of the impressive building, waiting for the center garage door to open. He'd sent Leonard Henderson, the guy in charge of the operation, a text a half hour ago with a short message:

Need to move the Range. Can you provide a new ride?

The answer was yes, of course.

The part Leonard hadn't added was "for the right price." This one's going to cost him, put a definite dent in his future plans. But he'll make up for it. So he's made a couple of mistakes recently. Madison and that new girl at the hotel. He's learned from those mistakes though, and he won't be making them again.

Sergio pulls onto the center of the concrete floor. On one side of him, guys in coveralls are searching a Mercedes-Benz S65 AMG Cabriolet, no doubt looking for personal items to remove. List $250,000. On the other side, two more guys are unbolting the front end of a BMW from the frame. He'd watched them take a car apart once, marveled at how they cut out the windshield, removed the doors and seats. They also cut the roof supports and sawed through the floor beneath the steering wheel. It's quite a production, and they are usually finished with the whole job within a few hours. If he didn't have his own line of work already established, it's something he could see himself doing.

Leonard walks through a side door, waves a hand in greeting. Sergio cuts the engine and gets out.

"You got heat?" Leonard asks.

"Maybe," Sergio admits.

Leonard reaches out to shake his hand, and they meet eyes for a moment. Sergio doesn't bother lying to him. Leonard isn't the kind of man you lie to. At six-three with boulder-wide shoulders and a grip that means business, he reminds Sergio of his employer. They have in common the same knack for reading people, eyes of steel culling truth from fiction, bullshit from reality.

"I've got some vehicles going overseas in a couple of days. The Range Rover can go with those. We'll get the location devices disabled first. What kind of ride you lookin' for?"

"Escalade would be nice."

"Got a nearly new, black one. The VIN plate's been switched with a junked car of the same make."

"How much?"

"With the trade on the Range Rover, thirty K."

"Twenty-five is deal."

"Twenty-eight, and cash, of course."

"Of course," Sergio says, realizing he's in no position to negotiate further.

"Wait here. We'll have the Escalade out in a few."

Sergio pats the envelope in his jacket pocket. He'd

brought thirty-five, so he'll have a bit left over. He loved the Range Rover, but he'd learned long ago that when something no longer serves you or has the potential to take you down, you simply part ways.

Emotional connection is for those who want to get caught. And he isn't getting caught. Ever. There is a life ahead of him that he fully intends to lead. Sooner rather than later.

Emory

CRAZY, BUT IT almost feels like we are on a date.

Not just crazy. Utterly crazy.

Sitting at a table for two, in the low-lit, romantically evocative restaurant of the Hotel California, we no doubt look like two people on a date. Neither of us has on a wedding band, so that negates the marriage assumption.

And, of course, I haven't missed the not-so-subtle glances of at least three women in the restaurant who have validated my own conclusion that Knox does indeed clean up well.

With a build like his, clothes aren't necessary to make the man, but the black blazer complements the width of his shoulders, and the white shirt, open at the neck, looks great against his tan neck.

"Emory?"

"Ah, yes?" I say quickly, realizing he has been saying something to me.

"Would you like a drink?"

"A glass of red wine would be nice."

He waves at a nearby waitress, who walks over with a smile on her pretty face, her eyes locked on Knox's face. "What can I get you?" she asks.

"Could we get a drink menu?" he says, returning her smile.

"Of course," she says, laughing self-consciously as she hands him one of the two she is holding, and then, as if remembering I'm at the table, hands me the other. "May I offer any suggestions?"

"A smooth red?" I say.

"We have a lovely Virginia wine that is full and smooth. It's a customer favorite."

"I'll try that," I say.

"Bourbon. Neat," Knox says.

We study the dinner menu in slightly awkward silence while she goes off to get our drinks. The words blur before my eyes, and I finally look up and say, "What exactly are we looking for here?"

"The next dot," he says, meeting my gaze with a level stare.

"How will we know it when we see it?"

"We might not. No sign of the Range Rover when we came in. So he might not come back here."

Just hearing the words makes my heart drop. We have no other lead. This one just has to pan out.

"While we're waiting for our drinks, I'm going to take a look around," Knox says. "You're good here?"

"Can't I come with you?"

"I think it's better if you stay here. I won't be long."

I want to argue, but I know he's right. This whole thing might be a wild goose chase, but on the off chance that it's not, we need to look as normal as possible. "Okay," I say. "Be careful."

He considers my words, as if they've surprised him. "I'll be back."

Knox

"Sooner or later the universe will serve you the revenge that you deserve."
—Jessica Brody

HE CAN'T PUT his finger on it, but something about this place gives him a weird feeling.

He walks out of the restaurant and heads down a hallway marked by a brass plate that reads GUEST ROOMS. The hall is wide, each room door a heavy walnut. The floor is made of wide wood boards with raised nail heads marking each corner. His steps make a not unpleasant squeak, the kind that defines a historic building.

He reaches the end of the hall and finds a wide set of stairs that lead to the next floor. He walks up and follows the hallway of the second floor. The doors are the same as those on the first floor. He's yet to hear sounds coming from any of the rooms, a television turned on or people talking. The place is eerily quiet.

At the end of the corridor, a woman appears. She's tall, over six feet in low heels. The word *imposing* pops into his head. Her black hair is pulled back in a bun at the nape of her neck, and her cheek bones are harshly prominent. She's dressed in a black suit with a dark-red blouse. She smiles at him, but it's a gesture that does not reach her eyes.

"Good evening," she says. "Is there something I can help you with?"

"No," he says, meeting her gaze with the awareness that

251

she has singled him out for questioning. "I was just looking around."

"You're not a guest at the hotel."

Statement, not question. "Just having dinner in the restaurant."

"Ah. And what is your conclusion of the place?"

"It's beautiful."

"Isn't it?"

"Lots of history here, I would imagine."

"Yes. When I bought the place, the bones were visible, but it took some vision to restore it to what it was."

"How long have you owned it?"

"Fifteen years."

"It's quite a jewel."

"Thank you. I hope you'll come back for a stay at some point."

"Definitely," he says, wondering why the owner of such a place would find his presence here concerning. Had she spotted him on a security camera? Or just happened to be walking his way?

"Well," he says, "I'd better get back to my dinner date."

"Enjoy," she says, waiting at the top of the stairs as he starts his descent.

He can feel her gaze on his back the entire way down. Security conscious management? Most likely. But he can't shake the feeling that there was something odd about the encounter. She'd been sizing him up, evaluating his presence and what it meant.

At the table, Emory looks up at him with a question in her eyes. "Find anything?"

He sits down, picks up the bourbon he'd ordered before leaving the table and takes a leveling sip. "I met the owner," he says.

"And?"

"I think she minded my looking around."

"Why?"

"Just the feeling I got."

"Did you ask her about Sergio?"

"No," he says, shaking his head. "Wasn't sure I should play that card with her yet."

Two men appear at the restaurant entrance, the hostess hurrying over to greet them. Knox notices, starts to look away, and then recognizes one of them. Senator Hagan. Shit.

"What is it?" Emory asks.

"Karma," he says. "Ready to order?"

The Senator

"… the devil doesn't come dressed in a red cape and pointy horns.
He comes as everything you've ever wished for …"
—Tucker Max

THERE WAS A limit to what one should be willing to do for one's country.

Hagan thought he was reaching his own limit tonight.

So maybe personal interest was first and foremost, but still, listening to this young windbag go on about his civic duty for the past hour was nearly enough to make him ditch the whole plan.

He wondered how this generation had gotten so full of itself. Maybe it was the fact that they'd taken so many selfies that they'd started to believe their own hype.

Arrington actually thought he had the answers to all of the country's problems. Hell, the world's problems, for that matter.

Arrington sat across the table, cutting his green salad with knife and fork, taking one delicate bite of arugula at a time, droning on and on in that annoyingly Harvard-educated voice of his, as if he actually had a prayer of changing his mind about the vote.

Hagan kept his own expression placidly interested, nodding when appropriate, trying not to let his gaze fall on the glass of red wine to the right of Arrington's plate. He did let himself glance at his phone screen, noting the time at the top. Twelve minutes from now, the waitress would

255

approach their table to let Arrington know there was a call for him on the hotel's house phone.

Once the arrogant ass exited the dining room, Tom would add the contents of the vial in his jacket pocket to the glass of red wine.

And only then would the night get interesting.

Knox

"It's choice – not chance – that determines your destiny. "
—Jean Nidetch

FORTUNATELY, THEIR TABLE sits at an angle that allows Knox a clear view of Senator Hagan without Hagan seeing him. Not that Hagan would have noticed, even if the tables had been angled differently. He seems quite focused on his dinner companion, a young, notably confident guy in an obviously expensive suit.

It seems an odd match. Business meeting, he supposes, but there is something interesting in the way Hagan appears so attentive to the other man's every word. His gaze barely leaves the man's face. He could wonder if there was something other than business going on, but Hagan doesn't seem the type.

The waitress has just placed Emory's entrée—a vegetable plate with mashed potatoes and creamed corn—in front of her when the younger man leaves the table to follow the hostess out of the dining area. Knox lets his gaze follow him out, then glances back at Hagan. The senator takes a sip from the wineglass in front of him, then sets it back down. He glances at the doorway through which the younger man has just disappeared, then reaches across the table for his wineglass.

This seems odd to Knox, so he continues watching. The senator reaches in his pocket. Knox can't see what he takes out. Whatever it is, he holds it beneath the table and then, lightning quick, raises his hand and flips something into the glass of wine.

What the hell? Did he just put something in the other man's drink?

"What is it?" Emory asks, noticing that Knox is staring across the room.

"I'm not sure," he says, shaking his head.

"Do you know him?" she asks, following his view to Hagan's table.

"Indirectly."

"What does that mean?"

He looks at Emory then, aware that he is about to change any positive opinion she might have begun to develop of him. "That's Senator Tom Hagan. His wife is the reason I'm on leave."

Her eyes widen as he watches her process what he's said, and it's clear this is the last thing she expects to hear. "Oh."

"Yeah. I have no idea how we both ended up here at the same time. But I'm fairly sure he just spiked his dinner companion's wine."

"What? Are you kidding?"

"No. I'm not."

"Why would he do that? Although I can understand why he would spike yours."

"At least you still have your sense of humor."

"Did you see him do it?"

"I did."

"Are you going to tell the guy?"

All decency dictates that he should, but he is going on gut here, and something isn't right. Not about what he just witnessed. And not about this place.

"Let's drag this dinner out as long as we need to see what happens from here."

"But this doesn't have anything to do with Mia and Grace."

"Almost for sure not."

"We're wasting time, Knox."

"Probably, but—"

"I know. The next dot."

"Two desserts then?"

"Why not?"

The Proprietor

"If the officers are leading from in front, watch out for an attack from the rear."
—Howard Tayler

SHE CHECKS THE security footage once she gets back to her office, looking for the time the man in the hallway came into the hotel.

Holding the iPad in one hand, she scrolls back and finds it at 7:05 p.m. A young woman is with him, pretty enough to be his date. They're not holding hands or touching though, so she's not sure whether it's a date or something else.

Odd that he'd been walking the halls of the hotel when he'd just come for dinner. Not that people don't check it out, but she likes to remain aware of who's looking around. He doesn't look like a typical tourist. He looks like military to her. Cut jawline. Formidable build. Keen eye.

She could be accused of paranoia, but one doesn't stay ahead of the odds by ignoring anything that looks suspicious. She isn't starting now.

She'll double-check the dining room in a bit to make sure he and his companion leave the premises once they've finished their dinner.

The Senator

"Be careful not to compromise what you want most for what you want now."
—Zig Ziglar

HE HASN'T FELT like this since before he'd found out Santa Claus wasn't real as a young boy. That excitement when he'd first woken and realized it was Christmas morning, and he couldn't wait to find out what was under the tree.

Sitting here at the table, watching Arrington saunter through the restaurant to their table, the anticipation of waiting for him to pick up the glass, it is all he can do to sit still in his chair, pushing his food with his fork to one side of the plate.

"Everything all right?" he asks as Arrington pulls his chair out with poorly concealed irritation.

"No idea what that was all about. Whoever called had already hung up when I got to the phone."

"Why wouldn't they call your cell?"

"Beats me."

"Well, while you were gone, I considered what you've said tonight. You have some excellent points that I will weigh in my own voting decision. Let's toast to that. Working things out." He raises his wineglass and waits for Arrington to do the same.

The younger senator hesitates, his expression reflecting his surprise that Hagan has wavered on his position. The surprise is quickly replaced with a pleased look.

Arrogance. Does it every time. Arrington reaches for his glass, clinks it against the rim of Hagan's, the crystal making a pleasant ding.

"To unexpected pleasures," Arrington says, taking a hefty sip of the red wine, as if intent on rewarding himself for the hard work he's done here tonight.

"Indeed," Hagan says softly. "Indeed."

Mia

"Beauty lies in the eyes of the beholder."
—Plato

THE CLOTHES MAKE her feel like throwing up.

Mia stares at herself in the mirror, tears welling in her eyes at the realization she has been made to look like a much younger version of herself.

No makeup except for a touch of pink lipstick. Her hair has been braided with a matching pink ribbon laced through the woven strands. Her dress is white with a high neckline and scalloped lacing. Her shoes are flat, ballet slippers.

When she'd asked the horrible Helga why they were dressing her this way, she had laughed and said, "For playtime. What else?"

Mia cannot imagine what man would be attracted to her in these clothes, but when she lets herself dare to follow that line of thought, she is afraid she does know what kind.

Despair floods through her veins, and she wants to rip the dress from her body, shred it into tiny pieces. Yank the ribbon from her hair and scrub the pink lipstick from her mouth. But then she thinks about the woman with the dead eyes and the promise she had made if Mia does not go along with her plans. She pictures the enormous man who escorted her to the spa room and the thought of him touching her makes nausea well up inside her so that she runs to the sink and gags. Nothing comes up though, her stomach aching from the physical retching.

She raises her head to stare at herself in the mirror again, recognizing herself as the caged animal she is. There will be no good end to this. How can there be? They will use her until she is either used up or no longer suitable for their needs. There is only one choice, really. Wait for them to end it. Or end it herself. As soon as she can find a way.

Knox

*"The scientific method actually correctly uses the most
direct evidence as the most reliable,
because that's the way you are least likely to get led
astray into dead ends and to misunderstand your data."*
—Aubrey de Grey

EMORY HAS GONE to the restroom, and Knox is checking his phone for messages when he glances back at Hagan's table. So he hadn't imagined it.

The guy with Hagan is starting to look stoned. He's staring down at his plate as if he's never seen food. He reaches for a piece of bread from the basket at the center of the table, picks it up and twirls it around, aims for his mouth and misses.

Knox watches as Hagan leans over and says something to him. The guy's lips work in an odd, puppet-like way. The two of them sit for another minute or two, Hagan glancing at his watch and then speaking to the man again.

He slides his chair back and stands, then walks over to the other man's chair, takes his arm and helps him up. The guy wobbles a bit. The waitress walks over and looks concerned. Knox hears her ask if there's anything she can do to help.

"Slight overindulgence in that wonderful wine," Hagan says, his voice carrying. "Better get him home. My driver will be outside."

"Certainly, Senator Hagan," she says, backing away and giving them room to maneuver through the dining room.

Some of the other guests have started to stare. Hagan shoulders the guy out of the room, disappearing through the doorway Knox had used earlier to check out the hotel.

He slides back his chair and gets up as casually as possible, following the two men. He spots Hagan ahead in the corridor, steps into a recessed doorway, and grabs a glance around the corner. Hagan is all but carrying the guy now, gone any pretense of two drunk buddies having a good time. He hears someone coming and ducks back into the doorway. The voices are low and urgent, but he recognizes the new one. It's the woman he met in the hallway earlier.

He leans over far enough to verify that he's right. Their backs are to him, but there's no mistaking the tall, imposing owner of the hotel. She's now helping Hagan with the man, pressing what looks like a remote in her right hand. To Knox's surprise, what had appeared to be part of the hallway wall slides open. He hears the sound of elevator doors opening. And then Hagan and the woman drag the other man inside. And the wall closes behind them.

~

HE WAITS WHERE he is for a minute or two in case they come back out. When there's no further sound coming from the end of the hall, he steps out and walks quickly back to the restaurant.

Emory is sitting at the table now, looking up at him with a curious expression. "I thought you left without me."

"We need to go," he says quickly, pulling his wallet from his jacket.

"What's wrong?" she asks, her voice low and alarmed.

"I'll tell you when we get outside. Let's just pay and go."

He waves for the waitress, and it seems as if it takes

forever for her to run his credit card and bring back the receipt for him to sign. But once they're outside and headed for the Jeep, Knox takes Emory's arm and leans in, as if they're an ordinary couple at the end of an ordinary date.

"Something's going on here," he says close to her ear. "We might be being watched. I just saw Senator Hagan drug his dinner date and basically carry him out of the restaurant. And then the owner of the place helped him get the guy into an elevator hidden behind a wall."

He feels Emory stiffen but she says nothing until he opens her door and waits for her to get in the Jeep, before going around and sliding in the driver's side.

"What?!" she says, her voice rising.

"I know. It sounds crazy, but something's going on here."

"But what could that possibly have to do with Mia?"

"Probably nothing. I don't know."

She leans back in her seat, releases a long sigh. "We don't have time to waste figuring out why the disgruntled husband of your lover is taking advantage of his dinner companion."

"Ouch," Knox says, noting the edge to her voice.

"This was just a dead end, wasn't it?"

"Emory, I don't have the answer from here. We're following a trail of breadcrumbs, and the only way I can determine whether what we've found has anything to do with Mia is for me to follow it through to a conclusion. Do you want me to call an Uber for you to go back to the city?"

"No," she says abruptly. "I'm not going anywhere until I know what you've found."

"Okay, but I need to come up with a plan first."

"To do what?"

"Get inside that elevator."

"How did they get in?"

"The woman had a remote control."

Emory stares out the windshield for a moment, silent, and then, "Think she might have a second one in her office?"

"It's possible."

"So how do we get in her office?"

"You sure you're up for that?"

"I'm positive."

"The young woman at the front desk. Let's see what we can find out from her. If it looks like I'm getting somewhere, you say you're going to the ladies room, and you'll be right back."

"Should I ask what you have in mind?"

"Probably not."

The Proprietor

"Seldom, very seldom, does complete truth belong to any human disclosure; seldom can it happen that something is not a little disguised or a little mistaken."
—Jane Austen

SHE STARES AT the senator, fury blazing from her eyes. The elevator has delivered them to the hidden bunker of the hotel. The younger senator can barely stand.

"I have no idea what you think you are doing, Senator Hagan, but do you have any idea what you have risked here tonight?"

"I'm sorry," he says, looking at her with a confidence that belies his words. "He had a little too much to drink."

"This looks like more than overindulging on wine."

"May I be honest with you?"

"I recommend it."

"There's something I need Senator Arrington to do regarding an upcoming vote. He hasn't responded to the normal leverage I like to employ. I believe a video clip of him with the date you've set up for him would change his mind."

She stares at him for several long seconds, aware that he is struggling to hold Arrington up now. Her fury has turned to steel, and her mind scrolls through her options like a computer searching through code. With a single photo released on Twitter, she could ruin him. But the game plays both ways. She can see his awareness of this in the way he

271

holds her gaze. They are two predators sizing each other up, weighing the reality of whose weapon will inflict the most damage.

She steps back, pulls a set of keys from her jacket pocket. "This way," she says, aware that he thinks he has won. The battle, maybe. But not the war.

Mia

*"No one will come and save you. No one will come riding
on a white horse
and take all your worries away. You have to save
yourself, little by little, day by day."*
—Charlotte Eriksson

SHE HEARS THE key turn in the lock, stiffens from her spot on the edge of the bed. The door swings in. She stands quickly, pressing her hands down the front of her silly, pink dress.

The woman enters first. Behind her is a tall man in a suit all but carrying a younger man also wearing a suit. Fear rises on a rush of bile in her throat.

The man drags the nearly unconscious man to the bed and drops him there.

"What is this?" Mia asks, raising her chin to offset the quiver in her voice.

"Your date," the woman says. "He's a bit out of it at the moment, but he likes little girls, so you should be able to bring him around."

Mia's face blazes red as the man standing next to her stares at her bare legs, the fitted waist of the dress, and finally at her face. "Very nice," he says.

The woman looks at him, her eyes narrowing. "Do you have any special instructions for her?"

"Wake him up. And just make sure he smiles for the camera," he says.

"Camera?" Mia asks, horror replacing her nausea.

273

"Of course," the woman says in a calm voice. "How else will I know you're following through on our agreement?"

"Please," Mia says. "Don't do this. I'm not—"

"You know what your options are," she says, her gaze as cold as her voice. "I'm sure you have concluded by now that this limp excuse for a man will be a walk in the park compared to what I have planned for you if you do not cooperate. You have one hour."

She walks out of the room then, the other man following along behind her. The door closes behind them with an ominous thunk of the lock.

The man on the bed makes a moaning sound. Mia turns to look at him, pushing back her own disgust for what she has agreed to do. She glances at the corners of the ceiling, looking for the camera she knows is hidden somewhere. But there is nothing obvious. She cannot tell where it has been placed.

Is it worth it? Doing this to stay alive? How much time will it buy her? Is it time to give up? Let whatever is going to happen, happen?

She thinks of Emory and the fact that she would be leaving her alone in this world. If their places were reversed, would Emory leave her?

She knows the answer. No. She wouldn't.

Mia walks over to the sink, staring at her reflection in the mirror. It's like looking at someone she doesn't know. Maybe that's how she can get through this. Pretend she's someone else. A person she'll never see again after tonight. She picks up the glass at the corner of the sink, fills it with water. And then she walks over to the bed and tosses it in the man's face.

Emory

*"Do not avert your eyes. It is important that you see this.
It is important that you feel this."*
—Kamand Kojouri

WE'RE STANDING AT the front desk, and Knox is working his magic with the woman now smiling at him and waiting to hear how it is she can help him. She is mid-twenties with a serious manner supported by her dark-gray suit and the severity of her hairstyle, a bun at the nape of her neck, pulled back so tightly that her eyes appear to squint a bit. She hardly looks like a pushover, but Knox has adapted a relaxed, easy-going posture that somehow manages to make him an even sexier version of the man I came to dinner with.

"I met the owner of this beautiful place earlier at dinner," he says, leaning one elbow on the mahogany reception desk. "We were chatting in the hallway, and I think I might have dropped my phone near there. We've searched the hallway, but I thought she might have picked it up and turned it in here."

The woman—whose name tag reads Sarah— shakes her head and says, "No. I've been here all night. No phones have been turned in."

"Is she still here? Or has she gone home for the evening?"

"Actually, she lives here on the property, but she's not available at this time of evening."

"Ah. Is there a chance she might have put the phone in her office?"

Sarah shakes her head. "I don't know. I can find out for you in the morning."

"Oh. Shoot. We were driving back to the city tonight. I really need to get that phone."

"You know, hon," Emory says, "while you're sorting this out, I'm going to the little girls room."

Knox nods without taking his eyes off Sarah. "Okay. You do that," he says.

And as ridiculous as she knows it to be, Emory feels a little stab of jealousy as she heads out of the lobby without looking back.

Knox

"Do what you can, with what you've got, where you are."
—Squire Bill Widener

AS SOON AS Emory is out of sight, Knox leans forward, elbows resting on the desk, his gaze set on Sarah's face. Her eyes have gone wide behind her black-frame glasses, her lips slightly parted.

He glances over his shoulder and then back at Sarah. "I was hoping she would give us a minute or two. May I tell you something?"

"Ah, yes, I suppose so," she says in barely more than a whisper.

"I noticed you earlier in the night when my girlfriend and I were having dinner. I haven't been able to take my eyes off you."

Her eyes widen a little more. "Really?"

"I'm sure I'm not the first man to visit this place who's told you that."

"Oh. No. Of course not."

"You know what else I've been wondering?"

"What?" Her gaze darts to the hallway down which Emory had disappeared a minute before and then returns to his.

He leans in closer, says the words close to her ear. "What your kiss would taste like."

Her intake of breath is audible. "But I don't even know your name."

"Knox." He glances at her name badge. "And you're Sarah. A favorite name of mine."

A small smile touches the corners of her mouth. "Thank you."

"Is there a place where we could be alone for a few minutes so I could test my theory?"

"What's your theory?"

"That you taste as good as you look."

The struggle between her disbelief that he's serious and her desire to find out is visible on her face. A full ten seconds pass while he determines to let her make up her mind. And then she says, "We could look for your phone in the owner's office. Just in case she found it and, like you said, left it there until tomorrow."

"Lead the way," he says, his voice low and intent.

She sticks her head around the wall behind the desk. "I'll be back in a few minutes," she says.

A male voice answers with, "Got it covered."

Sarah steps around the reception desk and beckons for him to follow her toward a hallway that is on the opposite side of the lobby from the women's restroom. Knox hopes Emory won't return before they're out of sight.

They make it to the office with Sarah leading the way. She sticks a key in the lock and turns the knob. He follows her inside, closing the door behind them.

The office is dimly lit by a lamp on the corner of a desk in the center of the room. At the back of the office, an open door reveals part of a bathroom. Knox is weighing his options when Sarah launches herself at him, throwing her arms around his neck and kissing him as if she's been on a deserted island without male company for a few years at least.

He follows her lead, backing her across the room until they bump the desk.

"Oh, my gosh," she says, pulling back for a moment to begin unbuttoning his shirt. "You are so beautiful. This isn't the kind of thing that ever happens to me."

"I find that hard to believe." He lowers his head to kiss her neck, untying the scarf at her throat. By the time he gets the knot undone, she has his shirt completely unbuttoned and is starting on his pants.

He pulls the scarf free from her blouse and spins her around to pin her against the desk.

"Whoa, cowboy," she says, laughing.

He slides his hands down her arms, grasps her wrists, and pulls them behind her back.

"Hey," she says, her laugh a little less certain now.

He quickly wraps the scarf around her wrists, whipping the fabric in a circle until he can secure it with a knot.

"Are we going Fifty Shades?" she asks on an uncertain giggle.

"Actually, Sarah," he says, swooping her up in his arms and holding her tight against him as he heads for the bathroom, "I'm going to have to put you on hold for a few minutes."

"What do you mean?"

"There's something I need to do, and I'll need you to wait in here."

He sets her down inside the shower stall, running his hands up and down her jacket and skirt in search of a phone. He finds it tucked inside a pocket, pulls it out and sets it on the sink before pulling the shower door closed. He reaches for the toilet brush beside the sink and wedges it through the door handles, effectively locking them.

Sarah stares at him in disbelief. "You can't leave me in here!"

"It's nothing personal."

"Why are you doing this? If she finds me here, I'll be fired!"

"I'd like to prevent that, but conflict of interest, I'm afraid."

"You ass!" she screams. "Let me out!"

He slams the door before the next expletive can reach his ears. Knowing he has limited time, he turns on the flashlight of his phone, not wanting to light up the office any more than necessary. He sits down on the chair behind the desk and begins opening drawers. The middle one holds nothing more than pens and paper clips. A side drawer contains some bland-looking files and envelopes.

The next two lower drawers are locked. He slides the chair back and drops to his knees to look under the center of the desk. He aims his phone flashlight at the corners, then slides his hand along the edges.

Bingo.

A small bracket holds what feels like a remote of some sort.

He tugs it free from the holder and pulls it out, recognizing it as similar to the one he'd watched the owner of the hotel open that elevator with.

He jumps to his feet. Now to find Emory.

Emory

"The more I see, the less I know for sure."
—John Lennon

I'M SITTING IN a chair in the lobby, looking at my phone and trying to act as if my nerves aren't leaping beneath their pulse points. Facebook isn't holding my interest though, and I throw another nervous glance at the lobby entryway, wondering what Knox has gotten himself into.

It's then that I see him standing just inside the archway that leads to the restaurant. He waves for me to follow him. I get up and walk casually across the wood floor, and by the time I reach the arch, he's already jogging down the hallway.

"Knox!"

"Come on," he says over his shoulder. "We don't have much time."

"For what?" I'm actually running to catch up with him, and when I do, he reaches back to grab my hand, pulling me now in an all-out run.

At the end of the hallway, he comes to an abrupt stop, pulling something from his pocket and aiming it at the wall. I hear a click and then the wall begins to separate, revealing an elevator door.

"Wow," I say.

Still holding my hand, Knox pulls me inside and hits the Close Door button. We stand for a moment, staring at the panel. There's only one button, marked B. Knox pushes it, and the elevator whispers into motion.

I look at Knox, notice his disheveled hair and the lipstick at the corner of his mouth. "What did you do?" I ask softly.

He lets go of my hand. "Persuade and detain. She'll be fine. A little mad at me for the moment, but no lasting damage."

"You might want to wipe off the evidence of your technique," I say, even as I wonder at the nudge of envy rooting somewhere near my heart.

Knox

THE ELEVATOR STOPS, and the doors slowly slide open onto a hallway dimly lit with sconce lighting. The room doors are some kind of heavy wood with keypad locks. Knox scans the walls for security cameras and spots them immediately.

"We're not going to have much time," he says, beckoning Emory to follow him.

"This is crazy. She can't be here."

"Maybe not, but while we're here, let's make sure," he says, grabbing her hand to pull her along behind him until they reach the end of the hall where the camera appears to have the least reach.

"What's your plan?" she asks. "We're just going to knock?"

"No need to reinvent the wheel here," he says, rapping on the door in front of them with his knuckles. They stand for a moment, Knox pressing his ear to the wood and closing his eyes.

"Anything?" she whispers.

He shakes his head, and they move to the next one. He knocks again, the sound echoing in the long hall. They wait, and still nothing. The third door yields the same. Knox is beginning to think he's overreached on this one as he pounds on the fourth door. This was an insane idea.

What had made him think whatever Senator Hagan was up to could have anything to do with Mia's disappearance?

But in the next instant, a scream rips through the room behind the door. "Help! Help me!"

"Oh, my God. That's Grace! That's Grace!" Emory pounds on the door with both fists. "Grace! Grace! Open the door."

"I can't!"

"Shut up, you little bitch!" A man's voice, and he's clearly not happy.

Is that the senator? Knox scans the hallway, spotting the fire extinguisher next to the elevator door. He runs down the hall, grabs it, and uses the end to pound away at the keypad lock on the door. It doesn't take long to prove his effort a waste of time.

"What are you going to do?" Emory says, barely getting the words out.

He checks to see which side of the door the hinges are on.

"You're not going to break that with your shoulder, are you?"

"That only works in movies," he says. "And it usually gets you a dislocated shoulder. The door's hung so that it swings inward, so I might have a shot at kicking it in."

Emory throws him a shocked glance. "Seriously?"

"Stand back from the door!" Knox yells to the girl inside. "Okay?"

"Okay!" Grace's voice is now muffled, barely audible.

Knox drives the heel of his foot near the keyhole, supposedly the weakest part of the door. The wood splinters slightly. He aims another kick in the same spot, making sure not to hit the lock itself. He kicks again. And then again. The wood cracks further. It's the seventh attempt that finally caves the bottom of the door in. He reaches through and turns the door handle from the other side.

He pulls the Glock from the holster on the back of his belt. He aims the gun at the center of the room. Huddled behind the corner of the bed's headboard, a teenage girl is sobbing. She has no clothes on, and Knox averts his eyes, grabbing a blanket from the bed and holding it out.

Emory runs to her and wraps her in the blanket, her voice breaking when she says, "Grace! Oh, thank God. Are you okay?"

Grace clamors out and throws her arms around Emory's neck. She is crying so hard, she cannot speak. Sobs engulf her. She nods hard against Emory's shoulder.

"Grace, where is Mia?" Emory asks, holding her by the shoulders now and staring into her face.

Grace shakes her head, her voice wobbly when she says, "I—I haven't seen her since the man took us."

"You don't know if she's here?" Emory asks, the words infused with fear.

"No," she says on a half-gasp, and then she's crying full force again, holding on to Emory as if she's afraid she'll melt and disappear.

"The man . . . he's in the bathroom."

Emory places her hands on Grace's shoulders, stares hard into her eyes. "Stay here with Detective Helmer. He'll make sure you're safe. Promise me you'll stay here, okay?"

She looks up at Emory, her eyes brimming with tears, the fear she's no doubt felt for days now reluctant to release its grip. "Where are you going?" she asks in a barely audible voice.

"I'm going to find Mia. She has to be here somewhere. I'll be back as soon as I can. All right?"

"Emory, wait for me," Knox throws out, but she's

already gone. "Damn it!" He aims his gun at the bathroom door. "Open up!"

A couple of seconds pass, and there's no answer. "Okay, then, I'll open it for you." He aims a solid kick beneath the door handle.

This door is less substantial than the room door, and it gives on the fourth kick. Knox sticks his hand through the hole and turns the lock, swinging the door fully open. He aims the gun at Senator Hagan's chest.

"No need for that," the senator says, his voice icy cool. "Let's make a deal, shall we?"

"An underage girl in your room? And there's the little matter of the drug you put in your friend's drink at dinner. No deals for you, Senator."

"Watch out!"

Knox turns at Grace's scream. Just in time to see the gun with a silencer on the end. He jumps sideways, but not in time to avoid the bullet.

Emory

I BANG ON every door in the hallway, praying I will somehow know which room my sister is in. I hammer each door as I go, pressing my ear to the wood in the hope of hearing Mia's voice. But there's nothing all the way to the end of the hall on the same side as the room where we'd found Grace.

I cross the hallway and start pounding on the door at the end. Again, nothing on the first, the second, the third. At the fourth door down, I bang as hard as I can, my fist now throbbing from the effort. I press my ear to the door, and it's then that I hear her voice. Unmistakable.

"Help. Please help." And then louder. "Please! Help me!"

Adrenaline hurls me into action. There's no way I can kick the door in. I pull the gun that Knox had given me from the waistband of my jeans, release the safety. I know I could kill myself using the gun to destroy the lock, but at this point, what other choice is there? I have to get it open.

I step to the side of the door and aim the muzzle directly above the keypad lock. I turn my head, close my eyes, and pull the trigger.

The lock shatters, a piece of the metal blowing out and hitting me in the side. I feel its jagged edge pierce my skin and gasp, stunned by the pain. But the lock is broken, dangling now as the other one had. I use my shoulder to shove the door inward, screaming out Mia's name as I go.

She is sitting on the bed in the middle of the room.

Her knees are drawn up tight against her chest, the expression on her face one of frozen fear. She's wearing a pink dress that looks like something a ten-year-old would wear. Her hair is braided, a pink ribbon on each end.

There's a man on the bed beside her, naked and seemingly unconscious. I look at his face and recognize him as the man from the restaurant. The one who left with the senator, looking as if he'd had too much to drink.

I run to Mia, dropping to my knees at the side of the bed and reaching for her. She falls into my arms, still saying nothing, as if she's unable to let herself believe I'm really here. Like it might all be a dream. "Mia," I say, wrapping my arms around her and hugging her so hard I'm afraid I'm actually hurting her.

She remains stiff for a few seconds, and then, all of a sudden, she throws her arms around my neck and starts to sob. She's crying so hard she can barely breathe. I'm crying too, trying to drag in gulps of air as I hold her against me, not sure I will ever be able to let her go.

"How did you find me?" she asks, looking into my eyes, her own pooling with fresh tears.

"It doesn't matter right now. All that matters is that we get out of here as fast as possible."

"Actually, I'm afraid that won't be at all possible."

The voice startles me, and I jump to my feet to find a very tall woman with ink-black hair pulled back in a tight bun at the nape of her neck, staring at me with hatred gleaming in those dark eyes.

"From here, I'm afraid there will only be one option for the two of you," she says in a deadly quiet voice. She lifts the gun in her right hand and points it directly at me.

"Sadly, you have created quite a messy situation for us to clean up, but these things do happen. We'll do what is necessary to get back to normal."

She looks at me then and says, "I think my mistake was in not listening to my initial feeling about you, dear girl. I have found that the only mistakes that arise here are the ones that occur after I have ignored my intuition. You have taught me a final lesson, and this will not happen again. Sergio has taken care of your other friends, so if you'll please come with me, we'll get this over with as quickly and as neatly as possible."

I stare at the woman, trying to process what she's just said, even as I realize I am listening to the words of a psychopath. "What have you done to Knox?" I scream.

"If his safety was your concern, you should have thought of that before trespassing where you do not belong."

"If you've hurt him or Grace—"

The woman laughs. "You'll what?" she asks. "You're hardly in a position to be making threats."

I frantically search my mind for a way to buy time and force myself not to glance at the gun I'd placed on the floor beside the bed. Can I reach for it fast enough, or will she shoot Mia or me before I can even get it in my hand? I'm afraid this is exactly what will happen so I aim for another tactic to stall her.

"You don't really think you're going to get away with this, do you?" I ask, locking my gaze with hers. My years of education suddenly make practical sense in a way I would never have imagined them doing. I know though that she has to see me as capable of besting her, that it is only this challenge that will give her pause.

"The police will be here at any moment," I say. "We called them when we broke into the other room."

"Oh, is that so?" she asks. "I do believe it will take them

a while to find us, considering no one knows about the secret bunker. Nonetheless, we should hurry along. Your gun. Kick it under the bed, please."

My heart drops to the floor. I hesitate, knowing that gun is the only chance we have.

"Now," she demands, aiming her gun at me, her finger on the trigger.

"Do it, Em," Mia says, her voice shaking.

With my thoughts racing for any branch of hope to grab on to, I find the gun with my left foot and push it under the bed.

"And so you know," the woman says, "this is my trap. It's a fact of life. Predator and prey. Our girl here being the latter. I suspect you would never have let it happen to you, am I right? You're the protector. The one who tries to keep away all of life's ugly unpleasantries. And let me guess, little sister here has hated you for it? It hardly seems fair, does it? That those of us in the protector roles aren't valued for those we save."

"Do not compare me to you," I say through gritted teeth. "You're evil. A vile, despicable—"

The woman laughs, as if truly amused. "Now, now. Continue seeing life through your rose-colored glasses, if you wish, but I'm afraid that doesn't change anything. The truth is undeniable. We each have our roles in this world. I'm under no illusions about my own. Do you think a year from now, if you were here to experience it, of course, that your younger sister would still be grateful for what you did for her in rescuing her here tonight? We both know the answer to that. Gratitude fades like smoke. And one day, you'll wake up to wonder what made you risk your own life to save one who sees you as the bane of her existence."

"That's not true!" Mia screams out. "You don't know what you're talking about."

"To the contrary," the woman says. "I am certain that I do. Now enough with the philosophy. Both of you, walk out the door. Now. Or I will shoot you here and simply have the extra mess to deal with once I go upstairs and assure the police there's nothing to be concerned about here at the Hotel California."

I swallow hard, reaching for Mia's hand, clasping her fingers between mine. My brain races for a plan, something, anything to delay, buy time. There are no police coming. This will be up to me. I have no idea if Sergio has actually gotten to Knox or not, but I can't wait for him. It's me against her. I have no gun. No weapon of any kind, and I have no doubt that she will shoot us.

I pull Mia in behind me and start to walk toward the door. She holds the gun out, pointed straight at Mia. She knows where my priorities are and that in controlling Mia, she has me. Keeping Mia tucked by my side, I step out into the hallway.

"Left, please," she orders, pressing the tip of the gun to my shoulder and pushing us forward.

I start walking, one foot in front of the other, closing my eyes for a moment, as I consider the only option I have. I open my eyes and focus on a point ahead in the hallway, the spot where a fire extinguisher hangs on the wall. I count my steps. One. Two. Three. Four. Five. Six. I turn, abruptly, ramming my shoulder into the woman's chest. I hear the gun go off, feel a blaze of pain ricochet through my left arm. A guttural scream comes from my throat, a sound I never imagined I could make. I shove her backward. She falls to the floor, the gun skittering across the hallway carpet.

Mia screams. "Emory!"

I straddle the woman's midsection and start to pummel her with my fists, first one, then the other, hitting her in the face and chest like someone who has gone mad. She's stronger than I would have thought, and she struggles, pushing at me until I fall over backward.

I sense Mia behind me, scrambling, and then look up to find her standing, her feet shoulder-width apart, her arms stretched out with the gun pointed directly at the woman now on top of me.

"Get. Off. Her." Mia's voice is steel, unrecognizable.

The woman looks up, snags her flinty gaze with Mia's. And then she laughs. "We both know you don't have what it takes."

"You're wrong about that," Mia says softly now. "This trap you've made here. You're a monster. A coward. You don't give your victims a chance for a fair fight. Anyone can lay a trap to catch someone who isn't expecting it. How do you think that makes you superior to anything? You don't have a heart. So how can you be human? You aren't."

"Mia. Give me the gun," I say. "Please. Hand me the gun."

Mia shakes her head. "No. Get up, Emory. Move away."

I get to my feet slowly, holding out one hand. "Give me the gun, Mia."

"No," she says again. "I won't let you carry this one. It's up to me to save myself. You gave me the chance. And now, for every other girl, animal, or God knows who you've preyed on, this is for them."

She points the gun directly at the woman's chest and pulls the trigger.

Knox

"Do not be afraid; our fate
Cannot be taken from us; it is a gift."
—Dante Alighieri

COMING OUT OF a hazy stupor, he hears the gunshot, his eyes trying to open themselves, even as his brain orders them to stay closed. He fights the pull back to unconsciousness, finally forcing his eyes to open. Nothing is clear at first, a cloudy haze at the edges of his vision. He hears himself groan, pain stabbing through his side. He presses his hand to the spot, stares at his palm now covered with blood.

He tries to remember where he is, what had happened. It comes to him in an abrupt jolt of clarity. He's scrambling to get up then, stumbling to his feet, swiping his gaze left, then right. He stumbles over to the bathroom door which is now closed, bangs hard with his fist. "Grace! Emory! Are you in there?"

He hears soft crying. It's the girl. "Grace, is Emory with you?"

"No! She went to find Mia."

"The senator? Where is he?"

"He left with the other guy. Sergio."

"You stay in there. Do not come out until I come back for you, okay?"

"Yes," she says, crying outright now.

Knox heads for the door, nearly falling into the hallway. At the end of the corridor, he sees Emory standing with a gun in her hand. On the floor, the woman who owns the hotel. Clearly, dead.

Bracing his hand against the wall, Knox makes his way slowly toward them. "Emory. Put down the gun."

He can see that she is frozen with shock. Blood is oozing from a wound on her shoulder.

The girl beside her looks stunned.

"I shot her," the girl says, looking at him with eyes now brimming with tears.

"Are you both okay?" he asks.

"Yes," Emory says, her gaze dropping to the bloodstain on his side. "You're hurt."

"So are you," he says.

He fumbles for the phone in his back pocket.

"Let me." She takes it from him and taps the screen. A moment later, she says, "Yes, we need an ambulance at the Hotel California. There's been a shooting. Please send the police too."

Emory

"The wound is the place where the Light enters you."
—Rumi

IN THE MONTHS following that awful night at the Hotel California, I put my focus on Mia and getting her the things she will need to feel safe again, among them the most highly recommended trauma therapist I can find.

Grace is in therapy as well. Mia talks with her on the phone for long stretches of time, and I know that they will have a lifetime bond that no one else will be able to truly understand.

For the first couple of months, Mia goes to therapy three days a week. She can't sleep at night, and it isn't unusual that she climbs in bed with me sometime after midnight. I don't mind though. Each time is a reminder to me that she is safe.

She decides to put college off for a year, and I make sure that we spend all my time off from work finding memorable things to do together.

In the initial weeks after she's told the police everything she knows, I agonize over whether charges will be brought against Mia for the death of that horrible woman. But after hours and hours of questioning, the police declare the shooting self defense, and Mia is left to focus on getting life back to normal.

And so we spend hours on the couch with Pounce, watching movies that offer little more than an opportunity to laugh and be somewhere else for a bit.

Mia loves the chickens, naming them Emma and Esther. Pounce is less fond of them, but with a good bit of encouragement from us, finally gives his approval to their presence in the form of completely ignoring them. We drive to the hardware store one morning and buy materials to make them a house in our back yard. Luckily, the fence we already have in place is high enough to keep them inside.

On another day, we decide to get out of the house and drive to Poplar Spring, an animal sanctuary in Poolesville, Maryland. It's an hour or so away, and we arrive in the middle of the afternoon when the cows and goats are lazing under the trees in front of the main house, napping and looking as close to a glimpse of what heaven will be like as I can imagine.

"Do you remember when we came here before?" I ask Mia, looking out at the pond where dozens of Canadian geese and white ducks are dunking for bugs.

"We found that goose with the broken wing," Mia says. "All the other places you called said she would have to be put to sleep. But you wouldn't accept that, so you kept calling places until you found this one. They said she could live her life here with the other ducks, and she would be protected, so not being able to fly really wouldn't matter."

I smile at the memory. "She was so happy when we put her in with the others."

Mia nods, her gaze on the ducks. "I guess we all need to be with those who get us, don't we?"

"Yeah," I say. "We do."

Mia is quiet for a moment, staring out at an older horse grazing near the fence. "What you did for me is what this place does for the animals that come here. You wouldn't give up until you found me. I knew you wouldn't. Emory, I'm so sorry for all the times I made you think I didn't appreciate you. I was horrible to you. I was awful. Can you ever forgive me?"

I feel a great rush of love for my sister and at the same time, gratitude that I had not given up on finding her.

"Mia, don't," I say. "You were just a girl trying to grow up. And I've been a sister who didn't always handle things the way I should have."

"You were there for me when Mama and Daddy died. If you hadn't been, I would have had nowhere to go. You gave up your life to take care of me. And I threw that back in your face. I thought about that so many times while I was in that nightmare, praying I would have the chance to make it up to you. I spent so much time acting like I didn't need you, Em. The truth is I always have. No one will ever be for me what you've been for me."

I reach out and put my hand on top of hers. "I don't know why horrible things happen in this life. What I do know is that we need to find a way to use what we go through to somehow put good back into the world."

"I want to," Mia says. "I don't want to let evil determine what I end up being."

"It won't," I say. "You're too strong for that."

Mia looks off across the pasture, a cloud crossing her face. "Do you think they'll ever find Sergio?"

Just the name sends a familiar chill through me. "I don't know."

"Probably not, right?"

I'd like to assure her that he will be found and punished for abducting Mia and Grace, but I can't do that. If Senator Hagan could get away with escaping to the Ivory Coast, then wasn't it true that bad people could get away with a lot of things? "Maybe one day he'll be found," I say.

"Sometimes, I'm afraid he'll find me again."

I reach out and squeeze her hand. "You're safe, Mia.

The Hotel California has been closed down. The other girls found there have been returned to their families. And everyone knowingly involved, arrested. That evil place doesn't exist anymore."

"My logical brain knows that, but I guess fear isn't logical."

"With time, it will fade."

"Will it?" she asks in a soft voice.

Again, I want to reassure her, but settle for, "I hope so."

We spend a wonderful day there at the sanctuary, holding chickens and turkeys, playing with baby pigs, rubbing the cows and horses. In most cases, the animals who come there have endured terrible lives, abuse, neglect, starvation. But they have been brought to this wonderful place to heal.

And sitting there on the grass of a green pasture, I want to believe that with time, the two of us will begin to heal as well.

Emory

"Life can only be understood backwards; but it must be lived forwards."
—Søren Kierkegaard

THE TRUTH IS I thought I would never hear from him again.

In the first weeks after we were both released from the hospital, I'd let myself hope that he would call. Reach out to say how he was doing, see how I was doing. But the days and months went by, one after the other, and I began to let the hope fade, slip away like threads of sunlight sliding from the horizon at dusk.

And then, out of the blue, late one night when I couldn't sleep, I received a text from him.

**I've been working on me. I think I might finally be someone worthy of giving a chance.
I haven't stopped thinking about you, and it's been nearly a year.
If that's where you are too, meet me at this address on Friday.
I hope you'll come.**

And so, here I am, stepping off the boat that has taken me from Saint Martin over to Anguilla, a place I've never been before, a beautiful island in the Caribbean, my heart pounding so hard that I can feel it against the wall of my chest.

At first, it had simply seemed too insane an idea to even consider. But I'd shown the text to Mia, and she had said I would be crazy not to go. And so, less than forty-eight hours later, here I am.

The driver of the boat helps carry my luggage into the customs office just up from the pier. He leaves me with a smiling, young woman with beautiful skin and a lilt in her voice who welcomes me to Anguilla. The process is quick by United States customs standards, and I walk outside of the building within minutes, pulling my luggage. An older man with graying hair is holding up a sign with my name on it. I lift a hand in recognition, and he smiles, taking my suitcase and pulling it toward a white van in the parking lot.

"Would you like a bottle of water, miss?" he asks, sliding into the driver's seat. "It'll take about twenty minutes to get there."

"Yes, please. Thank you." I sit back and take in the sights outside the window. Incredible resort hotels are interspersed with small, stucco-type houses where goats mow the front yards. As we go, the houses are fewer and farther between, and in just under twenty minutes, the driver turns the van onto an unpaved road. At the top of a small knoll, I can see the ocean in the distance. Within a couple of minutes, he makes another turn and stops the van at a house that sits just off the beach.

It's not enormous, but it is charming with bright pink stucco walls. Beautiful flowers in an abundance of colors climb the frame surrounding the front door.

The driver gets out and walks around to my side of the van. "The fare has already been taken care of, miss," he says. "I hope you enjoy your stay in Anguilla."

"Thank you so much," I say, and then watch him back out of the driveway and pull away. The front door of the house opens, and there stands Knox, tan and more gorgeous than I remember. He's wearing a white T-shirt and some kind of hip-looking swim trunks.

"You came," he says.

"I did," I manage, unable to censor the smile on my face. I'm happy to see him, and I see no point in trying to act cool about it.

He walks toward me, and we stand there for a moment, just looking at each other, the seconds ticking by. I take him in as fully as he takes me in. And I see in his eyes the same thing I'm feeling, pure gladness to rest my eyes on him. I realize now that memory had softened my grief at the thought of never seeing him again by letting me forget how completely beautiful he is.

"How are you?" I ask, my voice barely making the words audible.

"Much better now that you're here," he says.

I smile then, because I don't know how to censor myself. "It's really good to see you, Knox."

"It's amazingly good to see you," he says.

We look at each other for a few long moments, and then he adds, "I was glad you said yes. I thought there was a very good chance that you wouldn't."

"I considered it," I admit. "It's a little out of my comfort zone, but I've kind of spent the last year redefining that, so it seemed like a good opportunity to put it into practice."

He laughs, softly, and then reaches out to brush the back of his hand across my cheek. And I swear the current of feeling that ripples through me is like nothing I've ever felt. I close my eyes for a moment, letting the feeling settle in, and then when I'm looking at him again, I say, "Whatever you've been doing has been good for you."

"Just coming to terms," he says, "with the things I can't

change and figuring out who I'm going to be now that I've accepted that."

"Who are you going to be?" I ask, meeting his gaze and holding it with the desire to see and hear his answer.

"Just a man who wants to live," he says, "and spend that life with someone who wants the same. Who can accept me with all my shortcomings, and my desire to do better, be better. I'm hoping that someone might be you, Emory."

My heart beats a note of pure gladness. And now, I touch him, my palm curving to his cheek. I lean forward, stretch up on my tiptoes, plant a soft kiss on his mouth. "That's why I'm here," I say.

He takes my suitcase, without letting go of my hand. We walk through the front door of the house. The main living area faces a white sand beach.

"Come on," he says, leading me through glass pane doors. "I want to show you something."

The sight before us takes my breath away. I've never seen anything so beautiful. The sand is a glistening white against an aqua sea.

"How did you find this?" I ask, tearing my gaze away from the beautiful sight to meet his.

"Basically luck," he says. "It's an investment property owned by a family out of England. They're currently in a squabble over whether to develop it or not. So far, the opposition is winning, and it's remaining as is for now. "I agreed to stay here for year, basically as a caretaker."

"Nice work, if you can get it."

"Nicer now that you're here," he says, smiling.

"About that," I say.

"Yeah, about that." He steps closer, loops his arm around my waist and reels me in a bit. "Hello."

I look up at him, smiling. "Hello."

"Confession?"

"I'm listening."

"I thought your Dr. Maverick might have ended up winning you over with his bedside manner."

"He was never *my* Dr. Maverick. And there was only one problem with him."

"Oh, yeah? What's that?"

"He wasn't you."

He smiles, looks undeniably pleased. "Were you this beautiful before, or am I like that guy who's been living out in the desert too long, and you're just a mirage?"

I feel the heat bloom in my cheeks. All of a sudden, I feel sixteen again, realizing the boy I've been crushing on likes me. "I think I'm real."

"So you are more beautiful?"

I shake my head, glancing down under a bout of ridiculous shyness.

He tips my chin up, and I am forced to meet his eyes. "You are. I don't think my memory even did you justice."

"You say that to all the girls?"

He swings a glance left and right. "What girls?"

I laugh.

"There is something I've been thinking about, here all by my lonesome."

"What is that?" I ask softly.

"What it would be like to kiss you. Really kiss you."

I feel the breath catch in my throat. My heart thumps once, hard. I feel a boldness I've never felt before. "I guess there's only one way to find out."

The heat in his gaze ignites something inside me. I slip my arms around his neck, and he lowers his mouth to mine. We kiss, and I all but dissolve in his arms. I've never been kissed like this, and all I know is that I want it to go on forever.

When he pulls back, he stares down at me, brushes

the back of his hand across my cheek. "Not even my imagination lived up to that."

"Mine either," I admit. We study each other, taking our time, and then I say, "Can I tell you something?"

He nods, rubbing his thumb against my lower lip.

I close my eyes for an instant and then open them to meet his gaze full force. "This past year, I've realized that life is to be lived. The desire I once had to make something of myself, become someone my parents would have ended up being proud of feels like something a little different these days, a need to really live, experience moments and places I know I will look back on one day and be grateful for having done."

He studies me in silence long enough that I begin to wonder if this sounds silly. But then he says, "I want what I do and who I'm with to be deliberate. My choice."

"Me too," I say softly.

He takes my hand and starts pulling me toward the sea in front of us. "Let's make that first memory."

I laugh, following him across the warm sand. "I can't swim in this," I say, waving a hand at the skirt and blouse I'd traveled in.

He loops an arm around my waist and lifts me up, walking into the water. "You sure can't," he says, setting me down at a point where the water laps at the back of my legs and reaching out to undo a button, pushes my blouse off my shoulders. He touches his thumb to the scar near my collar bone, leans in and gently presses his lips against it.

I lift his T-shirt, run my hand along his waist and find the scar from the bullet he'd taken in helping me save Mia. I lean down and press my lips to it, lingering for a long moment.

I hear his intake of breath, raise my head to look up at him.

"I can help you with this clothes problem you seem to be having," he says in a voice laced with desire.

"You're a master problem solver, aren't you?"

"So I've been told. How am I doing?"

"So far, very good." I reach out to pull his face to mine, kissing him, deep and full while the Caribbean Sea laps at the back of my legs and a blazing sun shines down upon us.

Dear Reader

I would like to thank you for taking the time to read my story. There are so many wonderful books to choose from these days, and I am hugely appreciative that you chose mine.

Please join my mailing list for updates on new releases and giveaways! Just go to http://www.inglathcooper.com – come check out my Facebook page for postings on books, dogs and things that make life good!

Wishing you many, many happy afternoons of reading pleasure.

All best,

Inglath

About Inglath Cooper

RITA® Award-winning author Inglath Cooper was born in Virginia. She is a graduate of Virginia Tech with a degree in English. She fell in love with books as soon as she learned how to read. "My mom read to us before bed, and I think that's how I started to love stories. It was like a little mini-vacation we looked forward to every night before going to sleep. I think I eventually read most of the books in my elementary school library."

That love for books translated into a natural love for writing and a desire to create stories that other readers could get lost in, just as she had gotten lost in her favorite books. Her stories focus on the dynamics of relationships, those between a man and a woman, mother and daughter, sisters, friends. They most often take place in small Virginia towns very much like the one where she grew up and are peopled with characters who reflect those values and traditions.

"There's something about small-town life that's just part of who I am. I've had the desire to live in other places, wondered what it would be like to be a true Manhattanite, but the thing I know I would miss is the familiarity of faces everywhere I go. There's a lot to be said for going in the grocery store and seeing ten people you know!"

Inglath Cooper is an avid supporter of companion animal rescue and is a volunteer and donor for the Franklin County Humane Society. She and her family have fostered many dogs and cats that have gone on to be adopted by other families. "The rewards are endless. It's an eye-opening moment to realize that what one person throws away can fill another person's life with love and joy."

Follow Inglath on Facebook

at www.facebook.com/inglathcooperbooks

Join her mailing list for news of new releases and giveaways at www.inglathcooper.com

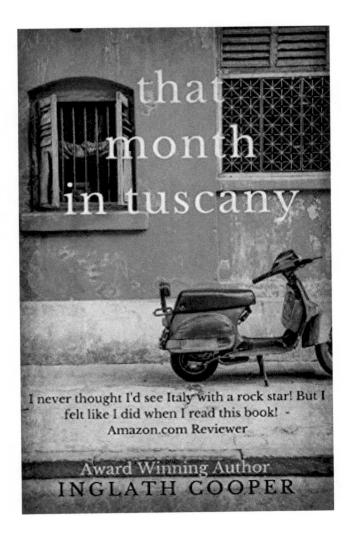

I never thought I'd see Italy with a rock star! But I
felt like I did when I read this book! -
Amazon.com Reviewer

Award Winning Author
INGLATH COOPER

Excerpt from That Month in Tuscany

Lizzy

IF I'M HONEST with myself, truly honest, I will admit I knew that in the end, he wouldn't go.

But to leave it until the night before: that surprises even me.

Here I sit on my over-packed suitcase in the foyer of this too large house I've spent the past five years decorating and fussing over — picking out paint colors and rugs, which include the exact same shade, and art that can only be hung on the walls if it looks like an original, even if it isn't.

I stare at the pair of tickets in my hand, open the folder and read the schedule as I have a dozen times before.

Departure Charlotte, North Carolina 3:45 PM
Arrival Rome, Italy 7:30 AM
Departure Rome, Italy 9:40 AM
Arrival Florence, Italy 10:45 AM

My name on one: Millicent Elizabeth Harper. His on the other: Tyler Fraiser Harper.

I bought the tickets six months ago. Plenty of time to plan how to get away from the office for a month. Make whatever arrangements had to be made. Didn't people do things like that now and then? Check out of their real lives for a bit? Let others take over in their absence?

Tyler's response would be, "Yeah, people who don't care about their careers. People who don't mind risking everything they've worked for by letting some Ivy League know-it-all step into their shoes long enough to prove that they can fill them."

Our twentieth anniversary is tomorrow. I'd imagined that we would arrive at the Hotel Savoy and celebrate with a bottle of Italian champagne in a room where we could spend the next month getting to know one another again — the way we had once known one another. Traveling around the Tuscan countryside on day trips and eating lunch in small town trattorias. Exploring art museums and local artisan shops.

I shared all of this with him, and he had done a fine job of making me believe that he found it as appealing as I did. It felt as if we again had a common interest after years of a life divided into his and hers, yours and mine.

Then, a little over a week ago, he'd begun to plant the seeds of backpedaling. I had just finished putting together a salad for our dinner when my cell phone rang.

It lay buzzing on the kitchen counter, and something in my stomach, even at that moment, told me that he would back out.

I started not to answer, as if that would change the course of the demolition he was about to execute on the trip I had been dreaming of our entire married life. Actually, maybe the trip was a metaphor for what I had hoped would be the resurrection of our marriage during a month away together. The two of us, Ty and me like it used to be when we first started dating, and it didn't matter what we were doing as long as we did it together.

Ironically, we've had the house to ourselves for almost two years now. It's hard to believe that Kylie's been away at college for that long, but she has. Almost two years during which I've continued to wait for Ty's promises of less time at the office and more time at home to actually bear fruit; only they never have.

And I guess this is what it has taken to make me see that they never will.

Me, sitting on a suitcase, alone in our house, waiting for something that's not going to happen. Waiting for Ty to realize that we hardly even know each other anymore; waiting for him to remember how much he had once loved me; waiting for him to miss me.

I feel my phone vibrate in the pocket of my jacket. I know without looking that it's Ty. Calling to make sure I've canceled our tickets and gotten as much of a refund as I can, considering that it's last minute. I know that he'll also want to make sure I'm back to my cheerful self. He'll be waiting for the note of impending forgiveness in my voice, the one that tells him he doesn't need to feel guilty. I'll be here, as I always have. Things happen. Plans get changed. Buck up, and move on.

I pull the phone from my pocket, stare at his name on the screen.

I lift my thumb to tap Answer. I'm poised to do every one of the things that Ty expects of me. I really am. Then I picture myself alone in this house every day from six-thirty to eight o'clock at night. And I just can't stand the thought of it.

I actually feel physically ill. I realize in that moment that I am at a crossroad. Stay and lose myself forever to someone I had never imagined I would be. Go and maybe, maybe, start to resurrect the real me. Or find out if she is actually gone forever.

The moment hangs. My stomach drops under the weight of my decision. I hit End Call and put the phone back in my pocket. And without looking back, I pick up my suitcase and walk out the door.

~

I PARK IN THE long-term lot and not in the back, either, where Ty would insist that I leave the BMW. I park it smack dab up front, tight in between a well-dented minivan and a Ford Taurus with peeling paint. It is the very last parking space Ty would pick and petty as it sounds, I get enormous pleasure from the fact that my door has to touch the other vehicle in order for me to squeeze out.

I get my suitcase out of the trunk, letting it drop to the pavement with a hard thunk. I roll it to the white airport shuttle waiting at the curb. An older man with a kind face gets out and takes my bag from me, lifting it up the stairs with enough effort that I wish he'd let me do it myself.

Then he smiles at me, and I realize he doesn't mind.

There are two people already on the shuttle, sitting in the back. They are absorbed in each other, the woman laughing at something the man has said. I deliberately don't look at them, keeping my gaze focused over the shoulder of the driver who is now whistling softly.

"What gate, ma'am?" he asks, looking up at me in the rearview mirror.

"United," I answer.

"You got it," he says, and goes back to his whistling.

I feel my phone vibrating in the pocket of my black coat. I try to resist the urge to look at who's calling, but my hand reaches for it automatically.

Ty. It's the third time he's called since I left the house. I put the phone back in my pocket.

When we arrive at the United gate, the whistling driver again helps me with my suitcase. I drop a tip in the cup by the door and thank him.

"You're most welcome, dear. Where you headed?"

"Italy," I say.

He lifts his eyebrows and says, "I always wanted to see that place. You going by yourself?"

"Yes," I answer. It's only then that I'm absolutely sure I am really doing this.

I am doing this.

~

THE CHECK-IN process is lengthy. When the woman behind the desk asks me about my husband's ticket, I tell her that he will be along shortly. Lying isn't something I'm in the habit of doing, but I don't think I can admit to her that he isn't coming without unraveling an explanation that might keep us both here way past the plane's departure time.

"Hopefully, he'll be here soon," she says. "Don't want to cut it too close. These international flights leave promptly."

I simply nod. She asks to see my passport, compares the picture with my face, and types a whole bunch of things into the computer. What, I cannot imagine because they already have all my information. A full five minutes tick by before she hands me the boarding pass.

Taking it from her feels like the closing of a door that I will not be able to reopen. As metaphors go, I have to think it's pretty accurate.

The security process is almost reason enough for me to stop flying altogether. If I could get to Italy by car, I would most certainly drive.

The underwire in my bra instigates a pat-down by a woman who looks as if she's no happier about the procedure than I am. She asks me in a cigarette-roughened voice if I would rather have this conducted in a private room. Since I suppose that means she and I would be the only two occupants, I choose public embarrassment instead.

Once my bra passes the feel-up check, I am directed through the booth where I have to spread my legs and raise my arms in the same posture criminals are told to take by their arresting officer. Not for the first time, I resent the heck out of the bad people who caused all of us trying-hard-to-be-good ones to have to go through this.

An oversize purse is my only carry-on and once my laptop and camera come through the conveyor belt, I stick them back inside.

I head for the concourse that my plane will be leaving from. Boarding begins in less than an hour, so I buy a few snacks and use the ladies room. I find a seat in the chairs by the gate. It looks as if the flight will be full, based on the number of people already here. The thought of an overbooked, way-too-full flight makes my stomach drop.

I cannot remember the last time I went anywhere by myself. I'm used to Ty carrying the tickets, checking in the luggage while Kylie and I hover in the background, handing over our identification when prompted, and checking email on our phones.

I pull out my phone now and glance at the screen, noticing a text message. I click in and see that it's from Winn.

Lizzy!!! U and Ty have the time of your lives. I CANNOT wait to hear all about it. I just know u 2 are going to come back like newlyweds. Shoot, Ty might even leave the firm, and y'all can travel around indefinitely the way u always dreamed about.

The message blurs before my eyes, the tears there before I can even think to will them away. I tap in a response.

Ty's not going.

I hit send, and it seems as if the reply is nearly instantaneous.

What?!!?

The phone vibrates. Winn's name pops up on the screen. I hit answer and put it to my ear. "Yes, I know. I was a fool to think he really would."

"Lizzy." My name is drawn out into at least six syllables. I hear her devastation. It's nearly as thick and heartbroken as my own. "What? Why?"

"A new case," I say.

"Are you kidding me?" she asks, the question lit with instant fury. While there's really nothing to be gained from it, it kind of feels nice to have someone see things from my point of view.

"I can't believe he would do this to you. It's your twentieth anniversary."

"Yes," I say. "It is."

"He doesn't deserve you, Lizzy. He never did."

"You're just saying that because you're mad. No one wanted us to be together more than you."

"Well, I was wrong. I'm a big enough person to admit that."

I almost smile at this. Ty has never had a bigger fan than Winn. In fact, I think she's been a little secretly in love with him since the day we both met him in English Lit at UVa.

"And what do you mean," she asks suddenly, "Ty's not going? Are *you* going?"

I glance around at the other passengers, and the whole thing feels surreal, like a dream I'm going to wake up from at any moment. "Yes," I say, again making my decision reality.

At least three seconds of silence tick by before she says, "Wow."

"You think I'm crazy."

"I think you're right. It's exactly what you should do. But I can't believe you're actually going to."

"There's something in there that should make me feel less than good."

"You know what I mean. How many times has he done this to you? That trip to the Caribbean after our ten-year reunion. The ski trip last winter—"

"I know," I say, stopping her. "I don't need to hear the list of times Ty has disappointed me. Because if I do, I'm also going to remember that I've pretty much been a doormat for him to wipe his feet on."

"I wish I could go with you," Winn says. "Are you staying the whole month?"

"That's my plan."

And then as if she remembers the reason I'm going alone, she says, "I'm really sorry, Lizzy. You don't deserve this. You deserve so much better."

"Spilled milk and all that," I say.

"It's his loss. One day, he's going to realize that. What did he say when you said you were going without him?"

"Um, he doesn't know yet."

Again, silence, processing, and then, "Are you sure this is Lizzy Harper?"

I actually laugh at this.

"I am incredulous. It's what you should have done a long time ago, you know," she says softly.

"Probably no denying that."

"He needs a good wake-up call."

"You know, Winn, it's not even about that. I'm doing this for me."

"Good. Good," she repeats. "How do I get in touch with you?"

"Once I leave the states, my phone will be useless. I didn't sign up for the international plan because I thought it would be nice for the two of us to cut off all communications from home for the time we were there. Ironic, isn't it?"

"But how will I know how you're doing?"

"I'll check in by email, if I have wireless."

"You promise?"

"I promise."

"I love you, Lizzy. I'm proud of you."

"You're just saying that because I'm so pathetic."

"Pathetic would be you canceling the trip."

"Yeah?"

"Yeah."

"And don't spend all of your time walking through museums and old churches and stuff. Find something fun to do. *Someone* fun to—"

"Winn!"

She laughs. "It would serve him right."

"You know that's not me."

"Maybe it should be you."

"Like that would fix my life."

"Might not fix your life, but it would definitely fix the moment."

I smile and shake my head. "You'd make a terrible shrink."

"But an excellent friend."

"I'll give you that."

"Roanoke won't be the same without you."

"It's only a month."

"Let me hear from you."

"I will," I say, adding, "Be good."

"Only if you promise not to be."

Books by Inglath Cooper

The Heart That Breaks
My Italian Lover
Fences – Book Three – Smith Mountain Lake Series
Dragonfly Summer – Book Two – Smith Mountain
Lake Series
Blue Wide Sky – Book One – Smith Mountain Lake
Series
That Month in Tuscany
And Then You Loved Me
Down a Country Road
Good Guys Love Dogs
Truths and Roses
Nashville – Part Ten – Not Without You
Nashville – Book Nine – You, Me and a Palm Tree
Nashville – Book Eight – R U Serious
Nashville – Book Seven – Commit
Nashville – Book Six – Sweet Tea and Me
Nashville – Book Five – Amazed
Nashville – Book Four – Pleasure in the Rain
Nashville – Book Three – What We Feel
Nashville – Book Two – Hammer and a Song
Nashville – Book One – Ready to Reach
A Gift of Grace
RITA® Award Winner John Riley's Girl
A Woman With Secrets
Unfinished Business
A Woman Like Annie
The Lost Daughter of Pigeon Hollow
A Year and a Day